# Spring in Promise Cove

by

# Casey Dawes

Mountain Vines Publishing

Copyright 2023 by Casey Dawes LLC.
All rights reserved.

No part of this book may be reproduced in any form or by any electronic or mechanical means, including information storage and retrieval systems, without permission in writing from the publisher, except by reviewers, who may quote brief passages in a review.

Some characters and events in this book are fictitious. Any similarity to real persons, living or dead, is coincidental and not intended by the author.

Book cover design by GetCovers
Edited by Beth Hicks
Interior design by Concierge Self-Publishing (www.ConciergeSelfPublishing.com)

Published by Mountain Vines Publishing
Missoula, MT
Contact email: info@ConciergeSelfPublishing.com

*Dedicated to Kathleen J. Morse.*

# Chapter One

"I'm going to Paris for the summer," Maggie's mother, Elaine, announced one especially fine day in late March, as she descended the stairs from the upstairs apartments to the floor of Culver's General Store. She was dressed in a blue skirt swirling with tropical flowers and birds and a white tank top. Her hair was covered with a bright scarf, while turquoise earrings dangled from her ears.

"What? No. You're joking," Maggie said with a laugh.

"I'm not."

"You can't go to Paris," Maggie said. "I need you here to cook and help run the store."

"Henri is already arranging my flight. I'll stay at his place. He's got an amazing apartment in the Latin Quarter. Lots of light. I've applied for a summer program at the Paris College of Art. It's all decided. I leave at the end of June."

"Henri? Who is Henri?"

"He's my very good friend from the internet." Her mother's tone was suggestive, but Maggie refused to think about what *that* meant.

"You know nothing about him. He could be an axe murderer."

"In Paris? No, he'd more likely use a stiletto," Elaine said with a smile. "But don't worry, your friend, the sheriff, did a full background check for me."

"Tom knew about this? And he didn't tell me?"

"I asked him not to."

This was insane. Her mother couldn't go to Paris and live with a stranger.

"You can't go. I need you. I can't run the store without you."

Elaine's expression became serious. "You are going to have to figure it out. I'm going to be seventy this summer. I think it's about time for me to follow my bliss, before it's too late."

Maggie gulped.

"Besides, Gregg can cook," Elaine added. "He's actually quite good. And he likes it. In fact, he'll be taking over today. I have work to do."

Elaine waved her slim fingers and headed back upstairs to her apartment.

Maggie sank to the stairs and stared blankly around the store. It was jammed with all the immediate needs of the local community of Promise Cove. While they did most of their shopping in the groceries of Whitefish and big box stores of Kalispell, they came in at least once a week for milk, coffee, and fresh vegetables when they could get them. In winter she stocked snow shovels; in the summer whimsical garden gloves were a hit.

A few years ago she and her mother had agreed to take advantage of the long unused commercial kitchen at the back of the store and serve a light breakfast and lunch to those who wanted it.

A service that was now going to be short a cook.

Her mother was right; Gregg could manage it. But who knew how long he would stay? Especially once Maggie's daughter Teagan left for college in late September. They'd been an item for about a year.

What if her mother stayed in Paris with Henri?

Maggie stood and strode to the counter where she'd left her phone. She was going to call the sheriff and find out exactly when he'd known about Elaine's scheme. Then she was going to give her childhood friend a good piece of her mind.

The bell over the front door chirped as she started dialing. Nancy Smith, the local mystery writer, slipped through the front door and headed to a far corner of the store without meeting Maggie's gaze.

An odd woman. The word that always came up in Maggie's mind was "vague." Nancy was hard to notice, and if no one did, it was almost as if she wasn't there. But under the pen name N.A. Nance, she wrote multiple-homicide suspense thrillers that routinely hit the best-seller list.

Maggie shook the thoughts from her head. She had more important things to think about than the peculiar behavior of one person in a town full of them.

A few moments later Nancy was standing in front of Maggie as if she'd appeared from thin air. Nancy looked around, then slid a box of tampons from under her jacket onto the table.

As she always did, Maggie quickly slipped them into a brown bag and rang up the sale.

Without saying a word, Nancy turned away.

Gregg held the door open for her as she left.

Maggie breathed a sigh of relief as he walked in. He was a little rough around the edges, but Gregg had turned out to be one of the good guys.

"Hey, glad to see you," she said as he approached the counter. "Got a minute?"

"Sure," he said. "There's something I need to run by you, too."

*Not more bad news.*

"I'm hoping you can work more hours this summer than we'd planned."

"Great. I can always use more hours. In fact, that's what I wanted to discuss with you. Mike asked me to work down at Moose's Tavern for the evening shift. He's setting up a grill for hamburgers and fries. Figures people need more options for dinner, especially with summer season coming up."

"You're going to be busy."

"Yeah, he wants me most nights."

"It's going to make it tough to spend much time with Teagan," Maggie pointed out.

"Yeah, about that." Gregg shifted his feet.

"If you're going to break up with her, you need to tell her first."

"Oh no. I figure it will be the other way around. She's going off to college. That'll change things. She wants more than life in a small town. Me? I'm happy here. In fact, I'm saving up to open my own restaurant." He must have seen the panic on her face. "But that won't be for a few years yet.

I'm sure you'll be able to hire someone between now and then."

"I certainly hope so. Sounds like you'll be very busy this summer. Because not only will you be working with Mike, you'll be the only cook here. My mother has announced she's going to Paris."

He nodded. "Yeah, I knew about that."

"How could you possibly know?"

"Elaine told me." The door chimed again, and a man strode in. "Well, I'd better get to work."

Gregg headed to the back, leaving Maggie feeling like everyone knew what was going on in this town except her.

And she was supposed to be the mayor.

# # #

Teagan arrived around two to give her a break, and she headed for the tiny space under the stairs where she'd carved out an office, ready to release some pent-up frustration.

She punched Tom's number.

"How dare you not tell me?" she began, knowing he would immediately recognize her voice. They'd been friends since elementary school when he used to share his Hostess cupcakes with her.

Elaine didn't believe in feeding sweets to children.

"Oh," Tom replied. "Your mother told you."

"Finally. After telling everyone *but* me."

"Who else knows?"

"Gregg, for one."

"I didn't realize she'd told him."

"Apparently." Maggie stressed the last syllable. "You should have stopped this harebrained scheme. Or told me so *I* could put an end to it."

"Elaine seems quite determined to go. And I checked out the man in Paris. Perfectly respectable."

"Don't you know that's what they say about serial killers? 'He was such a *nice* man.'"

Tom laughed. "You're being melodramatic."

"Don't you dare laugh at me, Tom Gerard. This is a crisis and you know it!"

"Calm down, Maggie. Everything will be fine. How about I take you out for a beer at Moose's after you close the store, and you can tell me what a rotten man I am."

"I'm not dating you, Tom. I've told you that."

"Hope springs eternal. I wish I could understand why not."

"You're my friend," she said.

"That's a great reason to date. They say friends make the best relationships."

"Until it goes south, and they never speak to each other again. I would lose both the relationship and the friendship. Nope. I'm not taking that risk."

"Well, the offer stands," he said.

"Why don't you go catch some bad guys," she said.

"I'll do that. See you." He disconnected right when she realized she wasn't done yelling at him.

She pulled a pile of scribbled notes in front of her. They were her effort to be a little more on top of the stock for the store. While she enjoyed the interaction with people, the minutiae of stocking, pricing, and the annual inventory ground her down. Fortunately, everyone, including her two closest friends, had joined in during winter's gloom, and their many hands had made light work of the chore.

Of course both of her friends had gone to Hawaii while she stayed home. Kelly had finally honeymooned with her new husband, Ryan. Alex had accompanied Julia Leonard, a talented musician they'd befriended in the fall, to a recording studio on Maui.

Instead of doing the work that needed doing, Maggie called Kelly.

"I need you," she said as soon as Kelly picked up. "Teagan has her own life, and my mother has gone temporarily insane."

"Teagan is almost eighteen and deserves her own life. But it is a difficult adjustment," Kelly said. She'd had her own nest empty out the year before. "But I've always thought your mother was merely eccentric, not insane."

Maggie outlined what she'd learned.

"That is a bit drastic. Is she happy about it?"

"Who cares if she's happy? It's nuts. Maybe it's early dementia."

Kelly dared to laugh.

"It's not funny. Why doesn't anyone get that this is a crisis?"

"Okay, okay. Tomorrow's Wednesday. Think you can hold off your breakdown until then? It's about time for a meeting of the Promise Cove Renewal Committee."

"I'd rather not wait."

"You're going to have to," Kelly said. "Ryan and I have plans for the evening."

"I guess."

"Good. Call Alex. I'll see you all tomorrow."

Maggie disconnected and put the phone down on the desk. Everyone else had somewhere better to be. When her dad had died the summer after her first year in college, Maggie had stepped up to run the store. Once she'd wound up pregnant, she permanently put her dreams aside to take care of her child. And now she was stuck in Promise Cove. Forever. Her life was over before she'd really had a chance to live ... or find true love.

## Chapter Two

Maggie handed the two bottles of chardonnay she'd brought to Kelly's as soon as she walked into the mudroom of the house.

"Really?" Kelly asked. "It's that bad?"

Maggie shrugged. "Alex here?"

"Yep, in the living room talking with Ryan."

"Ryan's not sticking around, is he?" She couldn't possibly have a meltdown in front of a man. And she so desperately needed to come unglued in the safe circle of friends.

"No, he's on his way to the quilting studio. He knows better. They're discussing ART business."

ART was the co-op gallery that was opposite the store on the main highway through town. It used to be the Art Center, but the other logs that had made up "Center" had fallen off years ago.

"All these talented people," Maggie said. "And I don't have anything remotely artistic in my body."

"You've got something better," Kelly said, handing her a glass of wine. "You are organized and a great leader. That counts for a lot."

"It's not the same. You know that."

Kelly shrugged. "We all have our talents. Maybe it's time you learned to honor yours."

Alex walked into the kitchen. "Oh good. The wine's here. How are you doing tonight madam mayor?"

"Oh, please don't call me that." Maggie cringed. She'd only run for the new town position as a lark.

"Why not?" Kelly asked, pouring a glass for Alex.

"I don't know. It makes me uncomfortable."

"Because of the recognition?" Alex asked.

"Because I don't really know what it means."

"I don't think anyone does," Kelly said. "Which is why it's important. You get to define the job for everyone else. Although Ryan did tell me that the artists associated with the co-op were hoping for a point person. Someone who could handle routine inquiries."

"Whatever those are," Maggie said with a sinking feeling. "This may turn out to be a great way to chew up more of my time."

"Perfect, then," Kelly said. "You'll have no hours to waste on moaning about being an empty-nester." She picked up the tray loaded with snacks in pretty bowls. Where Maggie would simply put bags of chips and jars of dip on a table, Kelly put things in attractive bowls and added flowers. It had taken a while to get used to.

"So your mother is off to Paris," Alex said as they headed into the living room. "Kelly told me when she called, but I also heard it at the post office. Apparently, Gregg mentioned it when he dropped off the store mail yesterday."

"Now everyone will know my mother has gone nuts." The post office was gossip central. "Why can't everything simply go on the way it has been?"

"Because it doesn't," Alex said bluntly.

Maggie took a gulp of wine in the awkward silence that followed. Alex knew better than anyone else how life could change in an instant. As a young woman, her husband had been killed in one of the endless wars in the Middle East.

"Help yourself, ladies," Kelly said as she sat in her favorite chair, an old-fashioned rocker. They clustered around the fireplace, the nighttime temperature still cold on the cusp of spring. Ryan had lit a fire before he'd left.

Maggie pulled her chair closer, feeling something more than the chill of evening. For so long being a mother was her purpose in life, her number one reason for getting past the shame of loving a man who got her pregnant and dumped her.

Her second reason had been to help her mother maintain the store. Her parents had given everything to create that business and now her mother was abandoning it.

Maggie's fingers gripped the stem of the wine glass.

"Careful," Kelly said gently.

Maggie forced herself to relax.

"Can we talk about my first official retreat?" Kelly asked. "The last one went well, and now that spring is here, I'm planning the next one. I'm going to invite some of my grandmother's regulars. But it would be nice to have one of you sit in again like Alex did last time. Maggie, are you up for that?"

"I couldn't possibly. Who's going to take care of the store? Do the mayoring that needs to be done?" Maggie waved the idea away.

"It might be good for you," Alex said. "I got a lot out of it."

"Non-starter," Maggie said firmly. "So what else do you need?"

Kelly outlined a few areas she wanted to change from the retreat she'd done in the fall. She'd inherited her grandmother's business providing support to artists from all different fields. After a trial run with locals, she was ready to move on to paying clients.

As they dipped into the snacks and another glass of wine, they sorted through the issues Kelly raised until she was satisfied that she had enough to move forward.

Neither Alex nor Kelly had broached the issue of Maggie going to the retreat again, which suited Maggie just fine.

While Alex helped Kelly refresh the snacks in the kitchen, Maggie poured a third glass of wine and wandered around the living room. Kelly had made only a few changes to the warm and welcoming space that her grandmother, Henrietta, had created. One addition was a bookshelf of her grandmother's poetry and journals. Idly, Maggie removed one and leafed through it.

When her friends returned to the room, she carried it to her chair and laid it on a nearby table.

"I think it's time to expand the renewal committee," Kelly said when they'd settled back down.

"What do you mean?" Maggie asked.

"We'll need more than just us to build an entire performing arts center," Alex said. "It's going to take money.

When they built the ART building, they used a lot of scrap lumber, but there were still things that had to be purchased, like wiring and plumbing. If we're going to have performances, we're going to need all of that on steroids."

"You're right. It's a big project. And is it the right one to begin with? I mean, there may be other things we should be doing for the town."

"No, I think this is a great idea," Alex said.

"What other things can you think of?" Kelly countered.

"Things for kids to do, some way of encouraging development of a few more places where people can stay and eat. Did you hear Mike is going to start serving hamburgers and fries at Moose's?"

"That will be great," Kelly said. "Ryan also heard from Larry that Mike was thinking about adding on a microbrewery. Apparently Mike has a home brewery going."

"How's Larry doing?" Maggie asked. The young contractor, who'd bartended at Moose's over the winter, had lost his home in a forest fire the previous fall.

"He's still staying at Ryan's place, but he may be taking a contracting job down by Billings for the summer," Kelly replied.

"I helped set up a GoFundMe account for all the victims of the fire," Maggie said. "There's quite a bit of money in it. Should be enough to cover what insurance doesn't for anyone who needs it."

"This is such a great place to live," Kelly said. "I'm glad I stayed."

"So are we," Maggie said with a smile. Having Kelly back completed the friendship ring. "Who else do you think should be on this committee?"

Maggie quickly wrote down the suggestions her friends threw out, and then the three of them hashed out a definitive list.

"When is your mother planning on leaving?" Kelly asked.

"Not until the end of June," Maggie said, refilling her glass. "That gives me plenty of time to convince her to stay here."

"Why would you want to do that?" Kelly asked as she

*Spring in Promise Cove*

refilled the bowls with snacks.

"Because it's dangerous out there! She's seventy years old. She has no idea what risks the modern world holds."

"Your mother has always seemed capable of handling herself," Alex said. She nodded to the glass. "And you should go easy on that stuff. It's not going to solve your problems for you."

"I'll do what I want." Defiantly, Maggie took another gulp. She would have drained the glass but wasn't that far gone ... yet.

Alex held up her hands in surrender.

Maggie placed the drink on a side table, sank into her chair, and put her head in her hands. "It's all too much. Everything around me is changing. I expect my mom to be there, just like she's always been. And a few weeks after she waltzes off to Paris, Teagan is leaving. Moose's Saloon won't be the same neighborhood dive it's always been. And what have I done with my life? Nothing. I'm an honorary mayor in a backwoods town. Whoop-de-do." She wanted another sip of wine, but her equilibrium was already a bit off balance. Alex had been right. It was time to stop, much as she wanted to numb herself to all that was happening around her.

"It *is* important," Kelly said.

Maggie defiantly shook her head. "Being governor matters. Being president matters. Heck, even being a big city mayor matters. But being number one in a small town doesn't really mean anything."

"Except to the people of that small town," Kelly said. "You made promises, Maggie. You have to keep them. We're excited about the performance space. It's a great idea. Now let's make it happen."

"I guess I'm kind of committed," Maggie said.

"Yep," Alex said.

"But you've got us with you ever step of the way. We'll help you out after your mother leaves. And we'll cry with you when Teagan takes off to live her own life," Kelly said.

"Thanks," Maggie said, fighting back the tears that were already threatening to spill.

No matter what, she was blessed with good friends.

# Chapter Three

The back room at Moose's Saloon was used for every community meeting and every retirement or anniversary party. It was the only space big enough to handle a decent-sized crowd. The plain room was sided with wood paneling and lit by a few Budweiser lights that had migrated from the bar in front. A plate glass window looked across a grassy strip to a group of pine trees. Behind those trees, lay one of the residential areas in town.

"Thanks for hosting us," she said to Mike, the owner of the tavern. He was a medium-sized man with close-cropped gray hair. "And for agreeing to be part of the committee."

"No problem," he said. "I'm glad you're doing this. Performances mean more people coming to town, as well as a chance to showcase some of the considerable talent we have. It will be a boost to the economy."

"You don't think it will be too much?" Maggie asked.

"Nah. Most of them won't make it past Whitefish. The ones who do will appreciate what we're trying to do here."

Two short and thin women came into the back room. Innkeeper Gabriella's dark hair was curled, evoking a feminine quality. Makalia's straight black hair capped her head in a sleek and stylish look, fitting her role as the artist co-op's webmaster.

Alex and Kelly followed right behind them.

"Looks like everyone's starting to arrive," Mike said. "I've set up some pitchers of water and glasses on that table for anyone who's thirsty." He picked up something that was sitting next to the row of empty glasses and handed it to Maggie. "Everyone who's in charge should have a gavel, even if they never use it."

"Thank you," Maggie said with a laugh. "I don't think it's going to be a problem."

"I'm here!" Ruth bellowed as she walked in. She was a lifelong knitter who ran the school cafeteria with an iron fist and a big heart.

Jim and James followed her. One was a painter and the other a sculptor, but Maggie could never remember who was what. They weren't brothers, and they lived separately, but they were never seen apart.

"Heard your mother's going to Paris," Jim said. "I'm so jealous."

"I went to Paris once," James said. "You can get into a lot of trouble there. A *lot* of trouble. Especially when you're young." A dreamy look drifted across his face.

"Her mother's seventy," Jim pointed out.

"You can still get into trouble at seventy," James said. "And I heard there's already a man involved."

Maggie strode to the front of the room and banged the gavel on the table. "I call this meeting to order," Maggie said as loudly as she could over her rapidly beating heart.

Everyone swiftly sat down. "You'll be fine," Kelly whispered as she headed to her chair. "You've got this."

Maggie didn't feel as confident as her friend. Not at all. Nonetheless, she forced a smile to her face. "Welcome to the expanded Promise Cove Renewal Committee."

"Here, here," Jim and James said together, slapping their hands on the table.

"Last fall," Maggie began, "Alex, Kelly, and I started talking about things our community could use. We've done a great job creating Promise Cove as a haven for visual artists. Thanks to Makalia, the town has become known even beyond the state. Last week I had two tourists from Germany stop by the store."

"Here, here," Jim and James cheered, raising their hands again.

She glared at them.

They put their hands down.

"All of this has enabled our artists, and even our writers, to make a good living yet still live in one of the best small towns in the country."

She glanced at the two men who quickly shut their mouths.

"But when my friend, Kelly, arrived in town, I realized we were missing something. What about performing artists? Musicians, dancers, even actors? Performances could draw people here to support places like Gabriella's inn, or the new sweet shop farther up the highway."

"Maybe we could get touring groups to come here, too," Mike suggested. "That would be a big draw to the town."

"Too big," Gabriella said. "And exactly opposite from what we want our town to be."

"I don't know," Mike said. "We've got to make a living. My work depends on people coming through town. No offense," he said to the general group. "But people who work at home don't come out for an after-work beer with the gang, and during the good weather, Friday night dates go to Whitefish. I'm hoping serving food will help, but ..." He shook his head.

"There might be a different solution to that," Ruth said. "We could do some events. You know like a trivia contest or something. Especially in the winter time, people get cabin fever. I bet they'd come down for something like that."

Mike nodded. "That's an interesting idea."

"And we could offer a special on those nights for people who didn't want to make a long drive back to their cabin up the mountain," Gabriella said.

"We could create a town website, separate from the ART stuff," Makalia said.

As others chimed in, the meeting slipped away from Maggie. She looked over at Alex and Kelly for help.

"Use the gavel," Alex mouthed.

Maggie slammed the wooden mallet down on the table.

Conversation stopped in mid-sentence as everyone turned back to her with expressions like disobedient grade-school students.

"These are all wonderful ideas," Maggie said. "But we need to focus." Suddenly, she was at a loss. She had no idea how to run a meeting. Why had she ever thought she could do this?

Eight expectant faces stared at her.

"I think we need a secretary," Kelly said slowly. "I'll volunteer for now. Then we can elect someone officially if we want."

"Oh no," Alex said. "That job is totally yours. But we should have a treasurer, too."

"Mike would be a good choice," Ruth said, looking at the saloon owner with a smile. "He's used to running a business."

"That's a great idea," Gabriella said. "I nominate Mike for treasurer."

"Second," said Alex.

"Wait a minute," Mike said. "Don't I get a say?"

"Well?" Ruth asked.

"Okay. I'll do it."

Everyone looked at Maggie again. In a panic, she looked at her friends.

"Vote," Alex said.

"Oh yes. All in favor say 'aye,'" Maggie said.

A chorus of "ayes" answered her.

"Mike is now our treasurer," she said, praying she was doing it correctly.

"Thanks, Mike," Ruth said.

"I've made notes of all the suggestions we had earlier," Kelly said. "Do you want to go back to talking about the performance space, Maggie?"

"Yes," Maggie said with a grateful sigh. Once this meeting was over she was going to grill Kelly on how she was supposed to run a meeting. Both her friends obviously knew more than she did.

For the next half hour suggestions flew back and forth about what the space should look like, how big it should be, and how practical it was to do it. Maggie's head was ready to explode with ideas, logistics, and possible problems. Kelly had steadily scribbled away in one of her notebooks.

Much to her amazement, the ideas began to take shape. All agreed that the stage was where they needed to expend their first efforts. The audience could bring folding chairs or blankets to sit on, much like they did for Shakespeare in the Park when it came to Whitefish. The large empty tract near to ART, already owned by the co-op, would be the perfect place for the events. The land had been cleared some time ago for an outdoor sports shop, but the owners had gone bankrupt before the foundation was poured.

"We're going to need a sound system," Jim said.

"A good one," James added.

"That costs money," Jim concluded.

"So do lights," Ruth said. "We're going to need a special kind of lights. It's light late in the summer, but we still want to be able to see the performer.

"Definitely," Mike agreed. "And that's another budget item." He, too, had started taking notes.

"What if it rains?" Makalia asked.

"For now," Maggie said, "we'll need to cancel. Later we can talk about adding a roof to the audience area."

"There's something nice about having the moon and stars overhead, though," Ruth said.

"Until they turn into clouds," Gabriella said.

Everyone chuckled.

By the end they had a plan and assignments.

"First thing we need are drawings and someone who can tell us what we need to build the thing," Jim said.

"I think I have someone," Mike was able to say before James could add a word. "A retired architect lives at the far end of the cove. He comes in for an afternoon once a week to watch the games and drink his beer. He's bored out of his mind, and he's spending too much time with his wife."

Another laugh made the rounds.

"Can you reach out to him?" Maggie asked.

"Will do."

"The next major item is fundraising," Gabriella said. "I know we can get donations for a lot of things, but we will need money, particularly for sound and lights." She looked at Maggie.

Maggie looked at Kelly who nodded.

"I'll take a look at that and come up with some ideas," Maggie said, an internal voice screaming "No!" as she did so.

But something inside her wanted her to make her mark. She'd never write the penultimate novel or create a lasting work of art, but she might be able to create a performance space.

## Chapter Four

"Glorious day," Tom said to Ryan who was coming down the stairs of Culver's. "Unusual for this early in April, but I'll take it after all the cold and snow we've had this winter."

"Could be global warming," Ryan said. "The weather's nothing like it's been for a long time. Sometimes it's hotter than usual, but remember that February cold snap, when it went below zero and just stayed there?"

"Yep. Seemed to go on forever."

"That's for sure."

"How's married life treating you?" Tom asked.

"Best thing that's ever happened. You know how you want a woman forever, even when you're young, and then suddenly she's totally in your life. It's a miracle." Ryan nodded toward the store. "When are you going to create your own? Everyone in town knows you like her."

"Even Maggie knows," Tom admitted. He kicked a small stone across the parking lot.

"Then what's the problem?"

"She wants to stay friends."

"What do you want?" Ryan prodded.

"I want to go out with her. But she's right. I don't want to lose what we've got either."

"I feel for you," Ryan said. "I'd suggest moving on, but I tried that, and it didn't turn out well. All I can do is hope she'll wake up to what's right in front of her and take you up on your offer."

"Thanks. You heading back to the point?" Tom gestured to the bag Ryan carried.

Ryan shook his head. "Back up to the studio—or at least that's where I'll start. Kelly has her weekly girls' night tonight. I'm banished. I'll do some work, then head upstairs. Larry and I are watching the latest Marvel movie. You should come, too. I've got more than enough snacks."

"I don't know."

"C'mon, man. It'll be fun. Better than moping after she turns you down again."

"How do you know I'm going to ask her out again? I could be picking up supplies."

"Instinct. Good luck with that." With a wave, Ryan got into his blue Explorer and headed for the road to his cabin.

Tom lingered in the parking lot for a few more moments, basking in the illusion that Maggie would finally say yes. Then he squared his shoulders and headed up the steps to the entrance.

There was a customer at the counter, so he wandered to the hardware section of the store. Maggie had put out the few gardening items she had, including some brightly flowered pink clogs for tiny feet. They made him smile. He had several nieces and nephews that he loved to spoil. He sent a quick text to one of his sisters asking for shoe sizes. As soon as he got her reply, he plucked a pair from the rack. He wandered down another aisle and picked up some aspirin and bandages. A third aisle brought a can of beef stew. By the time he made it back to Maggie, his arms were loaded.

"Oh hi, Tom," she said.

"Mike said you had a good meeting yesterday. It sounds like the performance space is really going to happen."

Maggie paled a bit. "I hope so. It seemed like a great idea when I thought of it. Now it feels like a mountain of work."

"But you've got a lot of people to help. You got them excited about it. It's going to be grand."

"Thanks." She smiled at him, looking directly into his eyes.

There was a connection there. He could have sworn it.

But she quickly looked away and held up the clogs. "These don't seem either your style or your size."

He laughed. "A niece."

"Lucky girl."

"She is. My sister is a great mom."

Maggie nodded. "She learned from a master. I always

wanted to trade mothers. My mother was so flakey. You got the one who actually had warm cookies waiting after school."

"But I also had chores, watching over my sisters, and maintaining my grades while you had the run of town. The grass is always greener."

She laughed.

He loved her laugh.

The door opened with a clang.

"Hi, Mom! I'm back!"

Teagan, Maggie's eighteen-year-old daughter came into the store, her footsteps barely making a sound as she walked toward them with a grin. "Two more months, and I'll be done with high school!"

He remembered that giddy feeling, that point in time when everything seemed possible, even marrying Maggie. As he watched her greet her daughter, he wondered what their life would have been like if it had turned out as he'd imagined it. She'd still run the store, and he'd still be a sheriff, but they'd have two or three kids and take annual vacations to Glacier or Yellowstone. They'd be the ones everyone admired: high school sweethearts who had made it.

Reality turned out to be quite different.

He threw his last few items into the bag Maggie had abandoned when she stopped to greet her daughter.

"Oh, I'm sorry," she said.

"No problem." He gave her a wave in preparation to leave.

"Tom, wait." Maggie turned to Teagan. "Can you watch the counter for a few? I need to talk to Tom."

"Sure. Let me dump my stuff on the stairs and grab a water."

"Want a cup of coffee?" Maggie asked Tom. "On the house. I'll meet you over by the tables."

"Sure." He had some time. In the town of Promise Cove, disasters rarely happened. That was fine by him. After pulling a sturdy cup from the stack, he dispensed the basic coffee Maggie kept brewed. No fancy blends or flavors. A pot of decaf was her only nod to other tastes.

He'd barely had time to contemplate the view out the window when she arrived, a large misshapen mug in her hands steaming with the coffee it contained.

"Bargain bin at ART?" he asked.

"Yep. Someone who'd taken a class or two, decided she wanted to be a potter, then gave it up after finding out her work wasn't getting rave reviews."

"I'm glad I never had the urge," he said.

"I wanted to be artistic," she said, her mouth drooping a bit at the corners. "While I wanted a *mother* who baked cookies and helped with the PTA, I also wanted to *be* Elaine. Her gift seemed so big, made it possible for someone as wonderful as my father to love her." She shook her head. "But no matter what I tried, I wasn't quite good enough. Someone always made sure to let me know that."

"Your mother?" He'd never thought Elaine was that cruel.

"Oh no. She always encouraged me to do whatever I wanted. Benign neglect. Probably how I wound up pregnant. I was doing what I wanted."

"Stop beating yourself up," he said. "It's a waste of time. You're a good mom, and you know it. Teagan's a great girl."

"Thanks, Tom. I just wish I was something more."

"You're enough for me," he said.

She looked away.

He cleared his throat. He'd crossed their unspoken line, a line he always wanted to vault across. She'd made it clear long ago, however, that he was supposed to stay firmly on his side.

Every once in a while, he slipped. Or his subconscious decided to test the waters. And every time he did, he achieved the same result.

Discomfort.

"So what did you want to talk about?" he asked.

"I need to find some extra help for the summer and beyond. I mean, what if my crazy mother never comes back from Paris?"

He laughed.

*Spring in Promise Cove*

"It's possible," she protested.

"Anything's possible, but I already have a job. I can't work for you."

"That's not what I mean, and you know it. I just thought, since you do a lot of work in the community, you might know a teenager looking for work. A good teenager. You know, the kind that shows up when they say they're going to. The kind that actually works instead of looking at their phone all day."

"Tall order," he said. As he sipped his coffee, he mentally went through the list of teens he knew. Unfortunately, the reason he knew them was they'd been in trouble of some sort, not the kind of worker Maggie was looking to hire.

"My cousin's kid," he said. "Sandy is looking for work. She's basically a good kid."

"Send her over," Maggie said. "I need to get this settled."

"Will do."

"Thanks."

"Anytime." He was tempted to tell her he'd do anything for her, but that would head into dangerous territory.

He was tired of this dance. Maybe he should take a risk.

"Would you like to go out for burgers sometime after Mike gets his grill up and running?"

Her expression read disappointment.

"We've been over this. We're just friends," she said.

"Friends can have dinner."

"Not in this town. And definitely not you and me."

"Lunch then."

"And where would that be?"

He shook his head. The only place to get lunch in town was right where they were sitting.

"We could go to Whitefish or Kalispell. No one would see us there."

"The answer is still, no. I'm sorry. I know you want more." She stood. "I just can't give it to you."

He watched her walk away, each of her steps increasing his desire for her.

# Chapter Five

Why did Tom continue to ask her out? Maggie had made it clear she wasn't interested.

She should be interested. He was the total opposite of the rich boy she'd fallen for, Teagan's father. Paul Lee had been rail thin, good-looking in an Eastern big-city kind of way. Elaine always said he had a "patrician nose." Maggie had interpreted that to mean "snooty."

Elaine hadn't liked him very much.

"He's phony," she'd said. "He'll hurt you, and then try to buy you off."

Paul had shown up one summer while Tom was away at law enforcement training. Paul had completed law school, and he'd wanted a break before starting in the family firm. As the summer had worn on, he told her he loved her and wanted to become a fishing guide instead of returning to Virginia.

The fool she'd been, she'd believed him. By the time she knew she was pregnant, he was long gone, back to his life as an attorney in the family firm in Richmond, Virginia.

But that hadn't been the worst of it.

She rolled a cart filled with boxes down the aisle, stopping at the cereal area. Deciding which brands to carry and which to leave off took far more of her mental energy than she wanted. There were certain staples: Betsy from the post office only ate Raisin Bran, and Rose Doolittle, who kept track of everyone's comings and goings from behind her living room curtain, lived off of Cheerios. In the summer, Maggie made sure to have plenty of packages of small boxes of cereal, the staple of most of the families who camped at the state park a half hour from town.

This is what her life had brought her to: contemplating the lives of people based on their choice of breakfast.

*Spring in Promise Cove*

Most of the afternoon rush—kids back from school, parents picking up something for dinner, and the after work crowd emptying the frozen meals she stocked—had already come and gone. Another hour of stocking and paperwork and it would be time to call it another day in the long series of such days.

Her only excitement was the development of a performing arts center. That project had her scared to death. She was so totally going to fail. And then everyone would hate her. They'd never come to the store again. She'd lose the business, the one her father had built, and her mother's heart would be broken.

Unless her mother never returned. Would she do such a thing? What had possessed her to decide to leave in the first place? Was the insanity hereditary? Would she book an African safari in her own dotage?

Maggie shook off her thoughts. She was being ridiculous.

She moved on to the crackers.

Teagan breezed back out from the upstairs apartment. "I'm done with my homework," she called. "I'm going to see what's up with Rebecca. I'll let you know if I'm staying for dinner."

Rebecca and Teagan had been best friends since junior high.

"Sure," Maggie said to Teagan as her daughter walked out the door.

Maggie had just finished with the cookies when the bell over the door clanged. She peered around the aisle.

A man about her age stood in the doorway. If he was younger, he'd look like one of the blond surfer dudes that were featured in half the television shows set in California. But his hair was graying at the temples, and his clothes spoke of wealth rather than water.

"Can I help you?" she said as she walked toward him.

His smile showed off his even white teeth.

"Hi, I'm Justin Thomas," he said. "I've just rented a vacation place near here for a few months. I'm looking to stock up on a few things."

"Hi." She put on her brightest smile. "I'm Maggie Marston, the newly elected mayor of Promise Cove. Welcome!"

"I can see I've come to the right place," he said, holding up a piece of paper with his left hand. "I've got a list."

No wedding band.

Of course that didn't mean anything.

And really, she shouldn't be looking in the first place.

"Well, that depends. If you need a few staples or emergency items, this is the perfect place. But if you want to outfit your house for the stay, you're better off going to Whitefish like most of the folks around here."

"Why would you send people somewhere else?" he asked.

"Because it's the right thing to do." Her brow wrinkled in puzzlement. "Why would you do anything else?"

"I don't know. The stores where I come from would offer to order things for you first. So they don't lose the business, you know."

"And you're from?"

"Southern California."

"You're not in California anymore. If you plan on staying long, you'll need to adopt Montana ways." She walked to the counter. As much as she expected him to be from the golden state, she was a little disappointed. Californians were a dime a dozen in Montana, and most Montanans wanted them to return south.

He laughed as he followed her. "So you're one of those who thinks Californians are a blight on the Montana landscape."

She forced a shrug. "Doesn't matter to me. Now, what do you need?"

"C'mon. Don't be like that. I don't bite. I'll be a good neighbor. Promise. Besides, I'm betting after a while I'll grow on you."

"So does fungus."

He laughed again. "I think I like you, Maggie Marston. Maybe I should ask you out for a drink. You do have a place to drink in this town, don't you?"

"Moose's Saloon is right up the road. Now what do you need?"

He handed over the list, releasing a pleasant aroma of ponderosa pine vanilla.

She starred at the block letters written in deep black ink, the writing of a take-charge, confident man. Looking up, she met his gaze, his pale blue eyes hinting of a summer sky over crashing surf. Heat rose in her body.

"Maggie, I need your help deciding which color to use." Elaine swooped in from the back of the store and came to a stop next to the counter.

The spell broke as Justin turned his attention to her mother.

"You must be new in town," Elaine said.

"Justin Thomas," he replied, holding out his hand. "I've got a vacation rental."

"Oh? Where?"

Justin described his rental property.

"Ah yes. The Scotts ... or was it the Lewises? Well, one of those families built it in the 1940s. Good solid construction. But there was some kind of feud, they had to sell, and some rich East Coast businessman bought it and never used it. Now his daughter rents it out." Elaine smiled with triumph at Justin. "How long are you staying?"

"I'm not sure about that right now. It depends on the business."

"And what business would that be?"

"I'm a developer."

"I see," Elaine said, her smile freezing on her face.

If Maggie didn't do something quickly, the situation was going to devolve. She grabbed a pen and rapidly checked items on the list. "You'll find these on our shelves," she said, handing the list back to him. "The rest you'll need to get in Kalispell or Whitefish, like I told you earlier." She picked up a basket from the floor next to her. "This should hold your shopping."

"Thank you," he said. "I appreciate the help." He nodded at Elaine. "And the info about my rental cabin. I'll get my things, and then maybe we can discuss that drink."

He headed to the first aisle.

"You're a fool if you go out with him," Elaine said.

"As foolish as running off to Paris to a man you don't know? Stay out of my life, Mom."

"He's just like Paul. He'll lead you on, hurt you, and leave."

"It's *my* business. And I'm not the same naïve girl I was back then. So drop it. Go paint or something."

"In some ways you haven't changed a bit. You still can't see the wolf in a high-priced suit. Why don't you go out with Tom? He's a good man."

"Tom, Tom, Tom!" Maggie hissed. "Everyone wants me to go out with Tom. Well, *I* don't want to go out with Tom. He's my best friend, and that's all he's ever going to be. If I want to have drinks with a man, I'm going to."

"You're making a mistake," Elaine said and left.

A few moments later Justin returned to the counter. "This is what I could find. I also found some razor blades that I needed. You didn't check them off."

"That's because I can't stock them as cheaply as the big box stores. You'd be better off getting a set at Costco or something."

He shook his head. "It's going to take me a while to understand what makes you people tick."

"Old fashioned values: lend a helping hand—especially if someone needs a pull from a ditch in the winter—and don't cheat. Not too difficult."

He laughed.

It was a nice laugh, not hidden or over the top. Like Baby Bear's chair, it was just right.

"So that will be all?" she asked.

"That and a commitment for a drink tonight. I obviously need more lessons on Montana culture since I'm going to be here a while."

Clearing her throat, she said, "I think you're all set."

"When does the store close?"

"Six p.m. on the dot." In the summer she'd stay open until nine, but she'd always closed at six to spend time with Teagan.

She wouldn't have that excuse anymore.

"Then that's when I'll pick you up," he said.

"Oh. Okay."

He nodded and headed out the door.

What had she just agreed to do? It was a small town. If they showed up at Moose's a little after six, the whole town would know she'd gone out with someone other than Tom by seven p.m.

By eight, everyone would have an opinion about Maggie's dating choices.

She was doomed.

# Chapter Six

Justin was as prompt as his word. The mud and dirt covering the lower third of his brand new GMC Yukon Denali testified to its off-road use.

"Nice car," she said, fastening her seatbelt. Warmth from the air in the car as well as the heated seat surrounded her in a cocoon.

"I spend a lot of time in it. Reliability and comfort are important. Where are we going?"

"About a half mile down the road."

He laughed. "We probably should have walked."

"It gets pretty cold once the sun goes down." *What were they going to talk about for an hour or so?* She hardly knew him.

"True. I've actually been in Montana for a few years, mostly down by Bozeman, working on a development near Big Sky. I'm used to the swings in temperature."

The vehicle rolled almost silently down the pavement. Moose's Saloon was easy to pick out, even in the approaching dusk, by the abundance of cars in its parking lot. The front of the building was rough planed wood stained a dark brown. Large circular lights pointed down on the sign spelling out the name in red letters.

Justin found a parking spot at the end of a row fairly close to the door. He got out and rapidly walked around the door, ready to help her out. He looked directly into her eyes as he took her hand.

"I'm quite sure you don't need the help," he said. "But I like the little courtesies. I hope you don't mind."

"Not at all." Her father had had the same gentle manner.

As soon as they walked in the door, she scanned the room for people she knew. She'd have had an easier time looking for people she didn't know.

*Spring in Promise Cove*

Kelly and Ryan were seated at the bar, each with a glass of red wine. Instinct must have made Kelly turn to Maggie just as the door closed behind her and Justin.

Kelly tilted her head and raised her finely shaped eyebrow.

As they walked to an empty table, a number of people nodded and waved. Soon—maybe in a half hour depending on how the text messages flew—the news that she was having drinks at Moose's with a stranger would be known to half the people in town.

Tom would be one of the first to know. He was well connected to all forms of communication in the town.

Guilt nudged at her. She pushed it away. There was nothing to feel guilty about. She was a free agent.

Justin held her chair for her as she sat.

"Nice, friendly place," he said, taking his own seat. "Is it the only one in town?"

"Pretty much. If people want something to eat locally, the store serves breakfast and lunch. Promise Cove Sweets serves great ice cream, but that's about it. Although Moose's is going to be adding burgers and fries soon."

"What do the tourists do for food?" he asked.

"Campers bring their own, and the inn up on the point serves both breakfast and dinner. It's not that far to Whitefish. That's where almost everyone goes for a serious date. But mostly, people cook at home. There are a few groups that gather together to have evening meals and try out new recipes, too."

"Sounds like a nice, relaxing town."

"We like it that way," she said, giving him a grin.

After looking around, presumably for a waitress, he asked, "What do you want to drink?"

"Beer will be fine, thanks."

"No chardonnay?"

"Not every woman drinks white wine," she said.

"I'm fonder of the ones that don't," he said, then rose to get their drinks.

She dug her phone out of her purse and studied it, praying the flush in her cheeks would quickly die down.

Around her the sounds of conversation—some murmurs, some rising in volume as drinks were consumed—rose. The aroma of hops permeated the wood of the place. Someone had put quarters in the old-fashioned jukebox, and Florida Georgia Line was making people tap their feet or fingers along to the beat.

"Mike seems like a great guy," Justin said, sliding the beers and a few napkins on the table. "He told me he wants to open a micro-brewery." Justin indicated the drinks. "These are a few samples I persuaded him to give us."

"You must be good," she said. "Mike doesn't hand out samples to just anyone."

"Well, I may have dropped a hint that I was here with the mayor."

She glanced at the bar. Wearing a grin that promised a grilling, Mike waved at her.

Trying not to think about the questions she'd have to answer later, she took a sip of the beer. Liquid with a slight hint of bitterness soothed by the sweet flavor of honey refreshed her taste buds. She took another.

Next to her, Justin was nodding. "If this is the quality of what he has to offer, I may have to invest in his start-up myself."

"I doubt he'll take investors," she said.

"He's got a GoFundMe page."

"Oh." Everyone had hopped on the fundraising bandwagon. "I may have to start one myself."

"Why? Is the store in trouble?"

"Oh no," she said. "We're building a performing art stage." She took another sip then continued. "You see, there are a lot of visual artists around. They formed a co-op and have a store."

"Yes, ART. Nice place."

"They even have a website."

"Smart."

"But that leaves the performing artists out in the cold," she said. "Kelly is a talented pianist who could have gone pro. And there's a singer-songwriter who just returned from doing a recording session in Hawaii. There have to be more in the area. We just haven't identified them, yet."

"It's got to be hard to find time alone for any length of time if you're a performing artist," Justin said.

"We've got a pretty good airport nearby. And actors have been buying second homes in Whitefish for decades. Julia Roberts owned a house up here for a while. It's a great place to renew and rest. Promise Cove is really good at protecting its residents, too."

"You don't blab," he said with a grin.

"Only to each other."

"And yet, here you are, blabbing to me."

Once again she looked straight into his eyes, and excitement pulsed in her veins. Her mother was right. Justin Thomas *was* dangerous. He reminded her of Paul.

Nonsense. She was older now. As long as she protected herself, she could enjoy his company. It had been too long since she'd had anyone to take her out.

Probably her own fault. Tom had certainly asked.

She looked over at Justin. He was observing the people around them, so he didn't notice her gaze.

He was so different from anyone in town. Did her attraction to his citified good looks and fancy car show how shallow she was? Or was there more to the man?

His gaze zeroed back in on her, and energy pulsed through her.

"How far have you gotten on this project to build a performing arts stage?" he asked.

"We've had a meeting."

"That far?"

"Yep." She grinned at him. "But we had good results. We have a list of things we need to do, and Mike is developing a budget for what we need to purchase. Most of the work will be done by volunteers."

"Tell me more," he said.

She did. He turned out to be a great listener, asking insightful questions, and adding good points to the plan. After a while she had to dig out a few scraps of paper from her purse to take notes. They'd finished the first set of beers and started on a second by the time the topic was finished.

"You know," he said, "I might be able to help you with the sound and lights."

"Really?"

"Let's just say I know people who know people. Sometimes theaters and concert spaces upgrade. We might be able to get what you need at a low cost or even for free."

"That would be amazing! You could do that?"

"I believe I can."

Then she paused. The performing arts venue was supposed to be a community project.

"Problem?"

"Um ..." She was the mayor, wasn't she? If it benefited the group, they shouldn't have any objection. "No. No problem."

"Hi there," Kelly said. She and Ryan stood by their table.

"Oh hi," Maggie said.

"We were headed out, and thought we'd stop to say hello." *Since you didn't bother to introduce us* was implied in Kelly's tone.

"Justin, this is one of my close friends and her husband, Kelly and Ryan Svoboda. Guys, this is Justin Thomas. He's renting a vacation place for a few months."

"Good to meet you both." Justin rose and shook hands with them. "Ryan Svoboda. Quilts?"

"Yep, that's me," Ryan said with a grin.

"I saw some of your work over at ART. Very impressive."

"Thanks," Ryan said.

"And Maggie says you're a talented pianist," Justin said to Kelly.

"I've trained to be a concert pianist," Kelly said with a professional smile. "I took some time off to raise a family, but I believe I'm ready to get back on a stage."

"I look forward to hearing you," Justin said. "Maggie was telling me about the plans for a performing arts center. Sounds ambitious."

"It is," Ryan said. "But it's amazing what people can do when they work together for a common purpose. Maggie's a great leader. If anyone can get it done, she can. And I can't wait for my wife's first concert." He gazed at Kelly with a sweet smile. "I feel like I've been waiting decades."

"Because you have." Kelly's glance at her new husband was equally heartfelt.

Their pleasure in each other seemed to solidify into a bubble around them, enclosing a secret known only to the two of them. After a few seconds, Ryan placed his arm around his wife's waist and said to Justin, "It's been a pleasure meeting you." He nodded at Maggie. "Take care."

"And call me as soon as you get a chance," Kelly said over her shoulder as they headed toward the door.

"Small towns," Justin said with a grin.

"Yep." Maggie moved her glass around the wet circle it had left on the table top, an ache forming below her breast bone. How she longed for what Kelly and Ryan had.

"What about you? What does a developer do, exactly?" she asked.

"Figure out the best way to use a piece of land."

"What if the land doesn't want to be used? Or the people around it don't want it to be developed?"

"Then the negotiations begin," he said. "Everyone has a say. Trust me. The feds, the state government, the largest landholder, even environmental groups weigh in. There are so many parties with opinions it's hard to keep track sometimes."

"And when everyone's done talking?"

"We have a solution that is satisfactory to everyone." He shrugged. "Or I walk away and find someplace else. It always turns out the way it's meant to be."

# Chapter Seven

Maggie dreaded her regular Wednesday get-together with Alex and Kelly. As she'd predicted, the entire town knew she'd been out with Justin Friday night. For days she'd fielded questions, some subtle, and some not-so-subtle, from people just "stopping by" the store for a few things.

With a sigh, she swiped some lip gloss over her lips and ran a brush through her hair. Justin had invited her to his place some evening for drinks and snacks, but so far she'd put him off. She wanted to go, but what was the etiquette for going to a man's place the first time? Especially, if she didn't want anything more than drinks, snacks, and a little conversation?

The whole thing would seem more intimate than it was.

"Thanks for taking over," she said to Elaine as she was getting ready to leave. "I do appreciate it." Maggie made a note that she'd taken a bottle of wine and some chips from the store inventory into her account book.

"It's fine," Elaine said. "I know how much you enjoy time with your friends. It's good for you. Will Ryan be there, too?"

"He's heading up to his quilting studio. Although he says he's going to work, he'll probably hang out with Larry and watch a show. Kelly says he enjoys being able to do things like that. They can still be their own people who want to be in a relationship, instead of a couple who doesn't know who they are when they're apart."

"Are you going out with Justin again?" Elaine asked.

"Maybe. I haven't decided."

"I take it he's asked."

"Yes."

"I know you don't want to hear this," Elaine began.

"Then don't say it."

"I have to. I saw what happened to you when Paul broke your heart. You are so much like your father. Both of you see the best in people and their potential: what they could become if they only took a different path or viewed things through an alternate lens. What you don't understand is that people are resistant to change. All of us. We're hardwired to do the same thing over and over again."

"And expect different results," Maggie said.

"No. That's the point. We don't really expect different results. We want the same ones."

"What you're saying has nothing to do with Justin. You just don't want me going out with him." Maggie picked up her bag. "You said it yourself. You think I need to have some fun. That's all I'm doing with him: having fun."

"What I'm talking about has everything to do with seeing Justin. You're picking the same kind of man that Paul was. At some level you must know you're going to get the same results."

"Justin is different."

"Oh, Maggie."

"Butt out, Mom. I'm in my forties. I think I can make my own decisions now, don't you?"

With a wave, Maggie left the store. It was all she could do not to stomp.

# # #

Maggie parked her car in the lot at Kelly's house. Taking the path around the side to the entryways, she paused where the path opened up into the central grounds. The late afternoon sun revealed sprouts of daffodils and a few crocuses already baring their purple heads. Buds swelled on the native bushes Kelly's grandmother, Henrietta, had planted. Next to the flower beds, a vegetable garden surrounded by a high deer fence sprouted early greens: chard, spinach, and leaf lettuce.

Beyond that garden, Maggie could see the edge of the first guest cabin, Athena, named for the goddess of art. Although she'd longed to inherit her mother's gift with a paintbrush, Maggie had only been blessed with her father's organizational skills. With a sigh, she headed for the kitchen door that headed into the mud room next to the kitchen.

"Hey, girlfriend," Kelly said, embracing her in a hug.

"Hey, yourself." Maggie held her friend for a few seconds. After not seeing each other for decades, their close childhood friendship had quickly warmed when Kelly returned to Promise Cove.

Alex burst through the door just as they went into the kitchen.

"Who is Justin, and why did you have drinks with him?" Alex demanded once she'd greeted them.

Kelly raised her palm. "All in good time. Let's get the feast together. Then we can interrogate the poor woman."

"But we have to talk about Kelly's next retreat first," Maggie said.

"And maybe the progress on the performing arts space," Kelly added.

"You two are awful!" Alex said. "What can I do to help?"

Kelly directed them to a picnic basket and cloth bag. She picked up a cold sack that clinked with bottles. "Serving dishes and tableware, including napkins, are already out there."

"Of course," Alex said.

"It's the way I am," Kelly said. "You ought to know that by now."

"Oh, we do," Maggie said. "And we bow down to your hostess prowess." She gave Kelly a mock bow.

"Just don't expect it at our house," Alex said.

With a laugh, they headed to the firepit. Mid-April was pushing the limits of when they could be outside after sunset, but Kelly had piled the chairs high with quilts. Soon wine would heat them from the inside.

Beyond the firepit the lake shimmered in the pale light of a sliver of an early moon and the fading sun. Maggie breathed in the pine scent around her, letting nature sate her before telling them everything she knew about Justin.

"I did meet him," Alex said. "He came into ART while I was doing my shift."

"You turkey," Maggie said. "What did you think?"

"He was born to be a surfer dude," Alex said.

"Certainly looks like one." Maggie tried to keep her attraction out of her voice.

"Yeah." Alex's voice took on the stubborn tone Maggie knew so well. She had something to say and was already prepared for Maggie not to like it.

Maggie wasn't ready to hear it yet. "You wanted to talk about the retreat," she said to Kelly. "The one you're planning for June."

"Yes," Kelly said, thankfully taking the hint. "I've sent out invitations to the women who've come to the retreats more than once in the past. I've told them there are only four slots, but the responses are coming in fast.

"I'm going to use the format like I did last time as a basis," Kelly continued. "I've made adjustments based on feedback I got from Ruth, Susan, and Alex. I was wondering, Maggie ..."

"Yes?"

"Would you like to come this time? I mean ... not that you can't handle it ... but with your mom going to Paris and Teagan leaving soon, you might want a place to express your feelings."

"Somewhere other than with Justin," Alex sniped.

"You can be a pain sometimes," Maggie shot back.

"I don't want you to get hurt. He's power hungry, just like the rest of them."

"You don't know anything about him."

"I know the type. Just don't trust him, Maggie. Okay?"

"He's fine. I'm fine. I don't need anyone's help. And I don't need the retreat. Thanks. But no thanks."

"I understand," Kelly said, her voice soothing. "Up to you. The offer stands. I won't be able to put you up, but you're welcome to attend the sessions."

"You should go," Alex said quietly. "It was more helpful than I thought it would be. Without that support, I might never have started dealing with Sean's death. I finally gave away the clothes that were in his closet and dresser. There's still more to do, but it's a start." When she looked over at

Maggie the toughness was gone, and a glimmer of vulnerability shown through.

Maggie clasped her lifelong friend's hand. Alex had always been prickly, but it had intensified after Sean had died in America's longest war. Alex's edges had hardened, and the spark of joy that had always been part of her had faded.

Could the retreat help her the way it had Alex? Or would Justin be the one who would finally jolt Maggie into fully living life again. Even if he only stayed for a little while, it might be worth the risk to see what the man had to offer.

She'd have to think about that some more, but not now.

"What about food?" Maggie asked.

"Ruth wants to cater the retreat. Since she doesn't work in the school kitchen in the summer, she thought she'd try her hand at creating menus and serving them. She's working with David to get some of his amazing vegetables to use in her recipes. So far it looks great. And Charlene Bird is going to supply the breads and sweet rolls we need for the morning."

"Sounds like you have everything in hand."

"Logistics are easy," Kelly said. "It's the emotional work that makes running these retreats so taxing. But now that I've settled into a daily routine of piano practice, I've remembered how much music fills me. It will give me strength to help people who are hurting or need to remember what's important."

Although it hadn't been her life's work, Kelly had slipped into her grandmother's shoes far more easily than she had first thought when presented with her unexpected inheritance. Maggie wasn't sure she'd have that much flexibility.

"Let's eat then," Maggie said. "I'm starved. Then we can talk about the performance center."

She'd do anything to prevent any more conversation about Justin.

## Chapter Eight

Things at home went on as normal. Elaine was in the store kitchen most mornings with Gregg coming in later to help out. Teagan moaned about school never ending, but participated fully in the rites of late senior year. She'd even been one of the officers of the class, helping to plan the prom and senior trip to Seattle.

Maggie was proud of her daughter. Teagan may have been raised by a single mom and a madcap grandmother in a small town in Western Montana, but she'd turned out okay. And she was going to get the full college experience. No family emergency was going to keep her in this little town. Maggie was determined to make sure of that.

But who could fault her father for dying that beautiful summer day? He'd been pottering in the backyard, creating his annual display of color when a heart attack made him lie down. He'd died before they could reach the hospital.

The garden had lay in neglect ever since. Occasionally, Elaine hired someone to bushwhack the tall grasses and try to assemble some order, but it quickly reverted to its wild nature.

Maggie stood on the back porch early Monday morning and imagined what her father had once created. It would be nice to build something like that again, only more in tune with nature. Maybe a small grouping of aspens surrounding a pool. She could almost imagine a she shed, a place solely hers, without her mother's prying or the need to tend to anyone else.

She'd get a rocking chair, a good music system, and spend her time reading and rocking.

Heaven.

With a sigh, she pushed off the post she'd been leaning against and walked inside to open the store. By noon she was bored. Even the regulars weren't stopping in. Apparently, their need for gossip had been satisfied. All the stocking was caught up, and she was going to have to resort to dusting the shelves.

Outside, the sun and blue sky taunted her. Within her, the turmoil over what to do about Justin Thomas churned.

She needed to get out of here. She called upstairs.

"Mom, I need to take a walk," she said. "Can you run the store for a while?"

"A walk? Where? Whatever for? You never take walks?"

"Can you just help me out without giving me the third degree?" Maggie asked.

"I want to protect you. It's a mother's job, you know."

"And who is going to do that while you're gallivanting around Paris?"

"Don't get snooty with me, young lady."

"Mom." Maggie drew out the word, exactly as she had as a teen. This time she left out the eye roll.

"I'll be down. Give me ten."

Maggie used the time to gather a bag of snacks and bottle of water, and to stuff them into the backpack that hung on the hooks at the back of the store. All her life they'd left their outerwear in the same spot.

Her hiking boots were below the pegs, and she pulled them on.

"Thanks," she said when Elaine finally reached the counter. "Everything's set. I'll be back in a few hours."

"Okay," Elaine said. She touched Maggie's arm. "Be safe."

"I will." Maggie felt the strength of her mother's love wrap around her. No matter what, she'd never had to question if her parents cared.

She burst through the front door and hustled down the steps like a kid running to recess. Playtime! Coaxing her old Yukon onto the road, she headed north. About ten miles from town, the space between the road and the lake widened, making room for a small but impressive craggy hill. A little-used trail went up its side. The final third was a difficult climb through rocky twists and turns, but the destination was worth it.

After parking at the trail head, she took a moment to inhale a lungful of air. Springtime in the Rockies was its own special part of heaven. Stilling, she listened, waiting to hear something beyond the caw of crows and ravens. A red-tail hawk made its classic screech in the far distance, the sound familiar to television audiences as a stand-in for every large bird swooping overhead.

Shouldering her pack, she began the trek. Mossy rocks and ferns lay at the edge of a swampy enclave where a few cedars held out next to a stream heading to the lake. Here and there, under the protection of a rotting log, fairy slippers peeked out, tiny patches of lilac and yellow. She took her time and concentrated on simply being where she was. It took some effort, but soon the daily chores, concerns about her daughter, and tangle of feelings about Justin faded.

The path followed the stream as it made a bend up the mountain, producing small waterfalls of crisp, clean liquid. She paused and took a photo of a sunlit water curtain flowing over smooth rock, as it had done for eons before she stood there.

Sliding the phone into her back pocket, she continued to follow the stream as it narrowed and poured from ledge to ledge before free flowing a dozen feet, only to tumble off another rock. This water was a spring miracle. In summer it was barely there, if at all. By fall, it was a dry canal waiting for the snowfall to amass, thaw, and fill it once again.

Nature's cycles. Uncomplicated cause and effect. Why couldn't human lives be so simple?

When she reached the twisty part of the trail, she stowed her phone inside the pack, and started to climb, often grabbing a tree trunk or rock outcropping to steady her legs. Her muscles complained about their use in unexpected ways. She'd be aching in the morning.

Finally she reached her destination: a fifteen-foot cataract that crashed to a deep pool below. A good flow of water already sped past. In another month it would be overwhelming.

Just like her life.

From the ledge by the pool, she could see a chunk of the lake stretching out in front of her. Here and there hard-to-get-to homes dotted the shore. Blackened trunks covered a swath of the forest to the west of the lake. The fire had only occurred a few years ago, but already the base of the burnt trees would be covered with new growth: grasses, deciduous shrubs, and tree shoots that had been waiting a long time for a little sunlight.

Maggie allowed her thoughts to return to her problems. Everything was changing, and she was going to have to change with it, no matter how much she didn't want to. She'd known she was going to have to let Teagan go on to her own life, and she had been mentally preparing for that.

It would be tough at first, but then life would right itself and continue with its inevitable routine. That should be enough, shouldn't it?

But her mother's decision to go to Europe had shown the first light on the fragility of that plan. Justin's arrival had shown her the cracks.

What ... exactly ... had she done with her life? Nothing she'd done made a hill of beans difference. Yes, she'd raised a good daughter and kept the store afloat for her mother and the rest of the townspeople, but was that enough?

That could be one of the reasons she'd resisted dating Tom. He was more of the same. Was love between two people a significant enough purpose to take up space on earth? Didn't there need to be some grander gesture?

Did someone like Justin have more to offer? He could expose her to the world outside of Montana, maybe prompt her to find a true calling. But was his work developing things for humans to use any more important than supplying the needs of everyday people?

A crow landed on a nearby rock and stared at her, tilting its head one way, then the other, as if trying to determine if she had anything good for him: a morsel of food or a shiny trinket.

"What do you think, guy?" she asked him. "Should I go out with the newcomer and risk a broken heart like my mom fears? Or will it turn into the most amazing relationship of

*Spring in Promise Cove*

my life?"

The crow hopped off the rock and stuck its beak in a cluster of stones, emerging with a tiny insect it gulped down. Then it turned its head to stare at her with one gold-rimmed eye. He cawed at her once more, then flew off, no longer bothering with her concerns.

She laughed. Maybe she was making too much of the whole thing. It was only drinks, not a lifetime commitment.

Digging into the pack, she pulled out her water and snack. As she munched, she stared at the lake. The few houses near the shore, along with their matchstick-sized decks in the water, looked like they belonged to a diorama an elementary school kid had crafted. Life sure had been simpler in elementary school. The hardest thing was stringing words together to make a complete sentence. Math had come easy to Maggie, and she'd loved to get lost in a book. But writing something her teacher praised took a while longer.

"It will come when you're ready," her mother had told her. "Don't worry. You're a wonderful girl."

Her mother had always been in her corner, supporting her through the tough times, explaining the changes that came with puberty well before they hit so she knew what to expect, and drying her tears when her first crush had broken her heart in fifth grade.

It had been some boy who'd only been there for a year, and his difference from the kids she knew had been honey to her. She'd never felt that way about Tom. He was her friend, a steady companion, not a boy to dream about when she lay awake in the middle of the night.

She'd tried to think of him that way, but it didn't work. Even in high school, she was grateful one of the football players asked her to the prom before Tom could get up the nerve. She never would have had the heart to turn him down, but she wanted to go to the most significant dance of her life with an exciting boy.

Not the friend who was steady and true.

# Chapter Nine

Tuesday afternoon, Maggie arrived at Moose's about fifteen minutes before the meeting was to start.

"Hey, Mike," she said as she walked into the bar. "What happened to spring?" Yesterday's warm tease had disappeared, and she'd needed to bundle back into her winter coat for the trip over.

"It's just Ma Nature's way of letting us know who's boss. At the end of the day she'll retake the planet, and we'll just be a footnote in the mud."

"My, you're gloomy today," she said.

"Ah, it's the clouds. I'm susceptible to the end of a long winter just like everyone else." He placed his fist on the edge of the polished bar and leaned on it. "Truthfully? I'm a bit lonely, too. It's hard to go home at the end of a good day and have no one to share it with."

"So why don't you have someone?" she asked.

"That's too long a story and will make a gray day even grayer. You go on in now, and I'll bring in some water and glasses."

She gave him a second glance as he went around the bar to the storeroom. He was on the short side with a muscular build, broad shoulders that narrowed to the thickened waist of middle age. His full mustache was still black, although his head was shaved, and his brown eyes usually glinted with humor.

Why *was* he still single?

She headed to the back room. She should be worried about her own lack of company instead of Mike's.

The committee arrived quickly, eager to get started with the next phase of the planning. Maggie had studied the book on running a meeting that Kelly had suggested, and she had her trusty gavel with her. A few minutes after two she called the meeting to order and had Kelly read the minutes from the previous meeting.

As her friend did so, she was amazed at how much they'd actually accomplished. Most of it was in terms of assignments, but it was a start.

"As for the treasurer's report," Mike said, "we started with nothing, we added nothing, we subtracted nothing, and we still got nothing."

Everyone laughed.

Ruth opened her purse and took out a dollar. She passed it to her left and indicated it should go to Mike.

"And now we have a dollar," he said with a smile directed to the cafeteria lady.

Ruth looked around. "Okay, folks. Cough it up."

There was a rustle of movement as everyone dug into their wallets and passed dollar bills to Mike.

"Gotta begin somewhere," Ruth said. "If you seed the kitty, more will come."

"Money attracts money," Jim said.

"And more money," James added.

"Okay, let's get to business," Maggie said. "What did your architect friend say?" she asked Mike who had finished stuffing the ones into an envelope.

"He actually created a draft plan," Mike said. "He was so excited to have something to do, he even went to Whitefish and got us copies." Mike passed around a stack of papers.

The set included an artist's rendering of what the center would look like as well as a blueprint of the structures.

"He realized that we'd need a building at the back of the audience for a sound system and lighting board," Mike said. "Don't want that stuff getting wet if it rains."

"We'll probably need poles to hang the speakers and lights," Makalia said.

"He mentioned that," Mike said, "but didn't want to add it until we'd approved the drawings. Then he'll also give us a materials list as well as more detailed drawings."

The group spent time looking at the drawings and making suggestions, but they were minor details. The concept Mike's friend had developed fit perfectly with what she'd envisioned. The stage area was spacious, allowing enough room to slide in an acoustical backdrop or curtains, as well as staging areas to the left and right of the performance space. Iron rods were available for side curtains, and more steel bars capable of holding heavy lights or sound equipment were snugged near the ceiling.

"Getting this built, as well as the equipment we need is going to require a good deal of capital."

"Kelly said she'd work with me on that," Gabriella said. "I understand she's really good at getting those with more than the rest of us to open their wallets and provide more than a dollar."

"Well, I don't know about that …" Kelly protested.

"According to her daughter," Alex said. "Her feats of fundraising are legendary in Palos Verdes Estates."

"Lisa talks too much," Kelly said. "But I'm happy to partner with Gabriella. As soon as Mike tells us how much money we need, we'll get started."

"I may have some news on that front as well," Maggie said.

"What?" asked Jim.

"How much?" James added.

"In a moment, gentlemen," Maggie said. "First, do I hear a motion to approve the drawings with the suggestions we've agreed on?"

"Oooh, listen to you, Madam Chairwoman," Alex teased. "I so move."

"Second," Ruth said.

The drawings were quickly approved, as well as a grateful thank you to be given to the man who'd created them.

As James discussed the prep they'd need to do on the land they were going to use, and Jim volunteered to get a crew together, Maggie ambled to the table to get some water. Running a meeting was more difficult than she'd realized, requiring ever-present vigilance so the group stayed on topic, but not losing some vital detail that was proffered by someone with a quiet voice.

"So what is this news you have, Maggie?" Jim asked

when they'd finished.

She took her seat again and told the group about Justin's connections and offer.

"Who is this Justin character?" James asked.

"He's staying for a while in one of the vacation homes," she answered. "He's exploring the area."

"Seems like a nice guy," Mike said. "Although he was seen having drinks with the mayor last Friday."

"You went out with him?" Ruth asked, voice rising in a feigned outrage that she hadn't heard about it yet.

She must have been the only one in town who hadn't heard it through the grapevine.

"It was drinks," Maggie said. "And just once. You are all making far too big a deal about it."

"He's a land developer," Makalia said.

Startled, Maggie looked over at her.

"He's renting the Scott's place. It's on the road up to my place." Makalia lived in a high steel and glass aerie overlooking Promise Cove. Before retreating to the woods, she'd run a successful web company in California, and still supported well-heeled clients from Montana. She was also the web developer for the ART center.

"Land developer?" Gabriella asked.

"He's just here to relax," Maggie said, trying not to sound defensive.

"Are you sure?"

"That's what he's told me."

"But he's not local," Jim said.

"This is a community project," James said.

"But Gabriella and Kelly are going to fundraise from people with deep pockets—probably the ones with second homes near the ski resort. They're not local either."

"We don't know him," James said.

"And—"

"Enough!" Maggie banged the gavel. "It's a generous offer, and I believe we should take advantage of it if it materializes."

"Here, here," Ruth said.

"I move we accept the offer," Gabriella said. With Kelly's

second, they agreed to accept anything anyone was willing to do for them, no matter what the source. Jim and James abstained.

After a few more items, Maggie gratefully called the meeting to a close.

"Whew," Kelly said as the participants left. "That was tough. You handled it marvelously."

"I'm going to strangle those two men if they keep talking like Tweedledum and Tweedledee."

"Oh, don't do that," Alex protested. "They're some of the best artists we have."

"Then get them to stop pushing me to the edge."

"We'll do what we can," Kelly soothed. "Now do something to relax before you go back to the store."

"Sure, I'll pop on over to the spa and get a massage," Maggie quipped, longing for the treat more than she would have thought possible.

Alex laughed. "You're right. We could use one of those here. Maybe Gabriella and Susan will add on."

Maggie and Kelly joined the chuckle.

"I think I'll chat with Mike a moment," Maggie said. "See you tomorrow."

Her friends nodded and left.

Mike whipped her up a mixture of orange juice, cranberry juice, and seltzer with a twist of lime, and left her alone as he prepped the space for the regulars who'd start drifting in around five. She sat on the stool and sipped, letting the tension of trying to corral too many people drift over her and slowly slip away.

The bar door opened.

She didn't have the strength to turn around.

"Drinking midday? It must be bad," Tom said as he slid on the stool next to her.

"It's non-alcoholic," she said. "And it was a long meeting."

"I have no doubt you triumphed." Tom nodded at Mike.

"Hah."

"Other than impossible meetings, how are things going?"

*Spring in Promise Cove*

"Fine." Was this a casual conversation, or was Tom going to get around to her few beers with Justin?

Mike slid a glass of Coke in front of Tim. "On the house."

"Thanks," Tom said. He turned back to Maggie. "Fine? In Maggie-speak that translates to 'just short of disaster.'"

"It wasn't that bad," she said, relaxing into their familiar companionship. "But tiring. I didn't know it took that much energy to keep people on track."

"It can be difficult. It takes a certain skill and not many people can do it well. You were born for the job."

"I'd rather have inherited my mother's artistic ability, or even some of it."

"Artists are great, but they need people like us to keep the world moving while they're lost in their muse."

She nodded and turned to look at him. He wasn't a bad looking man, although he didn't have Justin's striking good looks. There was more of a teddy bear quality to him, not the girth, but a high snuggle ability.

If a woman were inclined that way.

Which she definitely wasn't.

He stared back at her, as if waiting for the moment to turn into something else. He'd done that off and on over the years, waiting for the spark that he obviously felt to strike her.

It never had.

"Yes," she said, turning back to her drink. "With my mother off the rails, someone needs to keep the store going."

Tom nodded. "I may be able to give you a hand. My niece is looking for a job. Her dad's work hours have been cut, and her grandmother moved in with them after her husband died last fall."

"I'm sorry to hear that."

"Sandy was looking to head over to the community college and get a nursing degree, but money got tight, and she stayed home to help out. They live about halfway between here and Whitefish, just off the main road, so it shouldn't be too hard to get here. She's a steady worker, and I think she'd fit right in with you and Teagan."

"Thanks, Tom. Send her over any time. I'll be glad to talk

to her. Thanks for thinking of her. You're a good friend."

She'd known him too long not to see the pain in his face, although he did his best to hide it.

He nodded, drained his soda, then waved. "See you around, Maggie."

She stared at the closed door for a moment.

Why couldn't things be different? Either she needed to fall in love with him, or he needed to fall out of love with her.

What would either of those things do to the friendship she treasured?

## Chapter Ten

*Weird.*

Maggie stared at the magnet display. She'd received a new shipment from the local company that produced them a few days ago. When she'd snapped them to the metallic board, she'd arranged them as she always did, a formation that looked random, but made sense to her. She could easily tell which ones she was running low on.

It was rare that locals bought merchandise meant for tourists. But there were several magnets missing. She didn't remember selling any, but she'd need to check with her mother and Teagan.

Grabbing a bright yellow feather duster, she started at the far end of the store, where she kept things that were out of season. Currently, it was stacked with inflatable floats, fins, and paper picnic supplies. Soon she'd switch them out for snow shovels and de-icers.

But not quite yet. Although it was April, freak snowstorms had arrived in May.

Plugging one earpiece in, she turned on her cleaning playlist and hummed along as she dusted. The only way to get through the dreaded chore was to dance her way through it. Soon she was stepping and twirling, raising the duster over head as she pretended she was on a crowded dance floor in New York.

She sashayed down the household supplies aisle, tapped along the frozen food chests, and swung with the cans. Juice caught the jitterbug, and rice required rock and roll. Between the nonsense she was making up in her head, the volume of the tunes, and the gyrations of her body, she missed the clang of the doorbell.

When the young woman appeared at the end of the prepared foods aisle, Maggie dropped her feather duster on the floor. She flicked off the music.

"Oh hello," Maggie said.

"I'm looking for the store owner," the woman said, the statement rising at the end like a question. "I think her name is Maggie. My name is Sandy. I'm Tom Gerard's niece."

Her prospective employee must think she was a stark raving lunatic.

"Oh hi. I'm not usually ... um ..." Maggie waved her arm down the aisle. "Dancing?" She took a deep breath and forged on. "But I hate dusting, so I try to make it fun. It's nice to meet you. Let me ... uh ... take care of this, and we can chat. Would you like a cup of coffee?" She scooped up the feather duster.

"Oh yes, please." Sandy was what her mother would have called a beanpole: tall, narrow, and curveless. But her hair and clothes were neat and tidy, her nails clean and trim, and her brown eyes appeared intelligent.

Grabbing one of the guest mugs, Maggie handed it to Sandy and indicated the urns. "That would be one of the jobs I'd need you to take care of—making sure those are always full. We can go hours with no one wanting a cup, then a rush comes in and it's gone in fifteen minutes."

The young woman nodded. "I can handle that."

"Good. Let's go over to the seating area and I'll tell you more about the job." Maggie picked the only table with a clear sightline to the front door. Her mother was prepping in the kitchen, and Teagan hadn't arrived back from her friend Rebecca's house, so she was on her own.

"Tell me about yourself," she said to Sandy after they were seated.

"I'm almost a year out of high school," Sandy began. "I got good grades, and I was planning to go to college, but things happened, and I couldn't."

"I know. Tom told me."

"You're good friends with Uncle Tom, my mom says."

"Yes. We are."

"Anyway. I'm responsible—at least that's what my mom always says. I work hard. And I really want this job. You see, I want to go back to school and become a nurse, or maybe a nurse-practitioner. I want to stay in the community, be near my folks. I'm not one of those kids who's going to leave and never come back. You can count on me."

That had been a hallmark of the Gerard family. A person could always count on them, from the grandparents to their descendants.

Maggie described the duties and the hours she expected Sandy to fill. "It will pick up after my mom leaves in June, and more when Teagan goes to Bozeman in the fall. Then it will depend when my mother comes back."

*If* she comes back.

"Sounds perfect," Sandy said. "I can work whenever you need me. Like I said, I want to earn money so I can go to school."

The young woman seemed older than her years. Life must have been difficult for her family over the past year.

"Let's give it a try then. I need to get some paperwork for you to fill out. Do you need any more coffee?"

"No thanks, I'm fine."

The doorbell jangled, and Maggie looked up. Gregg waved as he came in. When he spotted Sandy, he strolled over to the tables.

"Hi," he said, holding out his hand. "I'm Gregg. I help out in the kitchen. Are you here for a job?"

"Yes," Sandy said, a light blush pinkening her cheeks. "Maggie just hired me."

"Great! You'll like working here. Maggie's the best. And her mother's a trip." Gregg had a big grin on his face.

A little tension left Maggie's back.

# # #

The morning may have been quiet, but everyone descended on the store as the clock struck eleven. The baked goods Charlene had delivered at ten disappeared off the shelves, clusters of neighbors chatted over coffee in the seating area, and a few people seemed to be stocking up for an apocalypse only they knew about. Elaine and Gregg started serving lunch about eleven-thirty, and the customers didn't let up until well after one.

Fortunately, Teagan had come home just as the rush was starting. Quickly taking in the situation, she dashed upstairs, cleaned up, and was ready to pitch in ten minutes later. They were perfectly synchronized during the chaos and kept things moving.

"Good job," Maggie told Teagan when the bulk of people left.

"Thanks. I love working with you." Teagan hugged her, and Maggie pulled her closer. No matter what else life had dished out, she had her daughter.

"Love you," she said and released Teagan.

"Can I go upstairs for a bit?" Teagan asked. "Rebecca and I worked on our history papers last night, but I want to go over mine one more time. It's a big grade, and I don't want to mess up."

"Sure. I've got this."

"Yell if you need me."

"Will do." Maggie watched her daughter head to their apartment. Interesting. Teagan hadn't stopped at the kitchen to say hi to Gregg. Maybe things were taking their course more rapidly than she'd thought.

She was ringing up a customer when the doorbell jangled. Her pulse quickened when she saw who it was.

Justin gave her a broad smile and a wave before heading down to one of the far aisles.

Her heart shouldn't be beating this quickly.

She nodded at whatever the customer was saying, bagged the groceries, and sent her on her way without understanding a word the woman said.

As soon as she left, Maggie smoothed her hair—even though it was a hopeless task. Checking her clothes, she whisked away a bit of dust that had clung to her blouse. Then she tidied up the counter while she waited for his return.

He was back with a package of frozen chicken breasts and a selection of leafy greens and asparagus.

"These vegetables look amazing," he said.

"We're lucky to get them. David runs an organic farm and greenhouse just south of here. He mainly supplies to the

Whitefish restaurants but always holds back some for the townspeople. They sell out pretty quick."

"I'll bet. Fresh vegetables in Montana in the winter and early spring are hard to find."

"Looks like you try to eat healthy," Maggie said.

"Yeah. I've done my share of carb binges. It worked when I was younger, but now all eating pasta or red meat does is sap my energy and make me feel bloated. Even my morning run doesn't change that. So I avoid them as much as I can." He grinned at her. "But that doesn't mean I don't love a good burger or a steak and potato piled high with sour cream now and then. I just can't do it very often anymore."

She nodded as if she, too, had considered the effect of what she ate on her body, as opposed to gobbling down whatever was handy to make for dinner that Teagan would eat. Working at the store had kept her metabolism high, but the reckoning would come.

"So ..." he said, leaning on the counter and staring at her with his deep blue eyes. "Have you thought any more about my offer of drinks?"

"I have." Her pulse picked up its pace again.

"And would you be open to having drinks with me next Friday at my humble abode?" His smile lessened, making him appear a gawky teenager asking out a girl for the first time.

She took a deep breath.

"Yes. I would love to have drinks with you."

# Chapter Eleven

During the week Maggie quickly realized Sandy was a godsend. She turned out to be everything she'd promised she was. Better still, she got along with Elaine and Teagan. In between the everyday chores, the meeting of the Promise Cove Renewal Committee, and running the store, Maggie floated about dreamily. She was going on a real date with a good-looking man. Not only that, but Justin was interesting to be with.

And he made her feel special. With someone like him, all the dreams she'd put on hold when she'd become pregnant with Teagan were possible.

She hadn't told her mother about her plans. No sense poking the beast unless it was necessary. With luck, her mother would miss her departure and assume she was doing something with friends, even though Maggie had spent most of her Friday nights home for the last eighteen years.

By Thursday Maggie wasn't sure what to do with herself. The end of April day was bright with sunshine and promise. The outside begged for her to come out and play. A hike was out of the question; she wanted to stay close in case someone needed something that Sandy couldn't figure out.

Maggie refreshed her cup of coffee and stared out her apartment window at the hills of the point that arced out into the lake, creating the cove that gave the town its name. It was there that the summer vacationers had first built homes, most of them sturdy log affairs, not the grandiose structures that dotted the mountain lifting across from it. Henrietta had created her retreat center there, and it was where Alex and Sean had made their home.

They'd been a perfect match, those two. Sean had smoothed Alex's rough edges, while she'd spurred him to be more open with his thoughts and feelings. When she'd gotten sick, he'd never left her side. When he'd died on his last tour of duty, Alex had sunk into a deep depression.

Maggie had never loved anyone to that depth. Although she'd been over the moon about Paul, when he'd denied the baby could possibly be his and refused to take a paternity test, her love had gone crashing to the ground.

Would she ever feel what Alex had felt, or what Kelly felt for Ryan? Would it be worth the cost at love's inevitable end?

Her gaze dropped to the tangled mess of the backyard. Physical work. That's what she needed. And the stretch behind the store was certainly in need of it. Wouldn't it be nice to spend a warm summer evening near her own firepit? She could put in a water feature. Hadn't her father had a small pond? There. She could still see the impression where it had been.

Energy pulsed through her. She dug out old jeans and a T-shirt, slid on some work boots, and headed downstairs.

# # #

An hour later she was sweaty, dirty, and unsure of what she'd really accomplished. Her first thought had been to cut the grass, but the old lawnmower had sputtered and died after a few feet, defeated by the tough western wheatgrass. Her father had tried to work with the native plants instead of imitating the green lawns of a city.

Maggie didn't have his skill.

But she did have his gardening books.

Eagerly, she charged up the back steps to the mudroom. Moving aside a stack of notebooks, numerous Mason jars, and broken clay pots, she uncovered what she was looking for, her father's copy of *The Montana's Gardener Companion*.

As she opened it, a sheaf of papers fluttered to the table. Quickly she scanned through them, her excitement growing as she looked. These were her father's notes outlining exactly where he'd planted what, the stones he'd placed, and the pond he'd dug.

The bones were there. All she had to do was unearth them and add a few touches of her own. The project would take much of the summer, but it would be hers. She wouldn't have to argue to achieve a consensus, or renounce part of her original vision to make everyone happy.

The backyard was hers to create, along with the ghost of her father.

"Thanks, Dad," she whispered to the heavens.

Grabbing one of the notebooks that still had blank pages and her father's master plan, she walked down the steps to the backyard. Starting from the area closest to the store, she walked the area, back and forth, uncovering more evidence of the old structure. With a trowel, she dug through a matted layer of dirt and exposed a section of one of the old slate stones her father had used for a pathway. Ridges of river rock, full of weeds, curved gracefully around raised flower beds. The pond she remembered had a stone cairn at one end that housed a pipe she could barely see. Maybe Tom could help her make sure it still worked.

Gradually she got to the back which seemed to be left undone. Checking her father's notes she could see that he'd planned a small arbor back there, just as she'd envisioned, although he hadn't made a space for the she shed she wanted to add. He must have run out of time.

They had all missed the signs. Would it have made a difference if he'd gone to the doctor for his growing fatigue, rather than simply thinking he was working too hard?

Would her own life have been different?

Water under the bridge, her mother would say.

That was true, but sometimes Maggie couldn't help but wonder, what if ... A life lived was a series of choices. Unlike a choose-your-own-adventure book, a person couldn't live the same years over again on a different path.

With a sigh, she looked around again. She'd plant bee- and butterfly-attracting flowers in the raised beds and add birdhouses near the shrubs against the house so small birds could hide from overhead predators if they needed to. There would be more in the back by the arbor she planned, but she was either going to need to figure out a way to get full-grown

*Spring in Promise Cove*

trees back there, or wait a long while for them to grow.

Her budget would never cover full-grown trees.

Best to start with the places that needed nothing other than elbow grease.

Strolling to where the pond had been, she wrote down a list of the things she'd need to do to get it running again. Her hand hesitated over Tom's name next to the plumbing. If she was going out with Justin, would Tom still be willing to help her?

Of course he would. He was her friend. No matter what. That's what they'd sworn to each other in fourth grade. Friends forever. Pinky swear.

She smiled when she thought of the innocent kids they'd been. Nothing had been more important than friendship. All the icky emotions about dating hadn't surfaced yet. What she'd give to go back to that naiveté, before she'd understood how duplicitous people could be.

When her dad, who'd loved her more than anyone in the whole wide world, had been alive.

She brushed off the stone bench he'd built by the pond and sat. She'd found a turtle by the side of the road once, she remembered. One of its flippers had been injured, run over by a car most likely. It had looked up at her with its beady eyes, and she knew she had to rescue it.

Carefully, picking it up by its shell, she'd raced home to Dad. The pond was only a few weeks old, but he'd suggested that might be a good place for the injured reptile.

"He'll be able to get insects there. I'll add a bit more mud to one end of the pond so he'll have room to burrow."

"How long will he live?" she'd asked.

"I don't know," Dad had told her. "That's the one thing about life we can't predict. Turtles like this one can live as long as 80 years."

"Wow. That's ancient!"

Dad had laughed.

They'd placed the turtle in the pond. He'd stayed for about ten years, then driven by some unknown urge, had climbed out of his home, found a hole under a fence board, and disappeared.

By that time, though, she wasn't really interested in turtles. She was off to college to take on the world.

The following year her father had died.

Maggie swept a tear from her eye and went to the toolshed for a pitchfork and some hand tools. The first step was to dig out the grass that had invaded the rocks around the pond. It was going to take dismantling part of the wall, but she'd do it right.

Just like her dad would have done.

### # # #

"What have you done to yourself?" Elaine asked when Maggie finally dragged herself into the house.

"I've been working in the back." Maggie pushed open the door to the space she and Teagan shared. Once her daughter had become a toddler and curious about everything, she and her mother had reconfigured the upstairs so Teagan and her mother's art supplies did not have to co-exist in the same space.

"I've been unearthing the pond," Maggie said with a grin, standing in her doorway. "I'm going to redo the whole backyard. Make it like Daddy had it. And maybe add a few changes of my own." Hard work had never felt so good. She was going to feel sore tomorrow, but now when she looked from her apartment to the back, she'd be able to see where the pond once was.

"Why on earth would you do that?" Elaine asked.

"Because I want to. You have your art and your trip to Paris. Teagan is starting her own life. The backyard will be my summer project." Something she could share with the ghost of her father. There were times she'd been working when she could sense him next to her.

"I never could understand your father's obsession with digging in the dirt, but I'm glad you have something to focus on besides the store … and that new man in town."

"I'm going out with Justin Friday night," Maggie announced.

"That is a bad idea. You are asking for it."

"Maybe I am. But it's my life, my choice, and from now on keep your disapproval to yourself!" She walked into her apartment and pulled the door hard behind her.

It closed with a satisfying thud.

# Chapter Twelve

How long had it been since she was on an official date?

Maggie got into her car and double-checked her face in the rearview mirror one more time. No smudges on her lipstick, and none of the color on her teeth. Check. No mascara clumps or drips; eye shadow had stayed where it was. Check. Hair as good as it got.

Check.

After searching the road for oncoming vehicles, she pulled out onto the main highway. With the warmer weather, tourists often sped up on the road on Friday nights, hurrying on their way to their summer retreats, not thinking about the people who actually lived in the small towns they whisked by, in spite of the slower speed limits.

She automatically checked for Tom's patrol car parked out of sight behind the ART building.

He was there, concentrating on the screen in front of him. He looked up for a moment when she passed and gave a wave.

She pretended she hadn't seen him, eyes straight in front of her, hands at two and ten. But her stomach knotted just the same.

Was she betraying him?

Elaine was wrong. Dating Justin was going to be the best thing that ever happened to her.

She turned off the highway onto the smaller paved road that led up the mountain. Here the pines came closer to the road, darkening the pavement so it was more difficult to see. She flicked on her headlights. The road curved as it ascended, and she slowed.

As she rounded the corner, a fawn was caught in her beams. It stared at her, unsteady on wobbly legs.

"Where's your mom, little one?" Maggie whispered.

The fawn continued to stare.

Maggie idled the car patiently. Mama had to be somewhere.

Sure enough, a doe popped her head out of the brush on the left. When she spotted her offspring in the middle of the pavement, she trotted over and nudged it, as if to say, "Come along, now."

The fawn roused itself and finally finished crossing the road.

Smiling, Maggie put her car in gear and continued up the road to Justin's house.

Like most of the recent structures in the area, the building was made of logs stained a dark brown. Sheets of glass lined the front, and stumps below indicated where trees had been felled to let in the light. A good-sized deck extended over the gradual slope below.

"Come on up," Justin said over the railing by the stairs leading to the deck. "I've got everything ready."

Climbing the stairs made her more winded than she normally was. At the top, Justin pulled her in for a brief hug.

"It's good to see you. I have everything set up here. I figured we could sit out here as long as we wanted, then move inside. Sound okay?"

"Absolutely fine. This is for you." She handed him the bottle of wine she'd selected from the store's pricier choices.

"Nice," he said, looking at the label. "You have good taste. Let me take your things. I'll put them inside while you get settled." He gestured to the well-padded metal chairs placed near a glass-topped table.

Instead of sitting, she walked to the edge of the deck and stared out at the view of the darkening lake. At its edge the sun was settling into the treetops, providing a sky full of pinks and yellows. The wind rustled the new leaves on nearby trees, probably chokecherry or aspens.

"Breathtaking," Justin said as he came up behind her. "I don't think I'll ever get tired of looking at that view. Especially this time of day. How can you get anything done around here?"

"Unfortunately," she said as he handed her a glass of

wine, "too often we stop seeing it. We can get stuck in the mud like everyone else."

"I suppose. We're always rushing around too much to stop and actually live our life."

She nodded.

"Tell me about yourself," he said. "What was it like to grow up here?"

"I suppose you could say it was magical."

"Did you go skiing a lot at Big Mountain in Whitefish?"

She laughed. "We had a few school trips there, but no, skiing downhill wasn't a big part of my life. It's pricy and requires an hour drive each way. My parents weren't skiers, so it was never a family thing. When I was a teen, I tried snowshoeing and cross-country skiing. I liked *that* kind of skiing, but I haven't been in years."

"Maybe we should try it come winter," he said.

"Are you going to be here in winter?"

"Could be. Depends on how everything works out."

How many layers were there to that statement?

"So cross country in the winter and …?" he asked.

"Working at the store, hanging out with my friends, school work … the usual. In the summer I still worked at the store. But we'd be at the beach almost every day. And a lot of kids had canoes and kayaks. We'd all trade off."

"Sounds idyllic."

"It was in some ways." She and Alex had always been together, except when they'd have one of their spats, usually brought on by her inability to tolerate her friend's sharp edges on a particular day. But there had been a group of them who would meet up at the beach. As she'd gotten older, the nights lingered, and there was often a campfire where pairs coupled off. Sometimes there were kisses in the dark of the night, and some of the bolder girls had snuck off into the woods with their partners.

Maggie hadn't been one of them.

"Hungry?" Justin asked, gesturing toward the platters and napkins he'd put on the table. There was even an ice bucket with a second bottle of wine at the ready.

Remembering the fawn on the twisty dark road, Maggie

doubted they'd open it.

"Yes, thanks." She sat and partook of the spread of cheeses, meats, nuts, olives, grapes, and figs. Rounds of crusty bread and multigrain crackers added to the feast.

"You've gone all out," she said. "This is wonderful."

"Nothing but the best for my guest."

"I hate to ask, but have you heard anything from your contacts in LA about the possibility of lights or sound equipment?"

"Not yet, but some of the leads sound promising. Have faith. It will happen. How's that coming by the way?"

She told him about the meetings and showed him the architect's drawings that she'd captured on her phone.

"Nicely done," Justin said. "Rustic enough to fit into the area, but it has everything you need to produce the versatile productions you're planning."

The warmth inside her wasn't only from the wine.

"Thank you. Now all we have to do is get it built."

"I'm really amazed you've been able to get this far," he said. "Doing things by committee can be difficult. Not everyone will be satisfied, but somehow they have to all pull together. If one person is marching to their own tune, it causes discomfort. If a group fights you all the way, the whole thing comes tumbling down like a house of cards. You have to be a strong leader to get it right. You should be proud of yourself."

As his words flowed over her, she glowed from within. People rarely understood what it took to run a committee.

"It can be exhausting," she admitted. "But I've done it before. Last year I put together the Promise Cove Summertime celebration."

"I bet it was a smashing success."

"We raised a lot of money, and everyone had fun, so yes, I'd call it a success." She smiled at Justin. "So what about you? What has your life been like?"

"Nothing as normal as yours. I was raised on the East Coast, went to a state school in Connecticut, then headed West. I'd always wanted to see California, but my parents never wanted to go. Family vacations were a house on the ocean in Maine or the odd trip to Orlando for the theme parks."

"Sounds nice."

He shrugged. "It was. My parents gave me a good childhood and a great start in life. They may not have had any desire to go to California, but they had plenty of connections. Once I was there, it was easy to find a job in the field I wanted."

"Land development."

"I know it sounds odd," he said. With a chuckle he added, "I can't imagine an elementary school kid saying he wants to be one when he grows up."

"Me either."

"I knew I wanted to build things on a grand scale, leverage the best in what the land had to offer, and provide recreation and homes for people. Once I learned more about the environment, I wanted to do it in a more sustainable way."

"I'm glad to hear that."

He nodded. "It's important. There's only so much earth to go around."

"What are you working on now?"

"Like I said, I finished a large project, and I've scheduled some down time. There are a number of potential projects people have contacted me about. I'm trying to decide my next move. It would be nice to stay in Montana, though. This state sure does have some nice people."

His gaze was steady on her, leaving no doubt of his meaning this time.

She sucked in a breath and looked away. With a will of their own, her fingers grabbed a grape and popped it in her mouth. Unable to speak, her hands went back into action, shredding one of the rounds of bread.

"Sorry. I didn't mean to make you nervous." Justin put one of his hands on hers.

She tingled from the warmth and stopped fidgeting.

"You intrigue me," he continued. "I'd like to get to know you better."

"You mean date more?"

"Yes. That's exactly what I mean."

"What did you have in mind?" She slipped her hand from his and managed to slide a slice of cheese on a cracker.

"Well," he said, his voice drifting down to a suggestive lower register. "I was thinking of dinner in Whitefish, perhaps next week? I've got a potential client I need to see—maybe you can borrow my car and take care of any shopping you need to do for an hour? Then I'll take you out to one of the fancy restaurants. How does that sound?"

"Sounds like a plan," she said, her insides tumbling with excitement.

She was going on a real date. Her life had gotten in gear again.

Hallelujah!

# Chapter Thirteen

"When did you notice it was missing?" Tom asked the woman who'd filed the complaint.

Mrs. Frank, a lifelong housewife who had moved to Promise Cove a decade ago with her retired husband, nodded. "I haven't used it since last May, so I only just noticed it. It's part of my Memorial Day decorations. I have things for each month's holiday, you see. Except August. August is always a problem." She looked at him earnestly as if it should be immediately clear to him why August was a problem.

His expression must not have given him the answer she wanted.

"August has no holidays," she said.

"Ahh. I see." Although he didn't see at all. "Where did you keep it when you didn't display it?" he asked.

"The vintage postcard was framed," Mrs. Frank said. "I kept it in the space where all my framed decorations go—in the closet by the guest bathroom. Sometimes I don't get them back right away, and last year was very busy. I had three grandchildren graduating, and I always do something nice for my sons on Father's Day. And the flag needed to be cleaned for Flag Day. June is an awfully hectic month." She shook her head.

He was exhausted even thinking about all the possible excuses a determined woman could use to decorate.

"And where do you keep things that you haven't quite put away?"

"Well, sometimes I lay them on the top of the washer. That's right next to the closet." She said it as if it should be obvious where they would be.

He jotted the note on his pad. "So it could have disappeared any time in the past year," he said.

"I'm afraid so."

"And how many people come in and out of your house during the year, besides family, I mean." While a family member certainly could be responsible, people tended to get their feathers ruffled if he suggested it.

"Oh dear. Lots of people. Let's see, the book club, sometimes the knitting club, then there's the garden club, and the parent-teacher group. I've had a few socials for my church. And there are my friends. They're always dropping by to have a cup of coffee. It's a busy house, sheriff."

"And your husband?"

"He's usually out fishing, or over at our son, Bud's, place. You see, Bud was the reason we originally moved here. He and my husband have always been close. Yes, my husband is often with Bud."

Smart man.

"Anything else you can remember? Anything that looked odd to you?"

"No, no. Everything last year was quite normal. Except for the fire, that is. I hope that doesn't become normal. I was scared out of my mind."

"Everyone was, Mrs. Frank." He stood. "Well, if you think of anything else, let me know, okay?"

"Do you think you'll find it?"

"I'll do my best," he said.

She escorted him to the door, closing it gently behind him. The large red, white, and blue wreath decorating the front barely quivered.

As he walked back to the patrol car, he mentally added this new theft to the few he already knew about. The community had a pilferer, that was clear. Odd things had gone missing. A wood carving, small coffee cup, and one of an expensive set of earrings had all been reported. It sounded like whoever was taking these things was an impulsive thief.

He got into the patrol car and checked for any new messages. Then he headed back to the highway and turned south toward Culver's General Store.

Someone there may have connected a particular woman

to the small thefts. And it probably was a woman. All of the groups Mrs. Frank mentioned tended to be female-centric.

A few minutes later he parked the car and walked up the steps to the store. Just prior to lunch, the place was busy for a Monday morning.

His niece, Sandy, was behind the counter with Teagan. The two young women were chatting with customers as they worked together to tame the line in front of them.

Wandering the aisles, he searched for anything he might need, denying who he was really looking for. No sign of the woman he still wanted, in spite of all of her rebuffs. No matter how hard he'd tried to date others, his heart still clung to hope that Maggie would reconsider.

By the time he worked his way back to the counter, the line was almost gone. He smiled while he watched Teagan and Sandy work. His niece seemed to fit right in, but Tom's gaze focused on Teagan.

He'd been a substitute for all the things fathers were supposed to do with their daughters, from cheering at her T-ball games to escorting her to a father-daughter dance. She confided in him when things weren't going well at home and let him in on her dreams for the future.

When she spotted him, she gave him a big grin. "Hey, Tom. Grandma's got an amazing panini going for lunch. You should stay."

His stomach rumbled in agreement.

"Put in my order," he called.

Teagan nodded as they finished up the last customer.

"How's it going?" he asked the pair when the lull finally came.

"Great," Sandy said. "Thanks for getting me the job, Uncle Tom."

"I didn't get the job for you," he said. "I only mentioned your name. You did the rest."

"Tom never takes credit for anything," Teagan said. "But he's the best."

"You almost ready to graduate?" he asked. "I'm looking forward to watching you get your diploma."

"Don't worry. I've already got your ticket," she said. "I'm

just hoping I don't have to beg for one for anyone else."

"What do you mean?" he asked, although he suspected he already knew.

"Mom's all goo-goo over this guy named Justin. She even went to his house on Friday for drinks. She came back all smiley and happy."

So that's where she'd been going Friday night. Part of his happiness bubbled deflated. He masked his unhappiness with a smile. "Well, good for her. I'm glad she's getting out."

"Why hasn't she ever gone out with you?" Teagan asked.

"Ah ... well ... she has her reasons. I've asked."

"I hope I'm not that dumb when I'm older." Teagan shook her head.

"Don't talk about your mother that way," he said.

She looked startled. "Sure, whatever."

"How's everyone doing?" Maggie breezed in from the corridor leading from the backyard. Her hair was tousled, and she had a smudge on her left check.

His heart leapt all over again.

"Hey, Maggie," he said.

"Oh, hi, Tom. Is everything okay?"

"Um, sure. Can I chat with you for a few moments?"

"Sure. I just came in to get some water and check on the girls. I'm working in the backyard. In fact, I have a question for you, too. Come on back."

She led the way down the hall to the porch that descended to the backyard, currently an overgrown feast of grasses and small shrubs.

"I'm going to make this back the way it was," she said, excitement filling her voice. "But I want to improve it—make it safe and attractive for birds, butterflies, and bees. All native, too. No foreign invaders in my backyard."

"Seems like a big job."

"Are you saying I'm not up to it?"

"Oh no. Not at all. You are the queen of big jobs."

"I am. And don't you forget that." She poked him in the chest. "Let me tell you what I have in mind."

As she described the changes she wanted to make, he began to see it in his imagination. His memory conjured up

*Casey Dawes*

past visits with her and her father, especially the long talks he'd had with Maggie's dad. Jack had been a patient and sweet man. His dream had been to have a general store in a small town. With Elaine's support, he'd made his dream come true.

"I need your help with something," Maggie said. "If you're willing."

"Sure. If I think I can do it, I'd be happy to help you."

"Great. It's over here."

She showed him the work she'd done on the pond area. Although she'd dug out a great deal, the places where the plastic lining for the pond was revealed showed a few cracks. She'd be best off replacing it.

When he suggested it to her, she nodded. "I may have to wait though," she said. "Those things can be pricy. But more than that, can you take a look at the pipe? It's buried in the rocks. I think Dad meant it to be a waterfall, but it never worked correctly."

He crouched down to look at the pipe. Jack may have been a great guy, but he wasn't a plumber. He could see where the water would leak from several joints that gapped open.

"I'm probably going to have to disassemble the whole structure to see what needs fixing." And most likely replace the bulk of the parts. But he'd do that for her. Anything to be the one to put a smile on her face.

"Oh," she said, frowning. "I can't ask you to do that. It sounds like a lot of work." The disappointment deepened the creases that would become wrinkles as she aged.

"Well, let me see what I can do in my spare time," he said. "It would be good to work with my hands." He stood and looked around. "It's a great vision, Maggie. When you get done, it will be beautiful."

"You think so?"

"I do."

"Thanks, Tom. Now what did you want to know?"

Briefly, without going into details, he outlined what he knew about the small items missing from shops and homes all over town. "It's got to be someone local. But someone who nobody really sees because she ... or he ... blends in."

"Now that you mention it, I thought I had a few magnets missing a month ago. I haven't had time to do inventory to check it out." She shrugged. "Besides, they don't cost much. I figured if someone took them, they needed some beauty in their life."

"You're a kind woman," Tom said.

She shrugged. "It's as much a practical matter. Shoplifting is an unfortunate fact of life for small town storeowners."

"Maybe, but I still believe you have a heart of gold." She looked up at him, and for a second, the air between them shimmered, but then the illusion disappeared.

## Chapter Fourteen

Maggie locked the door behind her when she went upstairs to change for her dinner date with Justin on Thursday evening. Although her mother had a key for emergencies, a locked door was respected by both of them.

With a sigh, Maggie pawed through her closet, trying to determine the right mix of casual and elegant. Justin was taking her to the restaurant inside the lodge, since that was where he was meeting his potential client. That meant jeans were out. Somewhere, she had a nice pair of khaki pants. Combined with her favorite coral blouse and some gold jewelry, it would have to do.

She also pulled out a dark tan jacket. Restaurants were unpredictable. The temperature could be perfect ... or icebox cold.

With a last glance in the mirror, she squared her shoulders and opened the door.

Her mother was standing in the hallway. She nodded.

"You do me proud," she unexpectedly said, "in so many ways. But it's nice to see you putting an effort into how you look. I just wish it wasn't for that man."

"Mom ..."

"I know." Elaine held up her hands. "I worry about you, Maggie. It's a mother's right. You were so hurt before. I don't want to see it happen again. And—" Elaine clamped her mouth closed.

"Thanks." Maggie gave her mom a hug. "I'll be okay. I promise. It's dinner, nothing more."

"I know. I'll worry all the same if you don't mind."

"Well, I do mind, but I can't do anything about it. Any more than I'll ever be able to stop worrying about Teagan."

Maggie's eyes watered a bit as she looked up at her mother's familiar face, so overwhelmed by love for this

*Spring in Promise Cove*

woman who had taken such good care of her. Aware of the moment as well, Elaine pulled her close, squeezed her tight, then released her. "Go have fun! I'll mind the store and your daughter."

Maggie gave a wave as she half ran down the stairs. Justin should be here any moment.

Elaine followed more slowly.

Maggie stopped at the counter. "Now you mind Grandma," she told Teagan. "And do your homework. Just because you're a senior, doesn't mean you can slack off."

Teagan laughed. "I've got it covered, Mom. Now have fun on your date."

Elaine walked over to Teagan.

Teagan put her arm around her grandmother and said in a fake whisper, "Did you tell the boys when to arrive?"

"I did. And the rum is hidden behind the aprons. Your mother will never find it."

"You two!" Maggie said with a chuckle. Out of the corner of her eye, she saw Justin's Denali pull up. "Got to go!" With a wave she walked with a light step to where her date waited.

"You look nice," he said as she settled into the passenger seat.

"Thanks. You clean up well yourself." Justin's khakis had a firm crease down the front, and his pale brown shirt had subtle lines of chocolate and gray woven into it. A dark brown sports coat lay across the back seat.

He smoothly pulled onto the two-lane and headed south.

It was a picture-perfect evening, the May sun still high in the sky in the late afternoon. In another month, summer solstice would keep it bright for the long Montana summer day. Solstice celebrations were becoming more popular. Maybe the town should put one on?

No. She didn't need one more thing to do.

"My meeting shouldn't last too long," he said. "Maybe forty-five minutes, an hour. Is that enough time to do your shopping?"

"I decided not to go shopping," she said. "I'm going to stop at the gift store, find a trashy magazine or gripping novel, and spend some quality time sitting with a glass of wine on their deck overlooking the lake. Who knows?" she teased. "Maybe someone will come along with a better offer."

"Be sure you give me a chance to counter it before you ride off into the sunset," he said.

"Will do," she said with a grin that matched the one he was giving her.

"It sounds like a fine plan," he said. "Other than that better offer idea. But I really don't mind if you want to borrow my car and get something you need."

"I work enough," she said. "What I don't get is time by myself. Thanks for the offer, though." Truthfully, this big vehicle intimidated her a bit, and some of the streets from the lodge to the stores were narrow. Parking would also be a nightmare.

"Suit yourself. I imagine you spend a lot of time traveling to get the things you need for the store and your family."

"I spend a lot of time *planning* so I don't have to be on the road," she said.

"Smart woman. What was your degree in?"

"You're assuming I finished college. I didn't. My dad got sick, and I came home. My mom didn't want me to quit, but it seemed more important to me to be here than in Kalispell. I was only in the community college anyway." Her plan had been to complete the two years, then transfer to one of the state universities.

"That's too bad," he said.

"Mmm." It wasn't a subject she wanted to go into. Letting the silence drift, she lost herself in the flashes of light and dark across the pavement, echoes of the sun filtering through the pine trees that lined the road.

Justin adjusted the volume of the music he had playing—a soft playlist including Secret Garden—and she relaxed back into the comfortable seat.

# # #

The time on the deck had been perfect. Maggie felt comfortably warm and satisfied. Her white wine had been delivered by an extremely polite young man who'd made her feel a bit ancient, but the book she'd picked up in the store had proved to be well-written and engaging.

When Justin had arrived to get her, she was glad for his appearance. As she stood, his gaze drifted over her, a slight smile of approval appearing on his face.

"Ready?" he asked.

"More than ready," she said. "It's amazing how much of an appetite I can work up sitting around."

He chuckled. "I'm glad you have a sense of humor. It's a very attractive quality in a woman."

Her insides warmed with the compliment.

They walked across the lobby to the restaurant. Like many Montana high-end resorts, the emphasis was on wood, Western-themed paintings, and a trophy elk or deer head or two. This place had a stuffed mountain goat on a ledge in one of the recesses. It's what the well-heeled tourists expected when they came to the state, and most places delivered.

The restaurant was as she'd thought it would be: white tablecloths and hushed voices. The maître d' led them to a corner table near a window overlooking the lake, then held her chair for her while she sat. After handing them both menus and telling them, "Abby, your server, will be with you shortly," he whisked off on rubber-soled shoes.

A young man totally dressed in black stopped by to fill their water glasses from the sweating pewter-colored pitcher he held.

"May I?" Justin held up the wine list.

"Go right ahead," she said. With his level of sophistication, his choice was bound to be better than hers, which tended toward a chardonnay under ten dollars.

Justin ran his well-manicured finger down the list. By the time Abby got to them, he'd already discussed his options with Maggie and selected one.

"Busy place for a Thursday night," Maggie said.

"There's always some meeting or another going on here.

The fellow I met with was here from Oklahoma. Apparently he wants to talk about a housing development near Tulsa."

"That country is too flat for me," she said.

"Oklahoma can be surprisingly hilly," he said, "at least the eastern part. Although the highest point in the state—about five thousand feet—is in the western panhandle."

"Still not up my alley. Will you take the job?"

"I'm not sure. Like I told you, I'm at that point in my life where I'm considering my options. I did a lot of traveling in the first half of my career. It's time to settle down, maybe."

"Did you pick up a wife along the way?" she asked. The question had been nagging at her ever since their first drink.

"Unfortunately for her, yes, I did. It was short-lived. She had dreams of a family living in one of the places I developed, and I was too much on the go for her liking. I think she was afraid it was too easy for me to cheat."

"And did you?"

"Cheat? No. Never. I took my vows seriously. But eventually the lack of trust led to a split. She's still in the development married to another construction guy who concentrates his work in the Dallas area where she lives. They're happy; they have a family. And I'm happy for them."

His hazel eyes studied her. "And how about you? Ever married?"

"No. Things between me and my daughter's father didn't work out."

"That's too bad. It must be tough raising a child on your own."

"I had my mother to help. But seeing Teagan grow has been one of the most rewarding parts of my life. You missed out on having kids."

"I guess I did."

Their food arrived, and the conversation drifted to other topics.

"I've been thinking about your venue," Justin said as their dessert, a fluffy chocolate mousse with a raspberry sauce, was delivered.

"Oh?"

"The drawings you showed me are great, but a little

limiting. I mean, what if you wanted to grow, become a destination? Think of the revenue it could bring to your little town."

Mike had suggested the same thing.

"I don't think people want Promise Cove to become a destination. It's a sleepy small town that no one knows about."

"I'm not sure I'd agree," he said. "One of the people I contacted about the lights knew about this place. His wife, a steady working actress, had come up her for some spa or retreat or something."

Maggie nodded. "It belonged to Kelly's grandmother. She's running it now. But that's an intimate gathering. Nothing like you're talking about."

"I see." A spoonful of mousse disappeared between his lips.

"While I'm grateful you're helping out," she said as gently as she could, "we're doing this as a community. That means staying with who we fundamentally are. You're used to big plans and enormous undertakings. We're one step up from a bake sale."

He nodded. "I get it. I'll try to keep my enthusiasm under control."

"Thanks." She glanced out the window. Somehow the bright afternoon had turned gray. As she looked, a few flakes of snow drifted down.

"Was there anything about snow in the forecast?" she asked.

"Snow? Isn't it a bit late for that? Even here?"

"It's snowed in August in the mountains. It's rare here, but that appears to be what it's doing."

He checked his phone. "Nothing significant. And I've got the car that can handle it."

She nodded, feeling confident that he'd get her home safe and sound.

## Chapter Fifteen

The snow barely stuck, and by Saturday morning—the first official work session of the Promise Cove Renewal Committee and their helpers—the temperature was back up to the mild fifties.

Justin had walked her to her door after their date and made sure she could get in. There had been no attempt at a kiss.

She was still working out whether she was happy or disappointed.

But there was no time to think about it now. A dozen people were standing around waiting for her to tell them what to do. Fortunately, she'd found someone who'd be far better at that than she would.

"Hi, everyone. I'm sure you all know George Small." She held her hand toward the six-foot grizzled builder next to her. His name got the usual chuckles. "He's been building in this area for about twenty-five years. He's agreed to help us out with the construction." She leaned forward and did the rest in a mock whisper. "He's doing it for free, too."

Everyone clapped. George was the go-to man for the big houses. He'd helped Makalia build her dream home on the mountain. And normally, he didn't come cheap. But best of all, he was a genuinely nice guy, and people liked working with him.

"Thanks, folks. I'm glad to be a part of this effort. Although, I have to admit, I have an ulterior motive. I play the drums in my spare time. In fact, I've even got a band. Some of you may have heard me play."

"Hear! Hear!" Mike yelled from the back.

"Ah yes. My favorite bartender."

More chuckles.

"Anyway, I've looked over the plans and talked to your

architect. He's proposed a solid, simple structure that it won't take us long to build. If everything works out right, you should be able to put on your first concert end of summer."

"That would be amazing," Maggie said.

"But it's going to take hard work from you all. I'm glad to see some of you here know how to get your hands dirty." He nodded at Susan Thomas, who carved animals using a chainsaw for ART.

Susan pumped her fist in the air.

With a broad grin, George continued. "Here's what we're going to do today. Mike and I were out last week staking out the space. You can see that all around you. Pink streamers are the outside edges, yellow marks the stage, and blue the sound booth. Please leave those stakes where they are. Right?"

"Right," the small group chorused back.

"Then we'll concentrate on clearing all the large rocks and small bushes from within the space and a perimeter of about three feet around the pink stakes to give us room to build. Some of those bushes are going to take a bit of work, especially to get the roots out. Susan, would you pick a few people and be on root duty."

"Will do," Susan called out.

"When we've cleared the area, I'll get my man with the backhoe in here to dig down for the foundations for the stage and sound booth. We'll need manual labor to make sure everything is squared. The audience area needs to be raked out and mowed. Mike, I think you said you've scheduled a cement truck to come in and pour?"

"Yep. He's coming Wednesday."

"Well then, folks, let's get this done."

Two young men joined Susan on root duty, while the others fanned out to move rocks. George had them build a couple of rock piles, rather than toss them indiscriminately, saying they could be used for future projects to spruce up the venue.

Maggie smiled at Makalia who took a few pictures of the activity, then pulled on her gloves and went to work.

### #

A little before noon, Elaine and Ruth arrived with sandwiches and two big jugs of lemonade and water. Maggie's stomach growled at the sight. She and Alex quickly set up a couple of tables, and food was laid out. Then Elaine set up a small station with a bucket of water, soap, and a bunch of towels.

"Wash your hands before you eat!" she called out as people noticed the spread and dropped what they were doing.

"Yes, ma'am," one of the helpers said with a grin.

Elaine gave him a gracious smile in return, and the young man's cheeks reddened.

Even at seventy, Elaine could still make men look twice, no matter what their age. That guy in Paris didn't stand a chance.

Ruth's laugh pealed out, and Maggie glanced over. Something Mike had said must have struck Ruth as funny. The pair started laughing together, and Maggie had a sudden sense that there might be more between the two of them than a joke.

Then Mike moved on to get his drink, and Ruth smiled equally broadly at the next worker.

Maggie was simply imagining things.

"It's going well, don't you think?" Kelly stepped next to her. She'd arrived shortly after the food; her morning practice had taken priority over the work party.

"You'd have to ask George about that, but he's bringing the backhoe over, so he must be ready to dig."

"He was smart to have us start at both ends and work toward the middle," Alex said, joining them. "It shouldn't take long to dig out the two spots that need it. The operator is pretty skilled from what Mike told me, so he should be able to get it close to square with the machine."

"That'll be good. I can't believe we're starting," Maggie said.

"There was never a doubt in my mind you'd get this built," Kelly said.

"Me either," Alex added.

"I'm not the only one picking up rocks," Maggie said.

"No, but you're the one who got us to this point. Leadership is not something everyone can do—especially leading volunteers."

Maggie opened her mouth to protest again.

Alex shook her head. "Someday you're going to have to accept that you're good at this. Kelly may be able to make beautiful music come out of a piano, but you get people to work in harmony. And that, my friend, is a talent."

Giving up the fight, Maggie shrugged. "Looks like the line's gone down. Let's eat. I'm starving."

The three of them got their food, then joined Ruth and Elaine.

"Thanks for pulling all this together," Maggie told them.

"Hey, I'd much rather make food than pull bushes," Ruth said with a smile.

"And I'm happy to help you out whatever way I can." Elaine put her arm around Maggie's shoulders and gave her a brief hug.

Justin's Denali pulled up on the far side of the work site. Stepping around the stakes, he walked to their small group. She stood up to greet him.

"I was hoping I'd catch you on a break," he said. "It looks like you've accomplished a lot."

"We have. Can I show you the space, at least as much as we have now?"

"Sure."

She led him out of earshot of her friends and mother. "This is where the stage will be," she said, pointing to the yellow stakes.

"It looks like you have room to make it bigger, if you want."

"Promise Cove isn't comfortable with 'big.' We tend to like 'just right.'"

"You and Goldilocks."

"Yep. Not too hot and not too cold."

"Ah yes. So was I 'just right' on our date night?"

"The perfect gentleman."

"Hmm. I'm not sure if that's a good thing or a bad thing. I do have a reputation to uphold."

"Not in this town. You'll be an outsider for the next ten years, so there are no expectations before then."

"Tough crowd," he said.

She laughed.

"The second reason I came by was to see if you wanted to come up to my place tomorrow. I feel like cooking and make a mean chicken Marsala when I put my mind to it."

"Sunday's a busy day at the store. Especially with the weather turning nice."

"Then it's a perfect day to have someone else wait on you."

"I suppose Teagan could finish out."

"Best take advantage while she's still around," he said with a grin.

"Okay, it's a date." Her stomach fluttered. Would he get around to kissing her this time?

"I'm glad. I really like you, Maggie. I'm interested to see where this can go." He looked around. "Mind if I lend a hand? It might take some time off those ten years."

"Does that mean you'll be staying long enough to get to ten years?"

"I'm certainly considering it." He caressed her arm. "There are many reasons to stay."

She tamped down her hope. Paul taught her that outsiders weren't to be trusted.

But she so very much wanted to believe Justin was the exception.

"No one will mind if you pick one of the more back-breaking jobs," she said. "They'll be needing people to get the ends ready for concrete after the backhoe does its job."

"Sounds like the perfect choice. Is George in charge?"

"He certainly is. Do you know him?"

"It's a small state," Justin said. "At least in terms of people. Everyone in building development has pretty much heard of everyone else. I'll ask him where he wants to put me. And I look forward to our dinner tomorrow evening."

She looked up at him, and the air between them sparked

with expectation. Then he dropped his hand from her arm and headed to where George was talking with the backhoe operator.

Heading back to the group, she noticed the smirks on Alex's and Kelly's faces, and the frown on her mother's.

"Not one word," she said when she got to the women. "Not a solitary word."

"I had no intention," Kelly said innocently.

"None at all," Alex added.

Then they both burst into laughter.

Maggie shook her head. "Time to get back to work."

"Yes, Mayor," all four of them chorused before breaking into laughter again.

She turned and walked away, waiting until they couldn't see her before busting out a big smile of her own.

It was a great day to be alive.

# Chapter Sixteen

For once Maggie was grateful for the old-fashioned claw foot tub in her apartment. Normally, it was simply an impediment to a daily shower, but with every muscle aching, she gratefully immersed herself in the warm water silky with lavender-scented Epsom salts.

She laid her head back on the sloping tub and closed her eyes.

They'd accomplished everything they'd set out to do. George had been a marvel, directing people where they were most useful. Just when energy was flagging, Charlene Bird arrived with a mound of cookies. Tom had even stopped by after his shift.

By that time Justin had left.

She shouldn't care. She and Tom were just friends. But having him and Justin together would have made her uncomfortable. She refused to think about why that was true.

Instead, she took the sponge Kelly had thoughtfully brought her after one of her trips to California and soaked it in the water. She smoothed it down her neck and around her shoulders, the heat and aroma loosening her muscles from their clenched protest.

The vision she'd had last fall was going to happen. She could imagine Kelly, regal in a full-length concert dress, picking out the notes that would baptize the stage. While getting a piano up there would be tricky, Mike had assured her it could be done. He even knew someone who would lend them a small concert grand for the evening.

Miracles could occur. She simply had to be open to them.

Was Justin one of her miracles? He could be if he stuck around, or at least spent the bulk of his time in Promise

Cove.

Sandy was definitely a miracle. When the time was right, Maggie could make her a manager. Then maybe she could take longer trips with Justin, visit the big cities she'd always longed to, and maybe some of the world's must-sees, like the Grand Canyon.

She stuck a leg out of the water, stretched it, and flexed her foot. Then she repeated the effort with her other leg.

Part of her knew she was getting ahead of herself, but dreaming was important. The work on the performing arts center was proof of that.

With a sigh, she swished the sponge and cleaned off the rest of her body.

# # #

After making the same fuss over her appearance, she arrived at Justin's at seven the next night. She got out of the car and stared up at the evening sky. Through the open windows of the house, she could hear the clank of dishes from somewhere in the back.

She had a moment.

Her eyes searched for the scattering of stars that were appearing, locating the bright speck of Venus near the moon. She sent a message to whatever higher being there was that she discover the right path to take with Justin. If a few nice dinners were all there were, she'd live with that. She wasn't going beyond a few kisses with him if it came to that. She'd already made that mistake once and repeating it seemed like madness.

But what if there was more? What would that even look like? He was a mover and shaker, used to traveling the country to impose his vision on a piece of land. He probably knew government officials, heck, even the president. Those were the circles he moved in.

What could she possibly add to his life? And if she became totally involved with him, what would happen to the world she knew and loved in Promise Cove?

*It's just dinner.*

After a deep breath, she climbed the stairs to the deck. "I'm here!" she called through the screen door.

"Come on in," Justin called from the state-of-the art kitchen at the far end of the great room that framed the deck side of the house.

She slid the screen door over and entered.

"Beautiful night," she said, dropping her purse on the nearest chair.

"It's even prettier now," he responded with a grin.

With a towel thrown over his shoulder and his sleeves rolled up on a pale blue button down shirt, he looked very much the executive turned chef. His blondish hair was tousled, as if he'd run his fingers through it more than once, and the color of the shirt accentuated the bright blue of his eyes.

Definitely a candidate for the cover of a trendy men's magazine.

Her crop pants and high-end T-shirt weren't up to the same standards.

"I'd properly great you," he said, holding up his hands, "but as I was prepping, something got away from me, and I had quite a mess to clean up.""

There was a smudge of greasy flour on his chin.

Nice to know he was human.

Nodding at the wine in the ice bucket, he said, "Go ahead and pour yourself a glass and head to the deck. I'll join you in a moment."

"Sure I can't help you do anything?"

"Quite sure. Add another person to this mix and true chaos will occur."

She poured the wine and went outside. Leaning against the rail, she sipped her wine and gazed at the lake. Other than that year in Kalispell, this was all the home she'd ever known. Did that make her a shallow person? Uneducated?

Plenty of city folk would say she was a hick, but from what Ryan had said at some of their gatherings, there were people in New York City that never went beyond the few blocks of their neighborhood. She'd always been a big reader. As far as current events, she'd made it a point to look

*Spring in Promise Cove*

beyond the headlines and the social media memes that people scattered like wind-blown pollen.

Inexperienced and untraveled, but she wasn't an idiot. So far, Justin hadn't made her feel that way.

"You must be having serious thoughts to produce that frown on those pretty lips," he said.

She laughed. "Do you always talk like that?"

"I only seem to do it when you're around."

"And why do you suppose that is?"

"Simple. I like you. You make me feel good." He held out his glass for a clink, the bright tingle loud in the evening air. "I don't invite just anyone to see the mess I can make in a perfectly good kitchen."

"I've always found messes make the best meals," she said. "At least judging by the way my mother cooks."

"You don't?"

"I'm real handy with a microwave." She took a sip. "I'm a basic cook. My kid never starved, nor did she live on boxed foods. Like every kid, she hated vegetables, but she got past that."

"She's good-looking like her mother," he said with a grin.

"Would you *stop* that?"

"What? Complimenting you? Probably not. You look like a woman who hasn't had nearly enough of it. I can't imagine what that fool was thinking when he let you go."

Intensity snapped between them.

"His loss. He never got to meet one of the greatest people in the world."

"I look forward to getting to know Teagan better." He slid his hand down and took hers. "And you." He kissed the top of her knuckles.

She slipped her hand from his and took a step away.

"I brought out a small antipasto. Not enough to stuff us, but to keep us going until the potatoes are done."

"Sounds good." As they seated themselves at the table, her mind skittered around for safe topics. "When does your rental end?"

"Are you trying to get rid of me?"

"Not at all. I was wondering what your plans were. You said you had a meeting with the guy from Oklahoma. Do you have anything else you're considering?"

"There are a few projects: the one you mentioned, a coastal development in Oregon, and a golf community near Dallas. But there's one more that I'm really hoping will come through. It would keep me in Montana. As I told you, I'd like to stay for a while."

"Mmm." She tried to keep non-committal, even though her insides were doing a bit of jumping up and down.

"So, tell me, if your life hadn't gone the way it did, if your father hadn't gotten ill, what were your plans?"

"My plans?"

"What would you have done after you graduated?"

"Oh, that." She tried to remember who she'd been those decades ago. "After community college, I was planning to go to Missoula. I thought I might major in business. I had visions of working in a big city—maybe Seattle—at a company that would immediately see how talented I was." She selected an olive and held it between her fingers. "Schoolgirl dreams." She popped the olive in her mouth.

"Dreams are essential. If we don't have them, how can we ever accomplish anything? You should see what goes on in my head when I'm thinking about a new project." He chuckled. "Or maybe you shouldn't. You've already seen what a mess I can make of a kitchen." A buzz came from the phone he'd laid on the table. "Speaking of which, I think we're about ready."

Dinner turned out to be amazing: chicken Marsala, scalloped potatoes, and perfectly seasoned Brussels sprouts. He kept her entertained with stories of things gone wrong at construction sites. They were finishing their meal as he related one about a staircase.

"You'd think the guy building it would have known what he was doing. He'd been in the field for twenty years. But he built it upside down! Anyone trying to go down it would have slid right down the steps."

"What did you do?"

"Made him do it over, of course. Took the materials out

of his paycheck."

"I bet he never did that again."

"Nope. But better yet, he went home that night and left the woman that had been driving him crazy. You never know why people make the mistakes they do. There's so little you can really take at face value."

"You're a kind man," she said.

"Don't count on it. I drive a hard bargain."

"Really?" she asked, sliding into the state where she felt out of her comfort zone. What were they talking about?

"Definitely." He stared at her. "I'd like to kiss you if you wouldn't mind."

She nodded. It was way too soon, but she wanted to know.

His lips were gentle and lingered on hers for mere seconds.

Was there a spark?

She couldn't tell.

## Chapter Seventeen

Alex led the way, her long legs striding over boulders that Maggie had to dance her way through.

Her friend had entirely too much energy. Already Maggie was starting to sweat, in spite of the cool morning weather.

"Ouch!" Maggie cried as a pointy twig scratched her arm. "Some days I hate hiking."

"It's good for you," Alex called out. "You need to do more aerobics."

"My body is fine, thank you!" she called back.

"Hiking can be fun," Kelly said. "Especially with the right person."

"Not you, too."

Kelly laughed.

The only benefit to this long, tiring uphill walk, was that they had to go single file. There was no chance for her friends to quiz her about her relationship with Justin.

After that kiss, he'd pulled back, as if sensing the timing wasn't right. She was still trying to decide if she'd felt a spark, like she had with Paul all those years ago.

Was she so used to being alone that her body no longer knew how to react when a good-looking man made a pass? Was it still too early to feel a spark? Or was there simply no chemical reaction between them?

That was hard to believe.

She stared at the boulder in front of her. How was she supposed to get over that?

"Go around to the right," Kelly said.

She looked to the right where a rough-barked pine struggled to grow from granite. "Where?"

"Put your left foot there." Kelly pointed. "Grab the tree, swing your right foot around, and put it there." Again she indicated the spot. "Alex!" she called. "Can you give Maggie a hand up?"

"Right there."

"I'll be behind you," Kelly told Maggie. "No need to worry."

Maggie stared at the proposed route. After shifting her backpack so it was square on her shoulders, she stretched her leg up and planted her foot, pushing off with the right to grab the tree trunk.

She was going to have scratches and bark burns for weeks.

Swinging around, she landed her right foot in the other spot and grabbed the hand Alex was holding out. One more push and she'd made the top of the rock.

"This is worse than labor," she muttered.

"You did it, Maggie. Good job!" Kelly said as she joined them.

"Only with the help of my friends."

"That's the way we get hard things done. We're lucky to have each other," Kelly said.

"Amen to that," Alex agreed.

"I'd suggest a group hug," said Maggie, "but I'm desperately afraid we're going to lose our balance and tumble down." She peered over the boulder at the twisty trail below them. The only thing that would stop a downward tumble was a large Douglas fir that had fallen. Someone had cut notches in it so people could climb over, but the bulk of the tree was sideways to the slope.

For a second, Maggie was overwhelmed by the force of nature. Douglas firs grew so tall and majestic, only to be felled by a combination of heavy snow and high winds. Her life was brief and fragile in comparison.

"Hey there," Alex said, putting her arm around her. "It's not too much farther. You can do it. Then we'll have our group hug."

Maggie nodded, afraid to speak because she'd break into tears. She reached down for a last bit of energy and they pushed on. In a few more feet a rush of water indicated they were getting close. The sound cooled her overheated body.

She climbed the last bit of the trail and caught up to where Alex stood. Kelly joined them.

Before them lay a stunning flume of tumbling rapids, cascading over rocks and tree limbs.

"Wow," Kelly said, although Maggie could barely hear her over the waterfall before them.

Alex nodded. "Follow me," she said loudly. She led them down between two massive granite boulders to a flatter slate gray rock. The water still rushed beside them, but the sound was quieter.

"Perfect," Kelly said.

Maggie looked at the two women, and her heart filled with the warmth of friendship. Stretching her arms, she stepped forward and embraced them. "Love you," she said, her throat closing, preventing her from saying anything else.

"Back at you," Alex said.

"Forever," Kelly added.

They stayed together for a few moments before separating.

"Let's eat," Maggie said. "I'm starving."

With the thunder of the cascade somewhat muted, they went about the business of unpacking. Ever the hostess, Kelly had brought a forest green woven tablecloth for their feast, along with hard plastic plates and matching napkins. She also had small containers of potato salad stowed in a cooler bag. Maggie had carried the chicken salad sandwiches her mother had prepared, while Alex brought a dessert she'd picked up from Charlene. They'd each carried their own water bottles.

"Now this is a feast," Kelly said.

"Nothing stokes the appetite like fresh air and exercise," Alex said. "We should do this more often."

"It's going to take me a year to recover from this one," Maggie added.

"Proof you need more of it," Alex said. "Exercise will help keep the aging at bay."

"I get enough at the store."

"How are things going?" Kelly asked. "Is Tom's niece working out?"

"Really well," Maggie said. "More important, she likes it. Sandy is eager to learn and really smart. That's great because Teagan's already got one foot out the door."

"Just like your Lisa. How are she and Peter doing?" Alex asked Kelly.

"Peter is firmly ensconced in Boston, much to his grandparents' delight. He's so much like his father that he fits right in. His only problem seems to be that the Richards are taking him to society events. He hates them."

"Business is a lot of who you know," Maggie said.

"True. But I think it's worse than that. They're trying to put the 'right' kind of woman in front of him."

Alex laughed. "He's only eighteen. Aren't they rushing things?"

Kelly shrugged. "My in-laws are massive control freaks. They're probably trying to make sure he doesn't stray with the wrong kind."

"Good grief," Alex said. "How did you ever stay married to John so long? I'd have killed him off as a surrogate for his parents."

"Always the violent choice," Maggie said.

"Comes from being a military wife," Alex retorted.

Maggie shook her head and took a bite of her sandwich. Sometimes not responding to Alex's efforts to bait her was the best way to go.

After finishing their sandwiches, they were quiet. The sun had come around to catch their rock in its rays, and Maggie's eyelids grew heavy with contentment. She leaned against a tree and put her face to the sun, letting herself drift in the moment. The others must have done the same because the only sound was the water coursing down the mountain.

She must have slept, because she slowly became aware of rustling beside her. Opening her eyes a slit, she noticed Kelly shooing away an over-inquisitive crow who was angling for the crumbs they'd left on their plates.

"Guess we'd better clean up," Maggie said, rousing herself.

"We've still got dessert," Kelly said.

"Dessert?" Alex's eyes popped open.

They laughed.

Using the same plates, they laid out the brownies Alex had brought. With the sweets, conversation picked up again.

"How is the retreat planning going?" Maggie asked Kelly.

"Going well. It's nice to feel I have a clue what I'm doing," she answered. "And it's scary to realize that there are perfect strangers paying me to pull this off. A dozen days I tell myself failure isn't an option."

"I still think you should go," Alex said to Maggie.

"No time."

"If you've got—"

"The work party for the performing arts center went well last Saturday," Kelly said, talking over Alex.

"We got a lot done," Maggie said with a grateful glance. "Mike said the cement truck is still on schedule to pour tomorrow."

"And then what happens?" Kelly asked.

"George said the next part is getting the framing done. He's lined up people who know how to use a hammer, but he's got a big job of his own to get done before he can schedule the next session."

"It's coming together fast," Kelly said. "And that's thanks to you."

"George is the one making it happen."

"Part of being a good leader is knowing who to choose to do things," Alex added.

Maggie smiled at Alex. Her friend could be prickly, but her heart was in the right place, and she always knew where she stood with Alex. "Thanks. It's easy to do when there is a supportive community. How do people get anything done if they're always fighting among themselves? In Promise Cove, we pull together. It's the best place to live."

"The best place in the last best place," Alex said, referring to what Montana was often called.

"I don't think I could live anywhere else anymore," Kelly said.

"Me either."

"That's because you both had a chance to have a life somewhere else," Maggie complained.

"Does that mean you'd leave if you could?" Alex asked.

"Well, not permanently. But it would be nice to spend some time in other places."

"Is that why you're interested in Justin?"

"No." Maggie squirmed. She'd have to give Alex some kind of answer or she'd never leave it alone. "We've had a few drinks, that's all."

"A few dinner dates is more like it," Alex said. "One at a swanky restaurant in Whitefish and one *in his house*."

"Don't you have better things to do than keep track of what I'm doing?"

"Alex, Maggie, let's *not* do this. It's a beautiful day. Let's enjoy it."

"But …" Maggie suddenly realized she did want to talk about it. What better way was there to figure out what was going on in her crazy brain than talking it out with her two best friends?

Alex and Kelly looked at her expectantly.

"I know you're worried about me," Maggie said to Alex. "You saw me after Paul dumped me. I was a mess."

Alex nodded.

"She came home while her husband was on deployment," Maggie explained to Kelly. "She was there for me, every step of the way. She even volunteered as my birth coach."

"Who else was going to do it?" Alex asked, her rigid posture finally relaxing. "Elaine would have wanted to spend time decorating the hospital room instead of counting time between contractions."

"Yes," Maggie said. "Mom always said she enjoyed the results of the birth, but not the experience."

"I can agree with that," Kelly said.

Maggie wet her fingertip and picked up brownie crumbs from her plate. "After that, Teagan took up what little time I had left after helping Mom with the store. I had no interest in going out with anyone."

"You certainly made that clear with Tom," Alex said.

Maggie sighed. "Look, I know Tom's a great guy. But he's my buddy, like a brother, you know what I mean?"

"You mean he's a good friend," Kelly said.

"Exactly."

"Hmm," Kelly said.

"What's that supposed to mean?" Maggie asked.

"Well, I've heard that people who are friends with each other first have the best marriages. Look at me. Ryan and I were friends a long time ago, but I don't think friendship was something John and I ever shared, if I'm honest with myself. We picked people we thought we should be with, not someone we had fun doing things with."

"Could be for some people," Maggie said. "But I don't feel a spark with Tom. And I want a spark. I want the fireworks, the champagne bubbles, and the big brass band!" She flung her arms wide.

"You may be asking a little too much from a man," Alex said.

They laughed.

"Have you kissed Justin?" Alex asked after they quieted.

Maggie looked over at the waterfall.

"She kissed him," Alex said. "She definitely kissed him."

"It wasn't a *kiss*," Maggie protested. "More like ... um ... testing the waters."

"And did those waters produce a spark?" Kelly asked.

"Um. I'm not sure," Maggie confessed.

"How can you not be sure?" Alex asked.

Maggie shrugged. "I'm just not." She gathered the plates together, shaking the crumbs onto her napkin and giving them a quick wipe before handing them to Kelly, who put them to the side.

"Where does he live?" Alex would not give it a rest.

"Here."

"That's a vacation house. Where does he actually live?"

Maggie searched her memory. He'd said his ex had a house in Dallas. But she didn't really know where he lived. Once again she shrugged. "The subject hasn't come up."

"That's because he's a land developer," Alex said, gathering the wrappers from their sandwiches and brownies and stuffing them in her bag. "He doesn't really live anywhere."

"Alex has a point," Kelly said, folding up the tablecloth and putting it at the bottom of her bag before adding in her plates and the salad containers. "He's probably not going to settle down in a place like Promise Cove."

"He might," Maggie said.

"He might," Kelly said. "But take it slow. Don't get serious too fast. Just have fun. That's what I think, but it's only my opinion."

"It's mine, too," Alex said. "We're your best friends, and we don't want you to get hurt again."

Maggie stretched out her arms and pulled them all close. Nothing matched good friends.

Nothing.

# Chapter Eighteen

Maggie broke down an old latticework fence she'd found in the shed. She could use the pieces the way George had used stakes to outline her vision of the backyard in its soil. Although she was starting with her dad's basic structure, she had a few changes she wanted to make. She wanted more curves in the paths and secret spots for a person to sit and listen to the fountain, read a book, or sketch a curious jay.

She was halfway through when the front gate closed with a clang.

Tom had arrived with a pitchfork and shovel. "I've got more tools in the truck," he said.

"Why are you here?"

"To help, of course. You said you needed it." His expression was earnest, and she remembered the same look on his face when he'd ask their third grade teacher if he could help clean the boards. He'd had such a crush on the newly minted teacher.

"Well, I'm certainly not going to turn you down," she said.

"Good. I know you want me to look at that pipe, but like I said, I think it needs to be replaced. You okay if I disassemble the rock tower your dad built? I'll mark down what went where so I should be able to get it pretty close to the way it was when I'm done."

"Sure. In fact, I might want to change it up a little. Maybe use a flower pot for the flow, and put in a couple of dirt areas where I can plant pansies in the spring."

"That would be pretty," he said. "I'll still keep track of what it looked like, but when I'm ready to put it back together, we can talk about what you want."

"Thanks."

"So what are all the stakes for?"

"It's my plan for the garden. I don't want to just replicate it; I want to change it up a little, put my stamp on it. Let me show you."

She led him down the path she envisioned from the back steps. "The path guides a walker through the experiences I plan to have. In here I'll put a raised bed with a few vegetables—David has said he'd help me plan a few easy maintenance things that are nice to have fresh during the summer months. I don't want a greenhouse. I'm not into vegetables that much."

"Besides, we have David to supply us."

"Yes." She grinned. The vision of their local organic grower arriving with piles of green, red, yellow, and all the other colors of the rainbow always made her happy. "Then over here, some cutting flowers. I do like a vase of fresh flowers on the table. Such a little thing that brings so much joy."

"Uh-huh."

"Then we arrive at the pond."

"With a turtle, I hope."

"Oh yes. I have to have a turtle." She frowned at the small area. "Is it big enough?"

"For a small turtle, yes. But you could expand it by digging more here and here. Makes it a much more interesting shape, too."

"And I could put in water plants, something for the turtle to hide under."

"You'll also need a log for him to sun himself."

"Maybe I should have two turtles, so one isn't lonely."

"You could name them Fred and Barney," he said with a grin.

"Or Fred and Wilma."

"Only if you want little baby turtles."

She laughed. "I'll worry about it after I actually have a pond." She led him around the pool to the area she'd designated for the bee and butterfly garden. Two delicate brown insects flew from the back of the yard and hovered nearby.

"Thicket Hairstreaks," Tom said.

"How do you know that?"

"I went through a butterfly identification phase. They're pretty common."

"But they seem to know what we've got planned."

He paused for a moment, but she wasn't sure why.

"Yes, they do." His voice was soft, so she turned to look at him.

His gaze was fixed on her. He held steady for a few brief seconds, then turned away. "If you build the wall about two feet high, it will give a nice sense of variety to the space, especially with the pond being at a low point."

She barely heard the words. Something had flickered between them, something unexpected. Had she imagined it? Or was she on overdrive because of Justin's kiss?

Giving her head a slight shake to clear it, she continued her tour. "The path crosses over here, behind the pond. I'm thinking native grasses and shrubs in here, something low maintenance."

"There's a new artist at ART," Tom said. "He's doing some cool outdoor sculptures of native animals and birds. Might be just the thing to add at one edge of the area."

"Not in my budget at the moment, but I see what you mean." She got to the final part of the backyard where her father had left a small grove of aspens. The wooden fence met the edge of the property, but the final span was strung wire. It wouldn't keep out a determined animal, but it deterred most humans.

"What are you planning for that?" Tom asked.

"In my dreams, I'd like a space for birds. A place for them to nest and hide. And a place for me to have for my very own."

"A she shed."

"How do you know about them?"

"I've got sisters. They're always complaining about wanting a space of their own."

"It's not complaining. It's a reasonable request. When Teagan was little, I couldn't even spend time in the bathroom."

He laughed. "But she's not little anymore."

"No. Now she takes over the bathroom for hours at a time."

Slowly, he looked around the space again. He nodded. "It's a great vision, Maggie. Where do you want to start?"

She led him back to the pond. "Tell me again what you have in mind to expand this."

He explained where he thought the boundaries should be and how deep the pit should be. "I know they have pond supplies in some of those big box stores down south. We'd need to line it, then I have to look at the pump and spigot to see what's gone wrong. In all likelihood, it's going to be best to replace the whole thing. It's been a long time since your dad put it in, and there will be more water to pump with the bigger basin."

She stared at it for a few moments, then nodded. "This is the most important spot for me. Can you dig it out? Are you sure you don't mind? It's hot and a lot of work."

"I don't mind at all."

"Let's say we work for about an hour, and then I'll get some lemonade and snacks."

"Sounds like a plan."

While he went to work on the pond, she gathered her stakes and finished laying out the space. Then she climbed the stairs to survey what she'd done. For a few seconds she watched Tom. He was methodically digging the edges of the future pond, tackling it like he did everything: slow and steady.

But there was something different as she watched him, almost like she was seeing him for the first time. What was happening to her? Tom was her best friend. She needed to keep it that way, especially while she was dating Justin.

Kelly's words echoed. *Don't get too serious.*

Would Justin stay like he'd indicated he wanted to do? If so, what happened then?

Take it one day at a time. That's what she needed to do. After Paul had dumped her, that's what she'd done. It had been the only way to make it through the day.

# # #

After an hour or so, she called a break. "Let me check on the girls and get us something," she said.

Tom wiped his brow with the back of his forearm. "Thanks. I feel like I could drink from a fire hose. It sure is getting hot." He looked at the pond. "You know, it might be nice to add a small tree here, something to provide shade for the pond and whoever is sitting next to it." He pointed to where he thought it should be.

It was a good point. She could see it the way he'd visualized it.

"I'll keep it in mind, but trees cost." She'd counted on revising the backyard being more of a labor project—something to keep her busy—than a money pit.

"You can put it in your plan and get it when you're ready," he said, following her to the stairs where she'd set a pitcher of lemonade, some glasses, and a plate of snacks on a rickety table.

She pulled over a pad and flipped to a page where she made a note. "I've started clearing away the space for the butterfly garden. Do you think I should get a load of dirt for it?"

"Probably. When I go down to Kalispell for the pond supplies, I'll stop at the landscaping place in Whitefish and see what they have. Could be they can put the dirt in the back of my truck while I'm there."

"Oh, you don't need to do that. Just tell me what I need to get. I don't want to trouble you. I'm thankful for what you're doing already."

"No problem. If I see an opportunity, I'll let you know and we can discuss it then." He picked up the lemonade glass and downed it. Then he refilled it and sipped more slowly. "Can you draw me a picture of what you think the waterfall on the pond should look like?"

"I can't draw," she said. "You know that. I made stick figures in high school."

He chuckled, and she joined in.

There it was again. That fleeting instant of something between them.

But wasn't it the same thing she felt with Alex and Kelly at times?

She pushed it to the back of her mind and picked up a pad.

"Draw circles and squares," he suggested. "Label them. That will help me visualize."

"Okay." She outlined what she saw in her mind as best she could.

He made a few suggestions, and when they were done, it was as close as they were going to get it.

When they'd finished, he glanced at his phone. "Hate to do this, but I've got to go. Got a late shift today." He held out his hand. "Can I have the drawing for a bit? I'll make a photocopy back at my place and return it. That way, whoever gets to Kalispell first can figure out what we need to make it happen. Okay?"

She tore off the page. "Thanks again, Tom. I really appreciate the help. It's above and beyond."

"It's what friends are for," he said.

"Regardless. Thanks."

He gathered his tools, waved good-bye, and headed out.

She stood there a few moments before heading back to the future butterfly garden. The Thicket Hairstreaks swept back into view, dancing in the air in front of her like they'd done it together forever.

# Chapter Nineteen

"It's such a stupid thing," Postmistress Betsy Wiznowski told Tom. "Just a bit of cactus kitsch I brought back from Tombstone when Harold and I went there years ago for a movie." Betsy's late husband had been a screenwriter in Hollywood. Over the years, he'd learned lots of stories as he picked up his mail in the small building.

"And it disappeared yesterday?"

"Yes. I know it was there when I opened up Monday morning, but when I cleaned off the desk at the end of the day, it was gone." The starch seemed to go out of her shoulders. "You'll probably never find it. That's okay. I need to get rid of all this stuff anyway. It's just taking up space."

Tom leaned across the counter. "I'll do my best to find it, Betsy. It's been there for years. Do you know who was in here yesterday?"

"Pretty much everyone," she said with a sigh. "Mondays are the busiest. People eager to catch up on what's what, you know. Once the school lets out, it's a madhouse."

"Anyone catch your eye? Maybe lingered too long in one spot after they got what they needed?"

Betsy shook her head. "I focus on the job in front of me. It's the fastest way to get through the line."

Inwardly, Tom sighed. He wished he could figure out who was committing these petty crimes. Whoever it was seemed to be getting bolder, as if the addiction to thieving was growing stronger. Because so many of the things taken were in houses, it had to be someone local, someone everyone knew and trusted.

That made it all the sadder.

"Okay. I'll keep looking."

"Thanks, Tom." Betsy was already back to sorting through mail.

As he went through the lobby where the mailboxes were, he ran into three of the townspeople in a cluster. The two women were stay-at-home moms, although both had remote jobs as well. The third was a long retired railroad man who loved to flirt with the younger women.

"Hey, Tom," the man said. "You see what's going on over at the ART center? Looks like it's going great guns on that performance space. They've got cement poured and everything."

"I haven't seen it recently, but I know they're working hard on it."

"How fast do you think they'll get it done?"

"Don't know. I think it depends as much on raising money for supplies as anything else. The labor is mostly voluntary, but some items need to be paid for."

"Like that sound system. I heard that new fella in town—Justin somebody—is trying to get us a deal."

"And I heard he's going out with Maggie," one of the women said.

"Weren't you sweet on Maggie?" the other asked.

"We're just friends," Tom said. He nodded and added, "Got to go solve crimes, folks. See you around." His footsteps were slower than they had been.

There had been moments on Saturday when he and Maggie had really connected with each other—at least that's how it had felt to him—moments of tension when the possibility of a kiss hovered in the air. Neither one of them had made a move, so the possibilities had melted away.

Helping her with the backyard would give them more time together, and that's what he wanted. If she'd realize how easy they were, maybe the rest would follow. Despite her protests, there *was* a spark. He'd felt it, and he knew she had, too, but she'd quickly pushed it away as it didn't fit into her worldview of how the two of them should be together.

Her plan was amazing. She'd definitely missed her calling, but she wouldn't have stumbled on it if she'd been able to stay in college. The Maggie who'd graduated high school was determined to get a business degree and escape to a big city. Her dad's death and her subsequent pregnancy had changed all that.

If Tom could have gotten his hands on Paul, he would have happily strangled him. How could a man turn his back on his own child? Or doubt the paternity? Anyone who knew Maggie for more than an hour knew she was incapable of a lie.

He grinned as a memory came back. She'd filched one of his action figures when they were in third grade. She was mad at him about something and wanted to get back at him. When he confronted her, she'd attempted to lie.

The result had been a red face and stutters.

He'd laughed at her, and she'd stomped to her cubby, pulled it from her backpack, and shoved it at him. "I hate you!" she'd yelled, then run to her chair, put her head on the table, and sobbed her heart out.

He wasn't able to stand her crying. He'd gone to her, put his arm around her, and begged her to stop, even offering to give her the figure.

Eventually, she'd stopped, wiped her eyes, turned her wet face to him, and smiled. "It's okay," she'd said. "You keep it. Sorry I was mad. We're still friends." Then she'd gotten up like nothing had happened and gone over to where Alex was playing with another friend.

Tom got into the squad car and put it into gear. Time to make his rounds and then he'd revisit the people who'd reported things stolen. There had to be some person they'd all noticed.

Although it might be difficult. People came to Promise Cove to fade from the limelight, not be in it. There were incredibly wealthy and famous artists, sports figures, and Hollywood celebrities scattered in the mountains and on the lakefront between here and Whitefish. There was an unwritten law in the town that nobody talked about anyone they'd seen.

As for the "little people," some of them were the characters one found in all small towns. The rest were ordinary people, not attracting much attention. Some were almost invisible.

By the end of his shift, he knew no more than when he'd

started. There was no common person everyone had had over. In detective shows it was always the cleaning lady or repairman, but real life was never that simple.

Discouraged, he headed to Mike's to grab a beer and burger before heading back to his house where he'd put up his feet and watch one of the British mysteries he'd become addicted to since the launch of BritBox.

The gravel crunched as he pulled into the lot. There were a few cars he recognized, including Ryan Svoboda's. Maybe he could snatch a bit of conversation with the quilter. Ryan, like many artists, was an observer. Additionally, he was a former cop, used to looking at a situation and analyzing what was going on in mere seconds.

"How's it going?" he asked Ryan, as he settled next to him on the comfortable bar chair, his heavy leather belt with all its required gadgets squeaking as he did so.

"Good," Ryan acknowledged. "You?"

"The usual."

"Maggie still won't go out with you."

Mike laughed as he slid a beer in front of Tom. "We'll see fireworks when Maggie Marston finally says yes to Tom."

"So your bet is on a yes."

"Absolutely. Maggie may be a lot of things, but she's no fool. Eventually she'll see what's right in front of her."

"Wait a minute," Tom said. "You guys don't have a pool going do you?"

Mike looked at Ryan and grinned. "Why would we ever do something like that?"

"Beats me."

"I can't believe it," Tom protested.

"Burger?" Mike asked.

"Yeah."

Mike headed toward the grill behind the bar.

"My bet's on a yes, too," Ryan said.

"Is that yes going to come some time in this decade?" Tom asked, half seriously.

"I have no idea. I have enough trouble figuring out one woman. You're on your own with Maggie. You've known her over forty years. I'd think you'd know how to get her to say yes by now."

"You'd think." Tom sipped his beer and looked around the familiar haunt. He'd spent a lot of time in this bar. As soon as they were legal, he and his friends would hang out, shooting darts, or making bad attempts at pool. It was pretty much the only place to take a date, so everyone in town knew who was going with whom.

And who wasn't.

"What do you make of this Justin Thomas character?" he asked Ryan.

"You mean other than always be suspicious of people with two first names?" Ryan turned toward him. "I'm going to bet you've done a background check."

"I may have."

"And?"

"Clean as a whistle. One marriage, amicable divorce, no kids. Lots of debt, but most of it's business, and that's how these guys roll. They're always moving money from one place to another. As a land developer, it makes sense that he'd borrow to fund the development, then pay it back as it's complete."

Ryan nodded. "Not a crook, but a sharp businessman."

"Very."

"And you're worried he's taking Maggie for a ride?"

"Who are you talking about?" Mike said as he placed a mounded plate of fries and an overloaded hamburger in front of Tom. "You good?" he asked Ryan.

"Got any more of those fries? Kelly will have my head if I don't eat whatever she's made for dinner, but I could use a snack before then."

"Coming right up." Mike turned back to the kitchen.

"I don't think Justin is intentionally fooling Maggie. It's more that he plays his cards close to his chest. He's not going to tell her until the very end what his plans are. And she's not willing to look deeply into what he's telling her. She wants to believe in the dream too much."

Ryan nodded. "She's always been a dreamer. Unfortunately, she never got a chance to follow them."

"They were the wrong ones anyway," Tom said.

"What do you mean?"

"I worked with her on Saturday on the backyard. She showed me what she had in mind. It was transformational. She could easily have been a master gardener."

"No one would have told her that in high school."

"Nope. Who would have even thought of that as a career?" Tom asked.

"She can still follow that path," Ryan said. "There's plenty of people in Whitefish who'd pay to get a beautiful landscape."

"She'd have to figure out that's what she wanted to do first."

"True." Tom dug into his hamburger.

"Here you go." Mike brought the fries to Ryan. "Another beer?"

"Nope. I'm good."

"Okay. I know Tom's a one-beer man. Something about being a cop and all that."

"Ha," Tom said.

"So who were you talking about before?"

"Justin Thomas," Ryan answered.

"He's a good guy. He's talking about investing in my brewing project."

"Is he?" Tom asked.

Mike nodded. "He's real impressed with my product."

"That's nice," Ryan said.

Justin Thomas knew how to play people. That was one thing Tom was sure of. He hoped he wouldn't hurt Maggie too badly when he left. Because that was another thing he was sure of.

Justin Thomas wouldn't stay in a small town like Promise Cove.

# Chapter Twenty

Justin had delivered.

"What he found," Maggie told the committee in front of her on Thursday, "was a recently refurbished little theater in the suburbs of LA. When they learned the land and building had been sold out from under them and their theater was slated to be demolished, they packed it in. Most of them were older folks, and they couldn't start over again."

"That's really sad," Gabriella said.

Heads nodded.

"It is, but it is great news for us. Justin figures he can get their equipment for a good price. And, he's willing to pay to ship it up here as his contribution to the community," Maggie announced with a smile.

"Well, I'm not sure he'd be contributing to our community," James said. "What do we know about him?" He glared at Maggie. "What do *you* know about him? He's a stranger. We keep to ourselves in Promise Cove."

"Now, James," Mike said, "You're being a little unfair. Justin seems to be a good guy. He's been nothing but helpful since he got here."

"I don't think we need to be looking a gift horse in the mouth," Kelly said. "I've spent some time with Justin, and like Mike said, he seems to be on the up and up."

"Ah yes. Any more discussion as to whether or not we should accept this offer from Justin, provided we can come up with the money to buy the equipment, of course?"

"How much is it?" Makalia asked.

Maggie told her.

"Seems reasonable. Mike had asked me to do some internet searches to help him come up with a budget, and that's the right amount for the equipment on this list." She held up the paper Maggie had provided each of them.

*Spring in Promise Cove*

"But where are we going to get that kind of money?" Jim asked.

"A bake sale isn't going to do it," James added.

She squashed the urge to bury her head in her hands.

"We've been talking about that," Alex said. "Most of the artists in the co-op, with a few exceptions ..." She looked pointedly at Jim and James. "Most of us have agreed to donate a portion of our proceeds from June and July to the fund. After all, the center will help us, too. It will bring more traffic to the store."

"That will cover about half, based on last year's sales," Mike said.

"And where do we get the rest?" Jim asked.

"With the same kind of logic, I'll throw in 10 percent of my June and July proceeds," Gabriella said. "Susan and I talked it over and we're really excited about it. We're thinking of adding a cottage to the inn property for larger parties to rent."

"That's still not going to be enough," James pointed out.

"How about a premier stage at the summertime celebration?" Kelly asked. "That's always a big draw in town. We can get a tent, set up a small platform, and charge admission."

"I'm not hauling a grand piano onto a platform in that field," Mike said with a grin.

"No, but I bet someone has a spinet or an old upright," Kelly said.

Mike groaned.

"Look, we're building this for performers," Kelly went on. "Let us put in some sweat equity. There's got to be someone really famous around here who would be willing to perform."

Makaila nodded. "I might know someone," she said softly.

"Can you ask them?" Maggie asked.

"If the opportunity arises. He's very protective of his privacy, but he loves Promise Cove, so there's a chance."

Maggie searched her memory for the person Makaila described. She couldn't come up with anyone. The man must be highly skilled at evading the public eye. She looked at Kelly. "Can you see if we can make this happen?"

"But the celebration is only a few months away."

"You pulled off a miracle last time. You can do it again," Maggie told her friend. "Okay, so we have some idea of how to get the funding."

"When do we have to have the money?" Mike asked.

"Justin said the theater would be ready to send up the equipment by late August. They're running their last few plays through July."

"I need time to crunch the numbers to see if we can really pull this off," Mike said. "If we don't have every penny, then how will we buy the equipment?"

"Justin said he'd float a loan," Maggie said.

"Nope," Jim said.

"Nope," James added. "That man's from outside. He's done enough interfering with our business now. We'll handle it ourselves."

"But how?" Mike asked.

"Like he said," Jim answered, "we'll handle it. James and I will make up the shortfall. You can pay us back over time."

"With healthy interest," James added.

"No interest." Jim shook his head. "That's just being petty."

"I suppose."

"That's very generous," Maggie said. "Thank you."

"I move we tell Justin to go ahead and make arrangements," Alex said.

"Second that," Mike said.

Everyone voted in favor of the motion. Even Jim and James.

# # #

Alex and Kelly joined Maggie for lunch back at the store. Gregg was on the grill, and he'd prepared some complicated vegetarian sandwich rich with mushrooms, peppers, and a dark, savory sauce with a little bit of a kick.

Maggie brought over three bottles of cold flavored seltzer water to go with the sandwiches.

"That boy is sure learning to cook," Kelly said after a bite.

"His talents are going to be wasted on Mike's hamburgers," Alex agreed.

They nodded and ate silently for a few moments.

"Is Teagan getting excited for school?" Kelly asked.

"The university is sending her all kinds of literature: recommendations on things she should read, social media groups to join, what to bring to college, that kind of thing." Maggie heard the wistfulness in her own voice.

"What would you do if you had the chance to start over? What's your passion?" Kelly asked gently.

Maggie took a bite of the delectable sandwich and chewed while she thought. If she didn't have anyone to support, what would she do? Mentally, she tried on a dozen different ideas, but none of them fit correctly.

"I have no idea," she admitted. "So it's probably a good idea I don't have that option." But it was something to think about. Like it or not, life was changing. Even if she went places with Justin or someone like him, she couldn't hang around all day while they worked. It sounded deadly.

Maybe she should go to the retreat Alex had been hounding her about. There had to be some way of sorting through her muddled thinking.

"And Justin?" Alex asked. "Where does he fit in your life?"

"Ahhh."

"What does that mean?" Alex asked.

"It means I like him. He's easy to be with, and he certainly takes care of me in a way I could get used to."

"But is there more than that?" Alex persisted.

"Yes." After debating for hours about Justin's kisses, Maggie had finally decided there was a spark. There had to be. Otherwise, why did she want to kiss him again?

"Is he staying in Promise Cove?" Kelly asked with a frown on her forehead.

"Like I said in the meeting, I'm not sure."

"What will happen if he doesn't?" Alex asked.

"I don't know that either," Maggie said, allowing an edge to creep into her voice. "Look, can't you let me enjoy myself? I'm having fun. There's no pressure from him to be more than a date."

"But he kissed you." Alex pressed on.

"So what?" She turned to her old friend to face her full on. "It's nice to be kissed. I'm not taking it any further. Can't you let me be? Why don't you work on your own love life instead of dragging yourself into mine?"

"Hush," Kelly said, patting Maggie's hand. "Alex is looking out for you. She cares. You know that."

"I do. I want her to care a little less."

Alex tensed and grabbed the table as if she were going to stand and leave. Then she uncoiled. "You're right. I want to be in your business, instead of looking at my own. It's easier. Sorry."

Maggie stared at her friend. Alex had never apologized that quickly in her life. Usually, there were several days, if not weeks, of a cooling off period. It had always amazed her how Alex could disappear for weeks on end in such a small town.

"Okay," she said. She sat up a little straighter. "All I know right now is I'm having fun with Justin. I don't know where it's going, but I'm hanging on for the ride to find out. So no more worry from either of you. My eyes are wide open. Let's talk about something more interesting. Who do you suppose Makalia has in mind to perform?"

With a laugh, they speculated about who might be hidden in the mountains. During the discussion, Maggie glanced over at her phone when it vibrated.

*Up for dinner? I'll pick you up at six?* Justin texted.

*Sounds good.*

Whatever happened, Maggie was going to spend the next few months having fun.

And maybe falling in love.

## Chapter Twenty-One

"I've got my flights," Elaine announced.

Maggie was double checking the schedule for Memorial Day Weekend, when the summer tourist madness would officially begin. While the number of people coming to Promise Cove was a fraction of those who descended on Whitefish and the other areas close to Glacier National Park, it was still double or triple the size of her regular traffic, depending on the weather.

"When do you leave?" Maggie asked. She didn't need to deal with this now. Her mother was a pro at picking the exact wrong time to discuss important items. It's as if she did it, knowing she'd push Maggie's buttons.

"June thirtieth," Elaine said. "It's a Thursday. I fly to Denver, then it's an overnight flight to Paris." Elaine practically danced around the counter. "Henri will pick me up at the airport." She spun around, acting like she was seventeen instead of seventy.

Maggie frowned for a second. Her mother was happy. Like she'd asked of Alex and Kelly, she needed to support Elaine, not give her grief. Her parents had been happy, but Dad had been gone a long time now.

Besides, who wouldn't want to go to Paris? Especially an artist?

Maggie forced a smile. "I'll be happy to take you to the airport. Sandy can manage the store."

Elaine stopped twirling. "How is she working out?"

"Really well. I think she has the capability and desire to manage the store."

"I'm so glad. That will give you more time to concentrate on the things you really want to do—like run the town." Elaine grinned.

"I do not want to run the town."

"Then why did you want to be mayor?"

"Because somebody needed to do it."

"Uh-huh."

"How did you know?" Maggie asked. "That Dad was the right one, I mean."

Elaine leaned with her back against the counter, the set of bangles she always wore clinking as she did so. Maggie thought her mother had studied a catalog of what artists were supposed to look like, chosen one, and donned the appearance and mannerisms like a suit of clothes.

"He didn't laugh at my desire to be an artist." Elaine looked over at Maggie. "And I was very, very bad back then. Pretentious and imitative. Most artists start out that way. We aren't confident enough to allow our inner vision to dominate. Your dad must have seen something in those terrible paintings. Or he saw something in me."

A half smile played on Elaine's face while her unfocused eyes gazed on something from long ago.

"And that was it?" Maggie asked.

"Oh no. It was only the first thing. He courted me ... beautifully. It was like it was his mission on earth to make me feel loved, secure, and still free enough to soar to whatever heights were possible."

"But you followed his dream."

Elaine nodded. "Women may have talked a good game about being free and just as good as a man in the 1970s, but it was difficult to break ties with the housewives who'd raised us. If a couple were both working, the man's job came first, even if no one talked about it. It was only later that began to change. Of course, the number of divorces rose as well."

It seemed like a faraway time to Maggie. Her mother had told her tales of how hard women fought for equal rights and opportunities, some of which still weren't there. As a single mom, Maggie hadn't had much time to worry about the niceties of equality. Survival was utmost on her mind.

"Even so," Elaine said, "I would have followed him anyway. Your dad ... well ... he fed my soul. That's the closest I can come to it. I'd never have become the artist I am without him."

"And now you think Henri will do that."

"Oh no." Elaine shook her head. "I'm under no such illusion. There was only one man in my life like that. And he's gone."

"Then why are you going to France?"

"For me. It's something I've wanted to do since I was a little girl and saw my first reproduction of a Picasso. I wanted to walk where he walked on Montmartre, and see what he saw, absorb the smells, sounds, and sights of Paris. Study art in the great museums—not only the Louvre, but the smaller ones like Jeu de Paume, and d'Orsay. Oh, to be able to stand in front of those masterpieces and breathe them into my soul."

Maggie had no reply; she didn't have that kind of passion.

"You'll be fine," Elaine said. "You have to accept who you are, and then you'll see the right path in front of you."

Teagan thumped down the stairs. "Hi, Grandma, Mom." She peered over Maggie's shoulder. "When am I scheduled today?"

"I gave you the early shift, so you could go to Whitefish with your friends."

"Any chance I can have tomorrow morning off?" Teagan asked. "Rebecca wants to go hiking. She says the trails are opening up."

"They are," Maggie said. "Alex dragged us up to the waterfall a few weeks ago."

"Was there water?" Teagan asked.

"Tons."

"Good, 'cause that's where Rebecca wants to go. So can I have the morning off? I'll be back by early afternoon."

"I don't know," Maggie said. "Memorial Day is next Monday, and you know how people get. They take off earlier and earlier every year. They're going to start pouring in this evening, making it a four-day weekend."

"I'll fill in for her," Elaine said.

"I guess," Maggie said. "But be careful. The snow is unstable in some areas. I've heard about avalanches on the news. Make sure you let me know if you two decide to go somewhere else."

"Sure, Mom. Thanks! Love you. What do you need me to do?"

Maggie set her to work in the back of the store, unpacking and stocking the canned goods that had been delivered on Friday.

"You'll make it through this," Elaine said as she pulled Maggie in for a quick hug.

"I know."

"It will all turn out okay, you'll see. Maybe not the way you intended, but maybe even better. Let things go. You don't have to control things all the time."

As she did when she was a child, Maggie let herself relax a bit into her mother's arms. If only she could stay here and let the small world of Promise Cove run itself. But she wasn't at that stage of life when she could indulge in whims like running off to Paris.

She was a woman of responsibility.

"Thanks, Mom. Love you."

The bell clanged over the door and Gregg's heavy footsteps thudded to the front. How he could make so much noise with tennis shoes was baffling.

"Hey, Gregg," Maggie called. "I have you down Friday, Saturday, Sunday, and Monday to do the lunch meals. Can you stay until 3 on Saturday and Sunday? Those will be our busiest days, and people may be hungry later."

"No can do," he said. "Mike wants me at the bar by two-thirty to start prepping for the dinner crowd. He's adding some salads to the menu to spruce it up."

Maggie dropped her pen. "But I need you here."

"Sorry, Maggie. I told you about this." Gregg's eyebrows formed a V over his nose. "It's important to me. You know that."

"Yeah, I know. I'll figure it out." Maybe Sandy could cook.

"I'll step in," Elaine said.

"I already had you down."

"Sorry," Gregg said again, then headed to the kitchen.

"How's the schedule today?" Elaine asked. "Are we staying open late?"

Maggie nodded. "Just a couple of hours later until eight. Sandy said she'd cover for me after five-thirty."

"What happens at five-thirty?"

"I get ready to go out with Justin."

"Again? Aren't you seeing too much of him?"

"I'm not twenty-something," Maggie said, the heat of anger building quickly. If one more person said they couldn't deliver ...

"I need some time to relax before this weekend, and Justin is providing it," she continued.

"Why not go out with your girlfriends?"

"Mom, I saw my girlfriends last night. They have their own lives."

"What about Tom?"

"What about him?" Maggie wanted to scream in exasperation. "He's a friend, but I have been invited on a date! Can't you just be happy for me?" Vaguely she heard the bell give a soft ring.

"Justin isn't good for you."

"Justin is fine for me." Without thinking, Maggie let her voice get louder. "I want to go out with him. I like Justin!"

When the bell chimed again, she whirled around to see who it was.

All she could see was Tom's back as he started down the stairs to his cruiser.

# Chapter Twenty-Two

He should just leave Promise Cove.

Tom slammed the door of the cruiser a little harder than necessary and left the parking lot of the general store.

He'd been waiting for twenty years and for what? To see the woman he loved going out with another man?

Once he left the town limits, he quickly hit the seventy-mile-hour speed limit of the winding two-lane. Trees blurred past and the occasional cottage or boarded-up business were just blinks of an eye.

The farther north he went, the more nature took back her territory. People who came up to Whitefish generally stayed there. Promise Cove had built a niche of artists that attracted some traffic, but most of the people made it work through the website designed by the amazing Makaila. They were never going to arrive in town in droves, which had suited him fine up to now.

He dodged a young deer that sprang across the road, fortunately far enough in front of him so he could react. But he didn't slow his speed.

If he did leave, where would he go? He couldn't imagine police work in a big city, or even a smaller one like Billings or Spokane. Maybe he could find a job in Paradise Valley close to Livingston, another enclave of stars, athletes, and notables who'd chosen a hidey-hole in Montana. They'd certainly pay more than what he was getting now.

And there were more people in that part of Montana, drawn by the nearness of Yellowstone Park and the world-class fly-fishing streams. A move would be a good chance to get over this foolishness with Maggie.

He hit the boundary of the next county and headed up a back road to one of the small fishing spots on Lake Koocanusa. It wasn't in his territory, but it was a good place to sit and think. The lack of cell service would only be a bonus.

He called dispatch and told them he was taking a late lunch, then grabbed an energy bar from the stack he always kept in the car. After he settled onto his favorite spot for fishing, a bark-stripped trunk of a tree that had wedged against one of the boulders, he opened the clear plastic wrapping from around the bar, and bit into the gooey nut and fruit snack.

Then he sat and stared, letting the sounds, smells, and touches of nature wash over him. He'd always wanted to bring Maggie here, teach her how to unwind from her responsibilities a little. With Teagan leaving for school, he'd hoped she'd have more time for herself, but it didn't look like she was going to get the chance. Elaine's escape and Maggie's job as mayor had piled on the stress.

But she was no longer his concern. Her choice was Justin, or another man like him. Justin was a wealthy, connected, athletic man, an older version of Paul. A small-town cop didn't stand a chance.

A bald eagle flew low over the narrow lake in front of him, its strong wings propelling it forward. The sun glinted on the white head and tail, silent beauty that could strike swiftly. It headed due north, intent on its journey, knowing its destination by some innate sense. Slowly it diminished in size, becoming a lonely black silhouette against the shimmering water.

Tom had always known what he wanted to do with his life, where he wanted to do it, and who he wanted to do it with. But he hadn't reckoned on the things—or people—beyond his control.

Picking up a nearby stone he arced it as high as he could overhead, until it descended into the lake with a satisfying plop. Ripples circled from the origin of its landing.

Every person was like that stone in the lake, their influence rippling away from them until it dissipated into a mere echo of itself. Tom liked being the proverbial small fish in a big pond. He liked knowing the people he was working for. And most of them were good people, which was why he was having trouble figuring out who was committing petty theft.

Another one had been reported as he drove up here. He'd have to stop by on his way back into town. Then he'd indulge himself in one of Mike's burgers and a plate stacked with fries for dinner. Heck, he might even have two beers.

He quickly chomped through the rest of his bar and stood up. There was no choice. He had to find work somewhere else.

# # #

Two hours later he was back at the small cement block building that passed as his office. There were two deputies to assist him with rotating shifts, as well as the dispatcher, a woman with two kids in high school and an iron will when it came to how things should be done in an office.

Tom had given up arguing with her decades ago.

He pulled up his notes from the interview with Fiona Lambert, a woman in her fifties who had hosted the knitting group the previous Monday night.

"We always meet Monday nights," she'd said. "It's a good way to start the week of right. We do our own pieces, of course, but we also knit baby caps for the hospitals in Whitefish and Kalispell. Those poor little ones come into this world with nothing to protect their heads."

He'd nodded while she'd explained the arrangement of the evening, including what she'd served for snacks. She'd given him a list of guests but stopped him as he was halfway down the steps of her house.

"Oh, I forgot someone. Nancy Smith was here, too."

"Nancy Smith?" he asked as he wrote down the name. He should know her, but he couldn't bring up a visual.

"Mystery writer ... kind of ... well ... I hate to say this ... but it's easy to forget her."

Now he had her. He'd never been able to remember her name. Whenever she was around it always took him a moment to distinguish her from whatever she was standing in front of.

He scribbled down her name and put a question mark next to it. How many of the other places that had had small thefts had failed to mention her name?

It was the only hopeful sign in this whole mess. He was developing a list of five or six people who had been in many of the places where the thefts had occurred. But it didn't make sense to him. None of these people needed money, and all were trusted members of the community.

He got into the squad car and headed back to his cabin near the lake shore. He'd picked it up at a reasonable price from an old friend of his parents. While it wasn't exactly on the shore, he preferred it that way. In his mind, the lake belonged to everyone. If a few people wanted to borrow his shoreline for a picnic, he didn't care, as long as they picked up after themselves.

He had a kayak and canoe stored by a shed a few yards from the lake. Early in the morning or late at night, when the weather cooperated, he would choose one or the other to glide out onto the water. He'd stay close to the shoreline, exploring inlets and coves, rewarded by sights of deer, eagles, great blue herons, and the occasional moose. Even more rare were the water critters like otters who he sometimes saw in the spring when the snow runoff rushed down the streams that fed the lake with icy cold water.

Once he'd locked eyes with a mountain lion who'd arrived with her two cubs for a drink.

He loved being this close to the wild and still able to be with a tight-knit community. How was he possibly going to leave?

Once he'd changed into his jeans and a comfortable blue work shirt, he drove his aging but serviceable blue Ford pickup down to the bar, his stomach already rumbling in anticipation. He backed his truck into a spot at the northern end of the parking lot, anticipating the space filling up as the long weekend approached. Only a smattering of pickups were in the lot now.

He stopped walking halfway between his truck and the door to the saloon.

What if Justin decided to take Maggie there for dinner?

Tom almost turned around.

No. He was not going to be chased out of town by the specter of Maggie with another man.

He marched to the door and went in.

"Hey, Tom," Mike called out in greeting.

Tom nodded, his gaze already shifting to the television to see what was on. The lens was zoomed in on a pitcher as he pawed the mound like a testy bull.

Baseball would do to distract him.

"So is the world of Promise Cove safe for another day?" Mike asked as he put a beer on a coaster in front of Tom.

"From major threats, yes." Tom picked up the beer and let the slow cool draft fill his mouth and slide down his throat.

"Means you still haven't figured out who's stealing all these little things."

"That would be right. It makes no sense to me. Why would someone do it?"

"Could be someone who can't help themselves," Mike said.

"You mean like a kleptomaniac?"

"Yeah."

"Huh." Tom took another long drink, his gaze drifting to the slow evolution of the game on television.

Mike headed off to another customer.

By the time the third player had struck out, Tom had finished his beer.

"When are you going to give Justin a run for his money?" Mike asked, standing in front of Tom once again.

"What do you mean?" Tom asked, pushing his glass toward the inside of the bar.

"It seems like Justin's getting a lot of time with the girl you've been stuck on your whole life. Don't get me wrong. Justin's a good guy, but I have the feeling he's not going to stay. He's too big for this town if you know what I mean."

"Maggie's only a friend."

"Right. And that's why you look at her the way you do. Remember, a bartender is an observer of human nature. I've been doing this a long time. I can tell you that the man in the red shirt over there is drinking with someone who isn't his wife. I'm going to have to keep an eye on the man with the black beard because he's spoiling for a fight. And those two women come in once a month, order two chardonnays each, and leave a generous tip. They're down-to-earth people who get tired of the attitudes of their regular friends."

"All that?" Tom asked.

"Yep. And that's how I know you are falling down on the job."

"What do you mean?"

"You're not working hard enough to get the woman you love."

"I've asked her out. She turns me down. Every single time."

"And?"

"I've tried hanging around with her and then asking her out, but that's a non-starter."

"No wonder she thinks of you as a friend."

"Well, Romeo," Tom said, letting a touch of sarcasm into his voice. "What do you suggest?"

"She needs a grand gesture, something to make her sit up and take notice."

"Like what?" Tom gestured at the television. "Say I love you at a stadium? Maggie doesn't even like sports."

"No. You start with flowers. There's not a woman alive who doesn't like flowers."

Tom shook his head. "Says the man whose last date was five years ago."

"I've been busy."

"Uh-huh. Can you get Gregg started on a hamburger and all the fixings? And a heaping plate of fries. I'm starved."

"Another beer?" Mike asked.

"Yep."

"Flowers," Mike said as he walked away.

Was the answer as simple as that? Did he really have a chance with Maggie?

Or was he fooling himself?

## Chapter Twenty-Three

An envelope with an unfamiliar return address in Virginia was at the bottom of the stack of mail Maggie was going through. It was a plain white envelope with a forever American Flag stamp.

Carefully crafted appeal for money? They were handwriting the addresses these days, becoming aware that many Americans tossed printed correspondence away without opening.

She held it in her hand, debating whether it deserved her attention or the circular file. Maybe a long-lost relative had left her money. She could indulge in a few seconds of financially secure daydreaming before tossing it where it belonged.

After slitting the envelope open, she withdrew the single typed page. She scanned the words, trying to string them together to have them make sense.

She balled it up and hurled it in the trash, then cradled her face in the palms of her hands.

*So not happening.*

She sat like that for a long time, memories flooding her brain. The slim young man with the patrician nose, shoulders never slumped, but an easy smile on his face. In his late twenties, his hair was already thinning. He always arrived with wildflowers in his hand and the most incredible ideas of how to spend their time that summer.

Her father's death and the upending of her future had finally become a dull ache, and she was ready to fly free as soon as she found someone to help her mother manage the store.

He promised her a life of joy. They'd spend it traveling until they found the perfect spot for him to become a fly-fishing guide, not too far from Promise Cove so she could check in on Elaine.

She'd gradually let her guard down, and kisses turned to something more. She'd been more physically free than she'd ever been in her life.

But somewhere along the way the protection they'd been using had failed as miserably as his reliability.

One fine summer day, Paul Lee had packed his bags, said he was sorry, and returned to take up his position in his family's law firm. When she'd called him a few months later to tell him she was pregnant, he told her it couldn't be possible. They'd used protection. She must have turned to someone else after he'd left.

Her answers had scaled up in anger and volume.

He'd hung up.

She was never able to reach him again.

Teagan had been born at the Whitefish hospital, and Elaine had been the best birthing coach a new mother could have.

Maggie should be grateful. She *was* grateful. They'd soldiered on—the Three Musketeers—without a man of any stripe in the picture. It had been hard.

And *now* Paul wanted to see if Teagan was his? After all the hard work was done?

With a groan, she reached into the garbage can, pulled out the ball of paper, and smoothed it out. It was one of those times when she wished she didn't feel so obligated to do the right thing.

# # #

"I made a warm cheese dip tonight," Kelly said as Maggie shook the raindrops from her coat and hung it on the peg in the mudroom.

Slipping off her shoes, she put on the slippers she'd brought from home and walked into the kitchen. "Where's Ryan?"

"Up at his studio. He's got a big commission due the end of the month, and it's not working out the way he'd planned it. I've learned to stay out of the way when that happens.

He's not bearable to be around."

"But you guys are okay, right?" The thought of her friend's second chance romance having any problems scared her.

"Oh yeah. Sure. I'm getting to know his moods, and he's getting to know mine. The nice thing about being older is I'm aware not everything is my fault, nor is it my responsibility to fix everything. It's very freeing."

"I'm not sure I could get there."

"You haven't really given yourself a chance."

"Justin and I are doing well. It might be for real. He made me dinner again on Thursday. And then we talked for hours. It was fun and easy, something I really needed before the chaos of the holiday weekend. People are cloning themselves, I swear it. This was the most traffic we've ever had."

"It's good that we're getting people to discover us."

"I hope it's not too much so we lose the character of the town."

The back door opened, and Alex stomped in.

"Whew!" she said. "It's coming down heavy out there."

"Supposed to rain solidly for the next three days," Kelly said.

"We need the rain," Alex said. "I brought the pie like you wanted. Charlene's using up the last of the strawberries she had, anticipating new ones arriving sometime in June."

"Some places have strawberries all year round," Maggie said.

"It's unnatural," Alex said. "Fruit should have a season, a flavor you only get to taste a few short months or weeks a year. It makes them special."

"I have three cheese dip, chips, and vegetables," Kelly said.

"And I brought wine and some small sandwiches Gregg was experimenting with," Maggie said.

Maggie uncorked the wine and poured it in the three glasses Alex placed next to her. The three women worked effortlessly together, as at ease in Kelly's kitchen as their own.

*Spring in Promise Cove*

As they served themselves and clinked glasses, they caught up on all of what had happened the week before.

Well, almost all.

"When do you think we'll get the stage done?" Alex asked. "I'm eager to hear Kelly's performance."

"I can wait," Kelly said.

"There's a lot to do," Maggie said. "The structure is the easy part. Now there's wiring, finishing, and all kinds of extras that stages require that I'd never even heard of. And this rain will delay things, too."

"There's bound to be more of it in June," Alex said, "before the rainy months end in July."

Maggie stuffed a cheese-laden broccoli floret in her mouth to prevent herself from saying anything about Paul's letter.

"These things always take longer than you think they should," Kelly said, taking a delicate bite from one of the sandwiches. When she'd finished swallowing, she said, "These are amazing."

"I got a letter from Paul," Maggie blurted out.

Kelly and Alex stared at her.

"*The* Paul?" Kelly asked.

Maggie nodded.

"You threw it away," Alex stated.

"Yes. But then I pulled it out of the trash. It's in my bag." She stared at her purse.

"Are you going to read it to us? I want to know what the jerk said."

"You don't have to," Kelly said, with a look toward Alex that said, "Back off."

Maggie got up and walked to her purse as if it were a ticking time bomb. After retrieving the letter, she leaned against the counter and read.

*Dear Maggie,*

*Don't throw this away. At least not until you hear me out.*

*I didn't act well when you told me you were pregnant. It was an action I will regret all my life, as short as it might* be.

*A cancer diagnosis makes a person rethink their life. While I've done some good things, I've made some mistakes. Before I leave this world, I want to make as much right as I can.*

*I'm ready to take that DNA test you asked me to do all those years ago. I'm sure your child is mine—you wouldn't lie to me. But I want this to be official in case anyone else has a question.*

*Will you do this for me?*

*I'd also like to meet your—our—child. I believe you had a daughter if my research is right. I know that's asking a lot, both of you and her. Please consider it.*

*Again, my heartfelt apologies for doing the wrong thing all those years ago.*
*Paul*

"He put in all his contact information," Maggie said as she folded up the letter and put it back in her purse.

"What are you going to do?" Kelly asked.

"I don't know."

"Ignore him," Alex said. "Just like he ignored you. Teagan doesn't need him. Why should she meet him and then lose him all over again because he's going to die?"

"Because it's the right thing to do." Kelly's voice was calm, but edged with steel. She sounded a lot like her grandmother, Henrietta.

Probably because it was exactly what Henrietta would have said. The original owner of the retreat center had had a high sense of morality and ethics, and made sure everyone thought about all the consequences of their actions.

And she was right.

Maggie returned to her chair, grabbed a chip, and mounded it with cheese. Once she'd munched it down, she took a good swallow of wine.

"Can we talk about something else?" she asked.

"Elaine told me you've decided to dig up the backyard. She thinks you're losing it," Alex announced.

Just once it would be nice to dissect Alex's life. The

problem was that there was no drama going on there. Alex spent her time creating amazing home decorations from wood. Nothing else was going on in her life.

"I'm trying to fix it up like my dad had it. Everyone else has a project. You guys are working on your art, Teagan's preparing to become an adult—at least she thinks she is—and my mother is flying to Europe. Why can't I have a project, too?"

"I'm just telling you what your mother said."

"My mother should keep her opinions to herself."

"Tell us about it. Big job?" Kelly glared at Alex.

"Bigger than I'd originally thought," Maggie said. "I want to start with the pond. Tom said I should make it bigger than my dad had it. He's going to tell me what I need and help me put it together. I may even get a turtle to put in there."

"A hawk will eat it," Alex said.

"We'll put in things so he can hide. We'll figure out something. Tom wouldn't let the turtle get hurt."

"No, he wouldn't," Kelly said softly. "He's a good man."

Maggie ignored the invitation to discuss Tom, and continued to talk about her plans for the back. "It's going to take time and a chunk of money, but it will be great. Something I can do to keep myself busy."

"I thought you had enough going on," Alex said. "I don't know how you do it. If I don't have my down time, I become pretty cranky."

Maggie and Kelly gave her a look.

"I know," Alex said. "I can be testy most of the time. That's why I love you guys. You put up with me."

"We love you, too," Maggie said.

"Dishes?" Kelly asked.

"Sounds good," Maggie said.

They went to work.

# Chapter Twenty-Four

"What's the problem?" Maggie asked George when she got to the site. He'd called her Thursday night to arrange the meeting. Mike was already there.

"There are a few. The simplest, but most annoying, is that things have gone missing. Little things, like three of a bunch of small wooden dowels we'd cut to make some connections. Some nuts and bolts we'd left to use the next time we got a chance to work here. Like I said, not much, but annoying and going to add extra time."

"I wonder if it's that same person Tom's chasing," Maggie said.

"You mean the one who's been taking all those little things like the trinket from the post office?" Mike asked.

Maggie nodded.

"Could be, but it's a bit out of character."

"I don't know. It's a thought."

"Yeah," George said. "Can you let Tom know? It might help find the person. My wife said one of the thimbles from her collection was missing after she'd had the church guild over a few weeks ago. It's downright annoying."

"What's he doing here?" Mike asked as he nodded toward Justin.

"I invited him," Maggie said. "I thought he might have some insights since he's a developer."

The man she was dating sauntered toward them, as put together and confident as possible. Where was the little leap of emotion she was supposed to feel for someone close?

What was wrong with her?

"Hi, everyone," Justin said. "Maggie said there were some problems. I'm here to help if I can."

"Thanks for coming by," George said.

Mike's hello was barely audible.

*Spring in Promise Cove*

What was up with him?

"As I was telling these two, there's some petty theft going on, but that's not the major problem. We ordered some wood from the lumberyard down in Columbia Falls. They didn't cut it right. All the pieces are at least an inch too short.

"They won't fit with the framework we've got," Justin said.

"Right. Here are the possibilities of what we can do." George continued on with his explanation, gesturing toward plans and places on the existing structures.

Mike and Justin asked questions, then Justin started making suggestions. George made counter suggestions that Justin swore weren't going to work.

"You're not from here!" Mike said, stepping forward with his barrel chest thrust out. "What George says goes. You don't get to act like you're in charge."

Whoa. She'd thought Mike and Justin got along.

Justin held up his hands as if to surrender. "Just trying to help, buddy."

"I'm not your buddy. You fooled me, coming in here friendly and helpful. But that's not really what you're after."

"I don't know what you're talking about." Justin turned so he was facing Mike head on.

"Oh, stop it!" Maggie said. "Both of you. Grow up." She turned to George. "Can you fix it?"

George stared at the plans, then at the tarped stack of wood the lumber company had delivered. "I think if we combine what I had in mind with one of Justin's suggestions, we can work around it. The alternative would be sending it back and asking for it to be recut. They probably wouldn't do it without a fight, and it would still cost us more money. The workaround will take some extra time, but we have more time than money, so that's what makes sense to me."

Justin and Mike had somehow moved back to their neutral corners without appearing to give ground.

Men. Why did she even bother trying to understand them?

"Okay then. We have a solution. Anything else?"

"Well ..." George said.

"Spill."

"One of the men keeps wanting to do things his way."

"Who?"

"James."

Of course. It had to be one of the joined-at-the-hip pair. The man was a brilliant painter, but she'd bet his elementary school report card had been filled with phrases like, "doesn't play well with others."

"I'll talk to him," she said.

"Okay then. We're set. See you Saturday," George said to Mike.

"I've got some time then, too," Justin said. "I'll be happy to lend a hand."

Mike opened his mouth.

Maggie glared at him.

He shut it.

"I've got to run," Justin said. "I've got a meeting in Whitefish. I'll call you later," he said to Maggie.

"Okay, thanks for stopping by," she said.

"I've got to go, too," George said. "Thanks for meeting me here. And talking to James. Justin had some good ideas." He patted her shoulder. "We'll get it done, Maggie. Don't you worry about it."

"Thanks, George.

As soon as George was out of earshot, she turned to Mike. "What's going on? I thought you liked Justin. He was going to invest in your brewery."

"I thought he was a good guy," Mike said. "But lately, I don't know. And I talked to a few of my friends in the microbrewery business. They said to be careful with investors. One of them even knew Justin from some other deal. He said Justin was a sharp businessman. And he didn't mean it in a nice way."

"I'm sure he is," Maggie said, unease taking a bit of her air away. "He wouldn't be as successful as he is if he didn't drive a hard bargain."

"You know," Mike said, his gaze steady on her, "people

*Spring in Promise Cove*

say those words, 'sharp businessman,' 'drive a hard bargain,' as if they're a good thing. And I suppose they are in a way. I mean, earning money, and lots of it, is the sign off success, isn't it?"

"Yes."

"But there's an edge to those phrases. For me, they mean that the person wins what he or she wants, but doesn't worry about the cost to the other person. There's also a feeling of shadiness about deals that may happen. I've known people—good people—who've been backed into a corner and made to do deals they didn't want to do, just because someone knew how to manipulate the law and the banks a little bit better than they did."

"Interesting observation," she said.

"Comes with the territory." He shrugged. "I'm a bartender. People tell me all kinds of stuff and I tend to think about it as I'm cleaning up at night."

"And you think Justin's that kind of man."

"I don't know anything, but be careful. We all care about you, Maggie. A man like Justin is always going to be looking for the next deal, the next opportunity."

Maggie nodded, unable to say anything because the air in her lungs seemed to have completely deserted her.

What if Mike was right?

"I could be totally off base, too," Mike said. "He could be perfect for you. And the town."

"I think he will be," she said.

"Anyway. Thanks for taking care of this. I'll buy you a beer next time you come in." With a wave, Mike grabbed his bike and headed down the road to the saloon.

Maggie walked across the street toward the general store, rehearsing what she'd say to James. Should she meet him in person? Probably.

But not now. She didn't have the strength.

A few people wandered around the store, most of whom she recognized, but at least one out-of-towner. As she walked to the counter, she automatically straightened things, placing a candy bar back in its rack, and taking an abandoned box of sugary cereal back to its shelf.

Sandy was at the counter chatting with one of the regulars as she rang up the order. The customer nodded and smiled as Sandy's efficient moves rapidly took care of the transaction.

Teagan came from the far side where the luncheon tables were located, a bottle of spray and rag in her hands. "Tables are all clean and set up," she announced to Sandy.

"Looking good, ladies," Maggie said after the customer left the counter.

"Thanks, Maggie," Sandy said.

"Think you can handle it for a few more hours?"

"Sure."

"Then I'm going to head down to Whitefish and pick up some of the plants I need for the backyard," she said. "I'll have my cell if anything comes up."

"Okay, Mom," Teagan said. "Have fun."

Maggie grabbed her purse and keys from the back office and headed to her Yukon. There was plenty of room in the back to bring home the shrubs she'd envisioned along the back of the house. Her dad had only planted a few, and about half of them had died.

Today the May weather was holding. Sun filtered through the trees, and she turned on the most relaxing playlist she owned, a combination of New Age and Native American. For several miles she tuned into the road and the music, leaving all other worries behind. But soon small thought tendrils made their way into the crooks and crannies of her brain matter. What would she say to James? Was Justin who she thought he was? And what was she going to do about Paul's request?

The tires ate up the pavement. Occasionally, crows and ravens swooped across the road, but the large animals, mostly deer, were enjoying a midday nap somewhere.

Why were there always problems she had to deal with?

Because she'd decided to run for mayor. Thankfully, Alex had demanded she give up the chairmanship of the summertime celebration. She and Kelly were running it jointly, with Gabriella and Susan Thomas providing substantial support.

Maggie smiled when she thought of Susan.

Over the past six months the woman had really become part of the community. She'd joined the volunteer fire department, right before the biggest fire the area had seen in a long time. While she'd been injured during the fight, that had only rallied people around her more. The community had finally seen past the tough exterior she displayed to the warmth and commitment of the person beneath it.

Kelly had been responsible for that. Susan had been a member at the first retreat Kelly had held.

If her friend could perform miracles like that, why was she being so stubborn about attending a retreat? She could certainly use the wisdom of other people. Instead of getting easier, life kept piling on problems: her mother, Teagan, James, Justin, the center, and now Paul.

Thankfully, Tom had stopped asking her out.

But was that really a good thing?

Of course it was. One less headache.

Maggie pulled into the parking lot of a nursery that specialized in native plants. She and her dad used to come here when it first opened, and he'd schooled her in the need to plant with as many native species as possible. "We never know what can be invasive," he'd told her. "Not until it takes hold and drives out the plants more suited to sustainability. Just look at the Russian olive. It was used for gardening, escaped, and now it crowds out native vegetation and uses up precious water near our rivers."

She'd taken his lessons to heart.

An older woman, graying hair captured in a braid, came out to meet her as she walked through the gate. "Hello, I'm Peggy. How are you doing?"

"I'm good," Maggie replied as she gazed around at the myriad of plants that seemed to stretch on for acres. "No, I'm better than good. This is more amazing than I remembered it."

Peggy smiled. "Plants are your happy place."

"Yes, I guess so. I don't think I'd realized it until I started reworking my dad's old garden."

"How long has he been gone?"

"Uh ... how did you know?"

"Dedicated gardeners don't give up until they have to. Besides, you look familiar, a family resemblance to someone I once saw often, I think."

"I used to come here a lot with my dad, Jack Marston. I'm Maggie."

"Oh yes! I remember Jack. He was a dear man. Gave us a lot of business when we were just starting out. And he was always referring people to me. Nice guy. I'm sorry to hear he passed."

"It was a while ago. I've been busy raising my daughter and handling the store." Something about Maggie made it easy to share details of her life. She followed the woman into the cool comfort of the store. Colorful pots lined the floor and some shelves, intermixed with garden ornaments. A pair of cast iron cranes caught her eye. They would be amazing by her pond.

"Did you bring your plans with you?" Peggy asked.

"No, sorry. I was so excited to get down here, I didn't think at all."

Peggy laughed. "Well, let's see what we can do about that. Tell me what you had in mind."

Maggie described the feeling she wanted to create when someone walked out the back door. "It's a small porch—more of a landing really—and I do need to paint it. There's an overhang my dad put in. It's big enough to keep the water off the porch."

"Are there eaves? Where does the water run?"

Maggie had to think about it for a moment. "To one of the front sides."

"Then you're going to want to be careful what you put there. Have you considered a rainwater barrel?"

"No, I hadn't even thought about it."

"With the weather getting drier, it's a good investment. That way you can capture the water in the rainy season and parse it out during the hot months. Let me show you what I mean."

Maggie leaned closer as Peggy explained the best way to

capture the water and direct it into an irrigation system. Then she helped Maggie decide the shrubs to use on the back end of the house. All were low-maintenance in terms of water and native to the area.

"I'll have to look into the rainwater later," Maggie said. "It's a good idea, but not in my budget right now." She gave a glance toward the cranes.

"Ah, you've fallen in love with our cranes," Peggy said. "Tell you what. You become as good a customer as your father was, and I'll sell them to you at cost."

"Oh, that would be too much," Maggie protested.

"Not in the least. Like I said, your dad was an early supporter. It's the least I can do for his daughter."

"Thank you," Maggie said, tears welling in her eyes.

"None of that. Now, let's get your plants loaded."

After stopping for supplies to strip and paint the back landing and steps, Maggie drove home with a contentment she hadn't felt in a long time. The problems that had been plaguing her were still there but seemed less strident than they had been on her way to Whitefish.

James would still have to wait until she got to a phone and arranged to see him.

But the more she thought about Paul's request, the more she felt she could give him what he needed for a paternity test. All it would take was a few hairs from Teagan's hairbrush. Her daughter didn't need to know.

And she never had to give Paul permission to see her.

Would he try to sidestep her and get to Teagan directly?

He could, but at some level she had to trust that he wouldn't. The man had cancer. She had to respect that. She'd take it one step at a time and pray she was doing the right thing.

Tomorrow.

Today she was going to enjoy the aroma of the plants in her vehicle, the soft music surrounding her, and the miles of Montana beauty ahead of her.

## Chapter Twenty-Five

Late Saturday morning, Maggie drove up to James's cabin. Her Yukon groaned and strained up the rocky, windy dirt road. About halfway up, a boulder had been left wedged into the dirt on the side of the road, forcing her into a tight turn around it. It was a wonder no one broke an axle on the thing.

Fifty yards before she got to her destination, a smaller, even more rutted road branched off to the right. Jim's house was up there. Such an odd pair. They'd each been married at one point or another, but the relationships hadn't lasted. Only their friendship survived.

When she reached the weathered-wood structure in the midst of tall pines, she parked in the only spot she could find—snug between two sturdy trunks. She squeezed out of the car, leaving her purse behind. Only a passing bear would be interested.

Climbing onto the front porch, she knocked on the once-varnished door.

No footsteps.

She knocked again, then looked around for a doorbell.

Nothing.

His vehicle was here, so he must be, unless he'd hiked over to Jim's on the worn path that headed away from the small clearing. She walked around the porch to the side of the house. No separate studio in the back; he must have a space inside his house.

She'd texted him she was coming. Had he forgotten?

After hesitating a bit more, she walked to the back of the house, where the clearing pushed back farther into the woods. Another pair of huge boulders hung over a cliff that dropped a few dozen feet. Light from the midday sun poured through the opening, highlighting the studio skylight and sliding glass doors at the back of the house.

Inside, James studied a canvas. The earbuds he wore explained why he hadn't heard her.

She knocked on the glass door.

He didn't move.

She tested the door.

Open.

She pushed the panel aside and walked into the studio.

"James?" she said, slowly walking into his vision.

"Oh!" He pulled out the earbuds. "Sorry. Van Halen. Helps me work but drowns out everything else." He wiped his hands on a paint-splattered rag. "Come into the kitchen. Coffee is on."

He led the way down a narrow hall to a wide open room that contained both kitchen and living space.

"Have a seat. Milk? Sugar?" He poured steaming coffee into a sturdy black mug.

"Plain. Thanks."

He placed the mug in front of her, then returned with his own bright red counterpart.

"So what can I do for you?" he asked.

"I appreciate the help you're giving us for the performing arts center," she said.

"No problem. It's good to help the community. Jim thinks so, too. Besides, I'm hoping we can get Van Halen to come play."

All she knew about Van Halen was that they were a rock band from a long time ago. "Are they still alive?"

His brow wrinkled. "I'm not sure. I know Eddie had cancer, but I thought he beat it. I better check."

"Well, if they're still together, I can check," she said with a smile.

James stared at the red mug, his brow still wrinkled.

"Um, James?"

"Oh. What? That's right. You said you wanted to talk about something."

"Yes." She drank a bit more of her coffee. "I was talking to George the other day. He's had a few problems on the site."

"I told him he shouldn't have gone with those crooks in Columbia Falls. They're always out to cheat people. Never listen. Always cut the wood wrong." James's head wagged back and forth like a Bassett hound after dunking its ears in a long drink of water.

"I don't think they're crooks, James. From what George said, these things happen. He usually insists on a sample before they run the wood, but he didn't have time. They've figured out how to fix that."

"Oh, well, that's good."

Nothing left but to bite the bullet. "But there's another problem, James."

"Oh, what's that?"

"You see, George is in charge of the whole building job."

"I *know* that."

"And I'm sure you have experience building."

"I sure do. I built this whole place myself. With a bit of help from Jim." James's head bobbled in the opposite direction.

"Well then, I'm sure you understand the importance of a team pulling together and doing things the same way."

"I sure do."

"That means that what George says, is the way things get done," she finished.

"Of course." He stopped moving. "Unless there's a better way to do it."

She took a swig of coffee and tried again.

"Then you talk to him about it."

"I always do."

"But if he says to do it his way, then …?" She raised an eyebrow and looked directly at him.

"I … oh … well … sometimes he's wrong."

"He's the one in charge. Everything needs to be done the same way. Don't you agree?"

"Well … yes, but … Maggie, sometimes he's just wrong."

"I understand. But at the end of the day, what George says goes. Okay? Can you do that for me, James?"

He put down his cup. "I suppose. You know I'd do anything for you, Maggie. The whole town would."

"Thanks," she said.

They finished their coffee, and James showed her his latest work before she headed back down the hill, carefully avoiding the axle-breaking boulder. James had assured her he would do things George's way. One problem solved.

Unease itched between her shoulder blades. Would the town do anything for her? And what kind of responsibility did that require from her? She'd run for mayor thinking it would be a symbolic position, providing press releases for Promise Cove events, and talking points during the stress of summer months.

Instead, it was turning out to be a whole lot more.

When she got back to the store, she spent a few moments checking that everything was running smoothly, ate lunch, then put on her gardening clothes.

In the back, she studied the area where she wanted to put the shrubs, then began to dig. Any bulbs she lifted out with the pitchfork, she put aside. She remembered how daffodils and crocus had come up faithfully every spring, followed by tulips. Later on less common flowers appeared, all chosen carefully by her father. Lately, they'd not been showing as much. As she dug, she realized they needed to be separated. There were more than enough to replant around the bushes and then add to areas around the garden.

By the end of the day, she was exhausted. She pushed herself up to standing and stepped back.

"It looks lovely." Elaine's voice startled her.

"I should have painted the porch before I did this. But I needed to get my hands in the dirt."

Elaine walked down the steps. "I brought you some iced tea." Ice cubes clinked as she handed Maggie the glass.

Maggie gulped half the glass down. "Thanks. I didn't realize how thirsty I was."

Elaine put her arm around Maggie's shoulders.

"Don't, I'm all sweaty," Maggie protested.

"That's never stopped me before. I'm so proud of you. In so many ways. I know I don't tell you nearly enough."

"Thanks, Mom."

Elaine gave Maggie a brief squeeze then let her go. She

studied the bushes, then turned to look around at the rest of the space. "It's going to take a lot of work, but I know it will be beautiful, just as it was when your father created it all those years ago." Her voice sounded wistful.

"Do you miss him?"

"Every day." Elaine sipped her own drink. "What happens over time is that the loss simply becomes part of your life. Jack is part of who I was and who I am. I feel him around me; sometimes I even talk to him."

"I miss him, too."

"I know you do. And I also know as you recreate this space, adding your own stamp, that you do it with him spiritually by your side."

Maggie put her arm around Elaine. "Love you, Mom."

At that moment she felt her father snuggling next to them, surrounding them in his soul's peace and love.

# # #

A light drizzle landed on the trees outside Justin's window, causing the needles to bend to end in a small droplet of water. Occasionally the sun would pop through and light up the forest like it was filled with diamonds.

She'd never be able to leave this land. It was too amazingly beautiful.

Shifting to watch Justin prepare their lunch, she wondered again what the end might be.

"You are a good cook," she said.

"Necessity. I like well-made meals, and there was no one else to create them for me."

The sounds of smooth jazz underscored the sizzle of onions sautéing in a shiny silver fry pan. He was making some kind of chard dish he planned to serve her along with a delicately baked trout.

She liked neither, but she wasn't going to say anything. At some level his savoir faire intimidated her.

"I'm sure if you ever get married again, your wife will appreciate that fact."

His glance was sharp, and for a second she caught a

glimpse of the astute businessman he was supposed to be.

"It smells delicious," she immediately said.

His shoulders relaxed enough to be noticeable.

"Can I do anything?"

"Not really. How do you like the wine?"

"It's really delightful. Um ... like lemons but not too tart."

He nodded. "Good description. I'd love to take you over to Washington for a long weekend. The vineyards around Walla Walla are finally coming into their own. Plus, it's a charming little town. Lots to shop for." He dumped a bunch of shredded chard into the pan, swirled it around, then covered the pan.

"Sounds fun."

"Great restaurants, too. There are dozens of places like that I'd love to show you."

She took another sip of the wine. It all sounded fantastic, everything she'd ever dreamed about seeing.

"Any place you've always wanted to see?" he asked.

"San Francisco. Henrietta—that's Kelly's grandmother—always talked about it like it was an enchanted place."

"Ah, the hippie dream of old. San Francisco isn't like that anymore though, except where they play for the tourists. Now it's high rents and tech companies, glitter and big money."

"You're not a fan."

"Not really. It's like LA, trying to be the image it invented for itself."

"I see."

He lifted the lid, swirled the greens again, then added a splash of Balsamic vinegar.

A timer buzzed, and he opened the oven. Putting on a mitt, he pulled out a pair of golden trout. Deftly, he slid the fish onto two white china plates, then added the greens.

"Can you bring the wine?"

"Sure."

They settled at a small dining room table near the plate glass windows. Everything outside was shrouded in fog and rain, but it still had a beauty that soothed.

Tentatively, she took a bite of the fish, ready to wash it down with the sauvignon blanc he'd provided.

Instead, she chewed thoughtfully. The man could cook. What was more impressive was that he could make it all come out at the same time without a big production.

"This is wonderful," she said. And without thinking, she repeated, "Some woman is going to be very happy."

He frowned, then put down his fork.

"Maggie, I need to make something clear. Marriage is not in my future. I tried it once and it didn't suit me."

"You'll never love anyone again?"

"Not what I said. I envision finding someone, maybe someone like you, that I can spend time with, make love to, and share life's journey for however it lasts."

"And when it's over?"

"We'll know it," he said. "And we'll part as friends."

"And you'll give her a gift to sweeten the ending."

"Don't be crass, Maggie. It doesn't suit you."

"Sorry."

But all the same, she felt like she was right.

## Chapter Twenty-Six

"This spring is bad already," Ben, one of the local forest rangers, said to Tom when he stopped by the office for their regular monthly meeting. "The heavy snowfall, followed by a dramatic increase in temperatures, is destabilizing everything. The warm weather is also increasing the number of people out on the trails." He took a sip from the thick white mug of coffee Ingrid, Tom's dispatcher, had poured him.

"And the bears are out and hungry," Tom said.

"Yep. But I'm more worried about the snow. This weather has gotten so crazy."

Tom nodded. While climate change may be heating the planet overall, shifting air streams made some cold places colder and others warmer. The reliable feeling he'd always had about Montana weather was being undermined as rapidly as the snow on the mountains.

Putting his mug on the counter, he walked over to the big county map he kept at the front of the office space he shared with the deputy sheriff. It was a topographical map, the curves showing the elevation of the mountains that swept north to Eureka and the Canadian border beyond, as well as the marked trails through the region. Next to it was a street map of Promise Cove and its immediate environs. It was dotted with black pins showing him where the petty thefts had occurred.

Not that it was helping him much.

Pointing to the topo map, he said, "Can you show me where the cornices are that make you most concerned for an avalanche. That way I can let folks know, particularly those who like to hike, what areas to stay away from."

"Good idea." Ben walked over to the map, and Tom handed him a box of red pins. "We've already put warnings at the trail heads, but any additional help to keep people off those trails is useful. There's always that one guy who thinks he knows better, or an out-of-towner who doesn't understand what an avalanche can do and how fast it can do it."

He studied the map, then placed five pins on scattered ridges. "I'd say these are the most likely to go in the next few weeks."

Tom looked at the pins and then traced a line of the most likely fall to see if there were trails in its path. "This is the only one that seems to be a problem to me."

Ben nodded. "Although these two could be in trouble, too."

"I see that."

After checking the round white clock on the wall above the maps, Ben said, "Got to go. Thanks for the coffee." He took a last sip and placed the empty mug back on the counter. "I'll keep you posted on the danger."

"Thanks."

After Ben left, Tom studied the town map. There was no rhyme or reason to the thefts. Most of the things taken were small items, usually only of sentimental value, although some expensive pieces had been snatched.

Could the person be doing it because they felt a need to take something? Kleptomania was rarer than crime shows would have the public believe, but these thefts felt like they were done by someone who had no impulse control. Someone who no one would ever notice.

Someone no one had noticed.

He sat at his desk and pulled up the list of victims he'd made on his computer. Then he picked up his phone and began calling.

### # # #

Two hours later he leaned back in his chair and studied the two names he'd added to several of the incident reports: Nancy Smith, a local mystery writer, and his own dispatcher, Ingrid Germundson.

He found it hard to believe Ingrid could be the culprit. She was so organized and methodical. Everything had to be in its place. But maybe taking little things was her true personality trying to get out? The compulsive opposite to the obsessive streak that made the office run as beautifully as it did?

His impression of Nancy was that there was none. She embodied the term "mousy."

Tapping his pen on the table, he stared at the two names. One of them was his thief, he could feel it in his bones. But who?

His cell phone tooted his cousin's ringtone, "Melodramma" by Andrea Bocelli. It suited his sister, Laura. He smiled.

"Hi there," he said.

"Hi, yourself. How are you? Maggie agree to go out with you yet?"

"Not yet."

"There's always hope. You're a good guy. Someday she'll open her eyes and see it."

"Uh-huh. So what can I do for you?"

"I'm mainly calling to find out how Sandy is doing at the store."

"Maggie loves her. She trusts her more every day, I think."

"Great," Laura said.

"And that ended that."

"Yep. She's really good at managing things. And I know she likes the store. She's a small town girl at heart. I hope some guy comes along and appreciates her, that's all."

"Sounds like Maggie when she was that age," Tom said.

Laura sighed. "Seriously, Tom, when are you going to shake that woman up and make her take a look at you?"

"That's not my style."

"Well, maybe it should be your style. She sees you as a friend. The only way she's going to see something different is if you *be* someone different."

"Ah, Laura, I wish that was true, but I think it's simply a lost cause. She wants someone totally different from me."

"Who? That Justin fellow?" Laura laughed. "He's a here today, gone tomorrow kind of guy. I know his type. They come into the real estate office all the time. Montana is a dream world to them. They buy property, thinking they own a piece of the last best place, then discover living in a remote state with a winter that lasts beyond reason isn't for them. They either sell outright, or use their property as a rental investment."

"Maggie seems to think he's going to stick."

"Maggie's wrong. You've got a chance, Tom. Take it."

"I'm going to look for another job," he blurted out. He couldn't stand being hounded about Maggie anymore. She wasn't his and she was never going to be his.

"Don't be ridiculous. You belong here."

"I'm not. I'm serious. I'm ready to start over."

"Tom, you're in your forties. Think of everything you'll lose if you leave the job you've worked for the last twenty years. Wait another five. Retire. Then go look for something else."

She was right. Laura had always been smart about financial decisions. But he didn't know if he could stay in the same town with Maggie for another five years.

"I'll think about it."

"And think about the other thing I said. Make a bold move. Something that makes her take notice. Women love big demonstrations."

"Uh-huh."

"Really, bro. I love you. I want to see you happy."

"Thanks. I know you do. But can we get off the subject?"

"Sure." She went on to catch him up on the status of her progeny, the real estate business, and the latest gossip she'd picked up at the post office. After they'd said goodbye, he pulled up his resume and made a few changes. As soon as he'd gotten it as good as he wanted, he clicked over to the application he'd found for a deputy sheriff's job in Park County. Carefully, he filled out the lines and attached his resume.

After he'd reviewed it, he let his mouse hover over the send button. He stared for a few moments. Park County was home to the rich and famous who were seeking peace and quiet, just like the Whitefish area was. He'd do well there. The salary was great. There were more things to do and more people to meet than there would ever be in Promise Cove.

He moved the mouse and clicked save.

Closing down his computer, he made sure everything was locked up tight and went out to his cruiser.

# # #

Saturday morning he got up early, threw a load of wash in, and made a shopping list while he ate his breakfast of egg, avocado, and whole wheat toast. Then he headed south to Columbia Falls for his monthly trip to stock up at a larger grocery store. Culver's General Store was great for more than most people would expect, but almost everyone in Promise Cove went to one of the larger towns or cities to buy in bulk. The same was true in small towns all across Montana.

Before the advent of online stores, families always planned a weekend trip to one of the big Montana cities or to nearby Coeur d'Alene or Spokane. Now everyone knew the name of their UPS and Fed-Ex drivers.

Before he hit the Super 1, he stopped by a few of the hardware and garden supply stores in the area, pricing the supplies he'd need to create the pond Maggie envisioned. He took measurements and wrote them down to determine how wide and how deep he was going to need to dig to make the hole based on the available lining sizes. Once he'd done that, he'd lay out the best way to arrange the circulating pump and pipes.

A few things at the garden store caught his eye. There were all sorts of urns and frogs, as well as other things that could be used to make the structure more interesting. As he looked, he wrote down possibilities and prices. He may not be the one to provide the flashy car or expensive dinner, but there might be another way to make Maggie see him for the man he was.

Once he finished his shopping and stowed perishables in the freezer bags he had for the purpose, he headed his truck back to Promise Cove. It was the beginning of June, and late spring was coming into full flower. Word was they'd have the Going to the Sun Road open by next weekend. He'd gotten his ticket for his annual trip over when they'd become available.

It was his favorite time to be in this part of the world. Everything seemed fresh and possible, as if nothing bad had ever happened in any corner of the world. Hope filled the air. New life was stirring. Being able to cruise the county and see newborn fawns, geese, and even a bear cub or two was one of the perks of the job.

He drove home, put the groceries away, moved the wash to the dryer, then headed back down to the store. When he peeked over the fence behind the store, he smiled. Maggie was hard at work.

"Need a hand?" he called out.

"Love one," she replied.

## Chapter Twenty-Seven

A bubble of happiness went through Maggie when Tom walked through the gate in his work clothes with his tools. She loved working on the garden by herself, but having a friend with her was even better.

"I'd like to start digging out the pond if that's okay by you," he said. "I went down to Columbia Falls this morning to do my shopping and stopped by a few stores to look at pond supplies. I know how big it has to be."

"That's wonderful! Sure!" Then she frowned. "But I'm not going to be able to afford the liner or pump or anything soon. Teagan's tuition is coming due. Even with her grants and loans, it's still a hefty amount. Mom started a fund when she was a kid, but tuition costs have gone up so much lately, it isn't covering as much as we'd hoped."

"Let's not get ahead of ourselves," Tom said. "All I'm doing is digging. Won't cost you a thing. Except maybe some of that lemonade you make. You know it's my favorite."

She laughed. "Sounds like a deal. And since you're in a digging mood, you can help me dig out this space over here. I'm planning some rocks and native grasses, with a dogwood to help provide shade and space for birds to build nests. But the dirt needs to be turned. You can use the soil you dig from the pond to help mound it."

He nodded. "Yes, ma'am," he said with a smile.

"Stop it."

"Nope," he said. "It's your garden, and I learned a long time ago not to argue with you when you have a plan, because you have a reason for doing everything you do."

She laughed. "Remember that time in fifth grade when we were doing that experiment? It was you and me and Jeff and Tony?"

"Yep." He grinned. "You told us we were doing it the

wrong way."

"But you wouldn't listen to me because I was a *girl*, and girls knew nothing about science."

"Boy were we dumb." He shook his head.

"Yep. But I had a good laugh when you guys stood there with slime all over you."

"You backed off in time."

"I knew what was coming." She smirked at him.

"That's when I knew that the only reaction to have when you are determined is to follow or get out of the way."

She laughed again, her ribcage releasing stress as she did so. It was a perfect moment. The sun in the sky, her dirty, sweaty efforts showing all over her body, and her dearest friend standing before her, ready to pitch in with a grin.

If only she could preserve this moment for the rest of her life.

Suddenly, she stopped laughing.

"What?" he asked.

"Oh … nothing." She smiled again, hiding the realization that had hit her. "Let's get to work."

He saluted and went off to dig the pond.

She stared at the future rock garden, but it wasn't what she was seeing. Instead, her memory was playing a film of a series of memories: times she and Tom had been together having fun, or adventures, or when he held her as she cried when her current crush had turned her down for the school dance.

He'd always been there for her, never asking much, only to be by her side. No matter how many times she'd turned him down for a date, he stuck by her.

Had she been a fool?

Without turning, she looked over at where he dug, his muscles visible as he attacked the ground with gusto.

Wasn't she supposed to feel something when she saw a man she loved using his body for her sake?

Nothing. No secret little softenings that were always too well described in her mother's torrid romances.

Maybe she was incapable of feeling anything anymore. Was she too old?

But she was only in her mid-forties. Weren't women supposed to be at the top of their sexual game when they turned fifty?

Was there something wrong with her?

"You working over there, or just daydreaming?" Tom yelled as he straightened and stretched his back.

"I'm on this." She pushed the tines of the pitchfork into the ground as far as she could. It went in about three inches and stopped. Pressing one foot on one side and then the other, she gained another inch. After wiggling it back and forth, she gave a little hop and got both feet on the edges.

A solid stop threw her off the tool.

She'd picked a good place for a rock garden.

Yanking out the pitchfork, she came back an inch and tried again.

Same problem.

It took two more tries before she was able to get the tines under the rock and push it toward the surface. Working her way around it, and digging out some of the dirt over it, she was finally able to bring it to the surface.

Not a very large stone for all that effort. She leveraged it from the hole with her gloved hands and tossed it to one side. She'd use it to build the rock retaining wall by the butterfly garden. She didn't have any clue how to build a wall, but somehow she'd figure it out.

"Got a wheelbarrow?" Tom called over.

"Yep. It's over there by the shed." She pointed to a far corner where her dad had built a makeshift structure. It was beyond weathered, with gaping holes, and it listed away from the fence, but it was still standing.

"Good. I'll use it for the soil once I get the really large rocks out of it. Where are you putting rocks by the way?"

"Can you stack them over there? I'll use them for the wall."

"Sure thing."

They went back to work. A little over an hour later she'd made discernable progress on the rock garden, and it looked like he was halfway through the pond hole. They each had good-sized piles of rocks started, and there was a cone of soft rich earth next to the rock garden.

"How about I get some lemonade?" she asked.

"Sounds good."

Brushing off her hands and jeans, she headed up the stairs that had finally dried after she'd scraped, primed, and painted them. At the top of the landing, she'd placed a couple of plastic chairs from the store's inventory and a foldable camp table. It was functional, but lacked the touches Kelly would have brought to any environment.

Before going into the kitchen, Maggie took a moment to look over the backyard, reimagining her garden in full bloom.

"Lemonade is ready," she called out when she returned to the porch.

"Great." Tom ran the back of his hand over his forehead, his gloves leaving a smudge. He yanked off his gloves and came up. Settling into a chair, he grabbed the glass and drank it down quickly. "Thirsty work, this gardening."

"Indeed. And messy." She pointed to his forehead.

"I'll be taking a shower as soon as I get home," he said. He glanced at the sun. "I have enough time to finish digging out the pond, then I'll need to get home."

"Hot date?" she said, keeping her tone light, to hide the unexpected hit of pain she felt.

"Nah. Dinner with Laura and the family. They have me over once a month. They're under this mistaken impression that a man can't cook for himself."

"Not that you correct that impression."

"Not in the least. A smart man never turns down a meal someone else cooks. And Laura's a really good cook."

"So's my mother. It's going to be tough when she leaves. I can do the basics, but it's not something that I enjoy. You can cook for hours, and it's gone in fifteen minutes. With the garden, it can last a long time."

"It's going to be beautiful. Just what you imagined."

"I hope so. It's going to take a while to bring together."

"Good things always do," he said.

The air between them shifted as he held her gaze a little longer than normal. She looked away. "More lemonade?"

"Sure." He held out his glass. "So I know you have the butterfly garden there, vegetables here, close to the house, and your rock garden over there. Paths in between?"

"Yes. I'm debating between slate or pebbles. Alex did a fabulous job with her walkway, lining it with rocks and fun things like fairies and frogs. I think there's even a dragon somewhere."

"Somehow I never thought of Alex as someone who went in for that kind of thing. She's always been a bit serious. I've worked hard never to get on her bad side."

"It got worse after her husband was killed," Maggie said.

Tom nodded. "I've never considered myself a pacifist—sometimes war is a necessary evil—but I sure wish we could live without it. Maybe if we spent as much time building peace as we do inventing weapons to kill each other, we could have fewer wars." He shrugged. "I don't know. I don't think anyone does."

She thought about his words. Time was changing her friend. The carefree young man was turning into someone who no longer took things for granted. It probably had something to do with his work.

"Any luck on the thefts?"

"Getting closer, I think. If there was only some way to be positive. I don't want to accuse anyone unjustly."

"What if you asked a few of us to keep a lookout of the few people you suspect?"

Tom shook his head. "Too intrusive, both for the person watching and the other. I want to keep us all together, not tear us apart."

"You're right."

He grinned. "Did I hear that? Did you actually say I was right?"

She gave him a mock punch in the arm. "I must have been mistaken."

"No doubt." His gaze locked in on hers again, and the light moment turned almost sweet. He placed his hand over hers, wrapping his fingers around hers.

Her pulse quickened.

"Come with me tonight," he said. "Laura wouldn't mind.

It wouldn't be a date. Not really. Just two friends going to a relative's house for dinner."

For a moment, a longing overtook her. She wanted to go with him. Laura's daughter, Sandy, was a joy to have around. Although she knew Laura only casually, the woman was always friendly.

Maggie took a deep breath, preparing to say yes for the first time.

Then she withdrew her hand.

"I can't. I promised Justin I'd watch a movie with him tonight."

"Oh." Tom looked away. "Maybe another time." He finished his lemonade and stood. "Time to get back to work."

Tightness took up residence in Maggie's chest as she returned the lemonade to the fridge and the glasses to the sink.

Her life was turning into a gigantic mess.

## Chapter Twenty-Eight

"So, give," Alex said to Maggie when they settled into Kelly's kitchen for another rainy Wednesday night. "What is Tom doing over at your house?"

"Helping me with my garden," Maggie replied. "I'm trying to make it come alive again. He saw me working, asked about it, and offered to help."

"And you, being no fool, took it," Kelly said, unwrapping Maggie's containers and adding them to the large kitchen table. They'd decided on a taco night. The fixings were on the table; all they had to do was dig in.

"Yeah."

"Why are you so glum about free labor?" Alex asked.

Maggie grabbed a warm flour tortilla with the tongs and laid it on her plate. She stalled as she added meat, cheese, guacamole, sour cream, lettuce, onion, and salsa. More time went by as she carefully folded to create the shape that would keep everything in, knowing that no matter how much care she took, juice would drip from the bottom and slide down her wrist.

Tacos were a messy business.

Like her life.

"Well?" Alex persisted.

"He's a good friend, that's all." Maggie took a big bite.

"I think you aren't telling us everything."

Maggie pointed to her mouth where she slowly chewed her food.

"I suspect the conflict between liking Tom and going out with Justin may be coming to a head," Kelly said, folding her own tortilla.

Kelly's tortillas never leaked.

Maggie shot her a glance. She'd never understand how Kelly knew what she did. Henrietta had been like that. It was eerie.

She finished chewing, put down her taco, and wiped her hand.

"Alright. I know you're not going to give up. Tom asked me to go with him to Laura's house for dinner. I already had a date with Justin. Tom wasn't happy about it. I haven't seen him for days."

"Well, what do you expect?" Alex asked. "He's been waiting for you to come to your senses for twenty some odd years. He's not going to last forever. In fact, there's a rumor going around town that he's applying for another sheriff's job."

"Somewhere else?" It couldn't be true.

Alex nodded.

Suddenly Maggie didn't feel like eating anymore. Tom couldn't leave. He was part of life in Promise Cove. Part of *her* life.

"I think it might not be the right time for this discussion," Kelly said. "How about we talk about the summer celebration instead. I've got a bunch of questions. I can't believe how much work goes into this. I know I saw it last year, but you made it seem so effortless, Maggie."

"Thanks." Maggie attempted to refold her tortilla and picked up the soggy mess again.

Tom was a friend, she insisted to herself. Love, true love, needed to come with magic: violins suddenly playing in the background and fireworks going off. The hero needed to be handsome, with a well-defined jaw and maybe a trace of stubble. A sexy British accent wouldn't hurt. Someone like Jude Law would be perfect.

So would Justin Thomas. He ticked all the boxes of what a hero was supposed to be: good-looking, smart, and comfortably well-off.

Not Tom Gerard. Tom was too familiar. Too comfortable. Like Maggie, the forties were making him a little bit squidgy around the edges. His jawline could no longer be defined as sharp, and his hair had drifted back from where it was in his twenties.

But was that all love was to her? A handsome man with

*Spring in Promise Cove*

good manners? She couldn't be that narrow, could she?

The memory of what she'd had with Paul haunted her. He'd definitely set off sparks all the way through her. Their time together had been all her fantasies come true. Justin was the one most like Paul. Even if she didn't feel the same spark, it would come in time. She wasn't young any more after all.

And Justin had indicated he was going to stay, at least part time, in Promise Cove. He was trying to become part of the community. Look at what he'd done to get the performing arts building off the ground.

"Earth to Maggie," Alex said, interrupting her vision of attending a red-carpet premier on Justin's arm.

"Oh." She refocused on the table before her. Her plate was covered with the remains of several tacos which she'd evidently devoured while daydreaming.

"We've asked you several times where you keep the list of vendors for the fair," Alex said. "You've nodded, but that's it. So where is it?"

"Where's what?"

"The list of vendors and their contact information."

Maggie became alert. Alex's voice had an edge to it, which meant she was on the verge of becoming totally sarcastic.

"It's on my computer—a spreadsheet. I'll send it to you."

"How about I send you an email and remind you?" Kelly asked gently.

"That would be good."

"Are you finished?" Kelly asked, looking at first Alex and then Maggie.

"Yes," they chorused.

Sometimes it was as if Kelly was the earth mother of the trio, guiding them to where they needed to go.

"How is the retreat planning going?" Maggie asked as they started cleaning up.

"The group is almost set," Kelly said. "And I have to say I'm nervous about them. They are all strong women with solid careers, and they all know each other. I have no idea why they think they need a retreat."

"Because every woman, no matter who she is or what she's accomplished, needs time alone to reflect on where her life is going," Maggie said. "Someplace where there are no other people asking for something or demanding attention."

"Like mothers, daughters, or customers?" Alex asked.

"Something like that," Maggie admitted.

"Which is exactly why you need to go to this retreat."

"I've got one spot open," Kelly said.

"Oh, you'll fill that," Maggie answered. "I'm too busy to go to a retreat. Besides, I don't have any real problems. Teagan's on a good path, and the store is doing well."

Alex and Kelly looked at each other and shook their head.

"And there's a river in Egypt," Alex said.

"Huh?"

"Denial," Kelly added with a grin.

"I'm not in denial. I'm totally realistic." Maggie's breath seemed to tighten. "I've been the one to pick up the pieces. Now that everyone else is set, it's my turn. If I want to have a little fun with Justin, it's my right."

"Okay," Kelly said, drawing out the word. "Anyway, back to the celebration. How about we take coffee into the living room. Alex and I still have plenty of questions."

Maggie filled her mug with the decaf Kelly always brewed at night, and ambled to the living room. The largest room in the house, it still managed to envelope her in its warmth, almost as if the ghost of Henrietta sat in the corner rocking chair, knitting needles arranging soft yarn into intricate patterns, her gaze missing nothing that went on around her. In the corner of the room, Henrietta's favorite flowers, yellow daffodils gleamed in a cobalt blue vase.

Taking the rocker, Maggie sat and longed for wisdom to descend. No bolt of insight found her, but when she wrapped herself in the shawl Kelly left on the chair, comfort swaddled her.

Alex and Kelly came in, Alex taking the overstuffed armchair, and Kelly arranging herself on the couch, a pad of paper and pen in her hands. For a moment they were all quiet, letting the peace of the room still them.

"I can feel her here," Alex said.

"Yes," Kelly agreed. "Whenever I need to sort things through, this is one of the places I come. Somehow, I can always find the answers I need. Even Ryan feels her presence."

"Mmm," Maggie said. "So what do you need to know?"

# # #

When Alex and Kelly finally got all the answers to the questions they had for the moment, Kelly had a list of things for Maggie to send them.

"I still don't know how you did this all by yourself," Kelly said.

"It was exhausting," Maggie admitted. "But once Alex came back, she helped a lot."

"By 'help,' she means she told me what to do, and I did it," Alex said.

"Best kind of help," Maggie said.

"Yep," Kelly agreed.

"So what about Justin?" Alex asked.

Maggie glared at her, then closed her eyes and rocked.

"I think you should let this go," Kelly said. "Maggie's a grown woman. She can make her own decisions."

"She hasn't shown the best judgment in the past," Alex said.

"'*She*' is right here," Maggie said. "And Kelly is right. I'm allowed to make my own decisions. Maybe Justin *is* the right man for me."

"Because he's exactly like Paul?" Alex said. "And Paul treated you so well. What did you ever do about that letter?"

"I sent him what he asked for."

"For heaven's sake, why? He never did anything for Teagan."

Maggie stood, all attempt at peace shattered. "Because he's dying of cancer! Isn't that enough? And what's more, I want to forgive him. I *need* to forgive him. We were obnoxiously young."

Alex shook her head.

"I think I'd better go," Maggie said.

"Don't leave angry," Kelly said. "You know by now, Alex likes to express her opinions."

"Sometimes she needs to keep them to herself."

"Mmm ... could be."

"Humph." Alex put her coffee mug down with a thud.

"Maybe a little more diplomacy," Kelly suggested.

"But she's going to get hurt."

"I don't think so," Maggie said, resettling herself in the rocking chair. "Justin isn't that kind of person. He's always said he isn't a settling down kind of person, but he likes it here. And he really likes me."

Alex frowned, but kept her mouth shut.

Thankfully.

"What will you do if he goes off to do another job permanently?" Kelly asked.

"Um ..." Maggie rocked harder. She had a vague idea of going with Justin to his next job, expanding her life beyond small town Montana. But if she did, who would handle the store or the performing arts center? Who would be mayor?

"I'm not sure," she finally admitted. "But I'll figure it out."

"And we'll be here to help you think it through," Kelly said.

"Thanks." Maggie looked at Alex.

"Yeah," Alex said. "Me, too."

"Love you guys," Maggie said.

"Back at you," Alex said.

Kelly added, "Always."

# Chapter Twenty-Nine

"Text me when you get this message." Maggie pressed send. Teagan had left to go hiking with her friend Rebecca a little after lunch, but Maggie had expected her back before she left to join Justin for dinner at his place. They'd been gone for five hours, which was a long time for the hike Teagan had said they were taking.

Maybe they'd gone back to Rebecca's house for dinner.

Maggie brushed her hair, threaded some earrings into her lobes, and reapplied her lipstick. She really should redo her makeup, but there'd been a rush at the store, and she was running late.

Gathering her purse and a light jacket for later, she ran down the stairs and headed for her car. How did all those glamorous people in Hollywood do it? It was a skill she was going to have to learn if she wanted to stay with Justin. Not that he'd ever said anything. It was simply a feeling Maggie had.

She drove almost mindlessly, used to taking the trip to the rental house. As she drove through the small town, she waved when she spotted Pamela Cuzins, a gifted photographer, emerging from the ART building. Mike was hauling trash to his bin when she went by. Farther on, Amanda was closing up Promise Cove Sweets.

All of it happened every day, the easy rhythm of a small town. *Her* small town.

She smiled and made the turn to head up the mountain to Justin's place.

After she parked the car, she checked her messages again. Nothing from Teagan.

Her daughter would be fine, wouldn't she? She and Rebecca were familiar with the rules of hiking, and their strong young bodies could handle anything that they encountered. They had bear spray.

But would they know how to use it? What if a snake appeared? Or a boulder rolled down from nowhere.

All the fears invented by mothers everywhere overwhelmed her for a moment.

She shook them off, picked up the pie she'd set aside when Charlene delivered, and headed up the stairs.

Justin stood and came to greet her when she got to the porch.

"You look lovely," he said, giving her a quick brush of his lips on hers. "And pie, too? I think I've gained about ten pounds knowing you."

"Liar," she teased.

"Probably." He grinned. "Have a seat. I'll put this in the kitchen and bring out some snacks. Pour yourself a glass of wine."

She pulled the bottle of expensive chardonnay from the wine cooler and filled her glass halfway. After returning it, she leaned back in the well-padded chair and stared up through the trees at the blue sky above. All she could hear was a dim clattering from the kitchen and the whoosh of the wind through the tops of the pines.

"How was your week?" Justin said as he put a platter of vegetables and dip on the table.

"Busy," she replied. "Tourists are starting to come up in numbers, it seems everyone in town has decided to clean up their landscaping, and grilling is in full swing."

He laughed. "A scenario being played out all across America."

"True. But I haven't seen all across America," she said.

"We'll change that." He put his hand on top of hers and gave it a brief squeeze. "I think I can even show you some treasured sites in Europe. A casita on the coast of Greece might suit you well."

"All that white and blue—I've seen pictures," she said, allowing herself to daydream of drifting in a swinging hammock while lithe young men served her drinks.

Justin laughed. "Spoken like a woman who truly needs a good rest."

She nodded and took another sip of wine. He knew her so well.

"And the performing arts center?" he asked.

"Slowly coming along. George has had some jobs of his own he needed to take care of, and he doesn't want people working without him there. Some of them get ideas of their own and deviate from the plan."

"That can be a problem with volunteers," Justin said. "But have faith. George is a good guy. I'd certainly hire him if the situation arose. He'll get it done before snow falls."

"But we want to have our inaugural performance in September," she said. "Kelly has been practicing like mad. Did you know she was almost a concert pianist?"

"I didn't. I suppose her marriage and family got in the way. It's tough to have all that if you're work involves a lot of travel. It's difficult enough when a man is gone all the time, but must be harder on a mother. And when you're away from home, there's always temptation."

The air between them lost its ease. He'd told her he'd never cheated while he was married, but when he wasn't? If they were together, but not married, would he be monogamous?

How well did she really know him?

"I guess you know that firsthand," she said.

"Like I told you, I never did anything while I was married. But when I wasn't, if it was offered, I took advantage if I was interested. No harm, no foul."

"Even if the woman was married?"

He didn't answer for a moment. "Are you sure you want to know?"

"I wouldn't have asked otherwise."

"Yeah. Once or twice. I figured any consequences were between her and her husband. Besides, if I hadn't said yes, someone else would have."

"I see."

"No, you probably don't," he said, turning to face her. "Being on the road is incredibly lonely. It's not the glamour of dining at fine restaurants and experiencing fun events. At the end of the day, no matter how beautiful the hotel room, it's an empty room. Day after day are meetings, being nice to people you may or may not like for way too long, bland hotel food, and too many drinks. At night, if there's no event, there's room service, a television set, and an obligatory phone call to someone you may still love."

"Sounds horrible."

"It can be."

"And still you do it. Why?"

"It's my job. Like your concert pianist friend, the concert is the reason to put up with all the other stuff. A deal coming together is my concert. The rest? It's what I have to do to make it happen."

"So, more important than a family?" Maggie asked.

"More important than anything. It has to be." He took her hand. "Otherwise I wouldn't be able to do it." He caressed the back of her hand with his thumb. "I really like you, Maggie. I think we could be good together. But it would take some work on both our parts. I know you want to travel, and that's great. I'd love not to be in that hotel room by myself." He smiled at her.

Her heart filled with cautious happiness. He wanted her. He was willing to make things work.

"But that would mean you'd have to give up managing the store."

"I couldn't do that."

"Why not?" he asked. "Teagan's off on her own soon. And your mother seems to be about to claim a new life for herself somewhere else. Why not just sell it and be free?"

"It's my *home*." Leave the place she'd grown up in? Her father's garden? Forever? "Sandy can manage while we're traveling. Then when we come back here in the summer, I can take over and tend the garden." Even as she said it, the impracticality of it took her breath away.

He shook his head. "I can't stay here."

"What do you mean?"

"I've tried to settle in here, but I'm too restless, too used to doing things my way. Even when I've tried to help out, I wind up butting heads with someone like Mike. The condo I have in LA suits me. It's as much permanence as I want." He paused, gazing deeply into her eyes. "It's beautiful there. You can see the ocean from the balconies. You'd love it. Give it a try. Come with me when I leave."

A sucker punch to her gut couldn't have hurt more.

"You want me to leave Promise Cove—my store, my town, and everything I've worked for— to come with you?"

"It's a big ask, I know. But we can be happy together. We enjoy each other's company. And when we get there, which I'm hoping will be soon, I know we'll enjoy each other's bodies as well. Think of all the things you could see and do. Things you've never done before."

"But what would I do for a living? I don't want to be dependent on anyone."

"You're a great manager. You'd fit right into my company with ease. It's work you'd be good at." He grinned. "You might even be in a position to boss people around."

She attempted a smile, but she couldn't quite grasp what he was saying. Oh, she understood the words, but the image he presented didn't make any sense. In no way could she picture herself standing in an office telling people what to do. The back room of a bar was a far different place.

Had it all been a fantasy? He was offering her exactly what she'd thought she wanted all her life. It was what she'd always told herself she'd missed out on by being a fool with Paul.

"What do you say?" he asked.

Her phone buzzed before she could even begin to answer.

Tom.

Alarm bells went off in her brain. In spite of the circumstances, she answered.

"Maggie, have you heard from Teagan?" Tom asked.

"Not since she went hiking with her friend Rebecca after lunch. I'm worried, but figured she went to Rebecca's for dinner or something."

"She didn't. Rebecca's mother contacted me. They were supposed to be back by six. Do you know what trail they took?"

"I think so. It's here in my phone." She scrambled to find

Teagan's text. It was a rule they both had about hiking, to let someone know where they were going. Maggie gave the information to Tom.

There was silence on the phone.

"Tom. Talk to me. What's going on?"

After another moment. Then he spoke. "There's been an avalanche."

Her baby could be trapped under the snow. Unable to breathe. Unable to ...

"Where are you?"

"Fire and rescue. They're coordinating with the forest service to send out teams. We'll find her, Maggie. I promise."

"You can't promise that," she sobbed. "No one can. I'm coming."

She shoved back her chair. "I need to go."

"Not like that," Justin said, standing. "I'll take you wherever you need to go as soon as you tell me what is going on."

"There's an avalanche. Teagan's missing—she may—she could be—I can't ..." Sobs overtook her.

Justin put his arm around her and held her close. "We'll find her. We will."

Maggie prayed he and Tom were right.

## Chapter Thirty

People milled about the command headquarters of the county fire and rescue building. The only space was at the back of the room. They leaned against the back wall, Maggie clutching Justin's hand as she listened to the dark-haired woman in the orange jacket speak, gesturing to the map behind her as she laid out the plan for search and rescue.

"As far as we know, there are six people who were on that trail who haven't returned yet," the woman said. "Two young women and a family of four: mother, father, and two teenage boys. Thankfully, the sun is still out and will be for a long time. We've got a helicopter up and searching, but it's tough to make out anything but snow and debris. Plus, a heavy wind is expected to move into the area as night falls, so we have limited time in the air." She paused. "Our best bet is search and rescue teams. The earlier we find them, the better."

Could Teagan hold out until they found her? Would she even know what to do in case of an avalanche?

"Gene Taylor, one of Whitefish Search and Rescue's most experienced members, will take one of our teams and begin the search where it is most likely the survivors will be found." The woman pointed at a man who looked to be in his late forties or early fifties, fit and with an air of confidence. "Another team will come with me. I'm Elizabeth Black Hawk, for those who don't know me. I've been doing search and rescue for the last fifteen years, so I know what I'm doing." She gestured to the side wall. "Sheriff Gerard, whom many of you already know, is our liaison and will take over the command center and coordinate the search effort.

"If you are here to help and—most importantly—have experience in tracking or rescue, talk to us. For the rest of you, there's coffee, and I understand sandwiches will be here soon."

"Who's making sandwiches?" Maggie mumbled. "I've always done that." It's what she should be doing now. She'd never felt so useless, so empty.

"Hang in there," Justin said. "They sound like they know what they're doing."

"But does Teagan? Rebecca? I don't know." Her voice caught again in her throat. This couldn't be happening.

People bustled in various directions. Gene Taylor gathered his group in one part of the room, and after a brief discussion with Tom, Elizabeth Black Hawk gathered hers in another.

Tom held up his hand, and the room quieted a bit. "Thank you all for coming to volunteer. The waiting part is hard, I know. This is a time when action feels better than standing around. But it's what needs to happen. I understand food will be here in fifteen minutes. Until then, enjoy your coffee. If there are any questions, please address them to me, so we can let Gene and Elizabeth do their jobs."

For a moment while he was speaking, his gaze caught Maggie's, and she could almost hear him whisper it would be alright. Then he looked at Justin, and his eyes ceased their communication.

"It's your fault you know."

Maggie turned.

"What are you talking about?" she asked Rebecca's mother, Beth.

"If Teagan hadn't persuaded her to go off this afternoon, she'd be safe. My little girl would be safe. Your daughter had no right to drag her up that trail. Those girls weren't experienced enough to go out into the wilderness."

"My understanding was Rebecca wanted to go on that trail," Maggie protested.

"You're wrong."

"Beth." A portly man took Rebecca's mom's arm. "Don't do this. We need to work together, not tear into each other."

"But it's her fault. She should have raised a responsible daughter. Just like we did."

"Wait a minute." Maggie's fear fueled her anger.

*Spring in Promise Cove*

"Teagan has been taught all her life to respect nature. She's an experienced hiker. I've met Rebecca a few times, and she told me she likes to hike a lot, too. It's not my fault. Or Teagan's. Not by a long shot. Now leave me alone!" Her voice rose in volume as she spoke.

"Shhh," Justin said, rubbing her back.

"I will not be quiet!" Maggie said. "Not while my daughter is out there, missing, hurt." This time when her voice caught, it produced a sob. Soon the tears were flowing.

Justin pulled her close as she cried into his shirt, murmuring into her hair, telling her the teams were on their way and that Rebecca's mom had gone.

Then another pair of arms pulled her close. Maggie fell apart once again as her mother soothed her, like she had when Maggie was little and something awful had happened. Even after she had stopped crying, she stayed in Elaine's embrace.

"Done?" her mother asked when Maggie finally stirred.

Maggie nodded.

"Good. There's work to do. Kelly and Alex are setting up the sandwiches, but you need to tend to the coffee." Elaine looked at Justin. "Come along. You can help, too."

Everything seemed slightly surreal. The solid cement walls provided a barrier to the wildness around them and contained the actions of the people within. Clusters gathered, talking and gesturing, but they could have been speaking in a foreign language. In the kitchen, Kelly and Alex moved efficiently, bringing trays to the serving window, and making sure they were continually replenished.

Her mother guided her to the coffee pots and their supplies. She went through the motions automatically, the acrid aroma of the grounds barely reaching her olfactory nerve. Off in the distance, Justin was put to work slapping mayo and mustard on slices of bread.

At one point Alex came up and hugged her, but all Maggie could do was nod. She needed to make coffee. That was her job. If she did it well enough, her daughter would come home safe.

Conversation went on around her, but she wasn't part of

it.

Pour a pot into an urn, fill it with water, pour the water into the reserve, put the pot back on the hot plate of the coffee maker. Clean out the grounds. Refill a paper holder with fresh coffee. Start the machine.

Then she stood while the coffee perked, waiting for the first drop to hit stained bottom of the coffee pot. Another drop. Then another. More rapidly they came until the drops became a steady stream, a brown waterfall to nourish the waiting crowd.

"How are you doing?" Tom asked.

She shrugged.

"They'll find her. These people are very, very good."

She nodded.

His walkie-talkie crackled. He turned and spoke into it. When he was done, he turned back to her. "I've got to go. Hang tough. We'll get through this."

He walked back to the main room, and she continued with the coffee.

### # # #

A buzz filled the building.

"They've located the family," someone shouted.

A cheer went up.

Maggie rushed out front. There was hope. Teagan couldn't be far away. Toward the front Tom nodded and spoke into the walkie-talkie before turning toward the small crowd and raising his hand.

Everyone settled with a final murmur.

"That was Gene's group. They've located the family northeast of the trail. One of the kids heard the thunder of the snow breaking off from the ridge. He was smart enough to get them to run across the mountain instead of trying to outpace the falling snow. They got caught in the edges, but not deep enough that they couldn't dig out. However, the father's leg was broken, so they had to stay where they were."

"Are they bringing them back here?" one person asked.

"They're putting the man on a stretcher and bringing him back down the trail. The others are pretty cold—no one was dressed for snow—so they're wrapped in emergency blankets. If someone could drive over to the trailhead with some coffee and blankets, that's what's needed now."

"I'll go," Ruth called out.

"And I'll go with her," Mike said. "We can take them down to the hospital to be checked out."

Tom nodded. "Good. That frees up the rescue team to get the guy to the hospital in the ambulance, regroup, and go back to the search."

Maggie wanted to ask, but she was afraid of the answer.

"Any word on Teagan and Rebecca?" Elaine asked.

"Not yet." Tom looked at Maggie. "We won't stop until we find them. You know that."

She nodded and watched him head to where Elizabeth was waiting.

Her lower lip trembled, but then her mother was at her side. "Help Ruth and Mike fill up thermoses and get blankets," Elaine said.

"Okay."

"I'll help, too." It was Rebecca's mother. "I'm sorry about earlier. I'm not like that. It's just I hurt so much it spilled out."

"I understand," Maggie said.

"Thank you."

Maggie showed Beth how the coffee worked, then went over to where Justin had been instructed to cut sandwiches. "How's it going?" she asked.

"I'm not feeling terribly useful," he admitted.

She nodded, then picked up a platter and arranged the triangles he'd cut onto its surface.

"Do you think if I asked Tom, he could find me a job doing something more fit to my skills?"

Shrugging her shoulders, she said, "Do what you want?" She was barely holding herself together. There was no room inside her for anyone else's problems.

Tom came into the kitchen. "One of the first teams to search is about ten minutes from here," he said. "They're going to need food. Do you have enough?"

She eyed the assembly line. "I'll get everyone moving."

"Say, Tom," Justin asked, moving closer to the sheriff. "Do you think you could find something else for me to do?"

"Like what?" Tom asked.

"I'm a good hiker. I've done a lot in the Sierras in California. I could help search."

"Do you have snowshoes?"

"No," Justin said.

"Have you done much hiking around here?"

"One or two hikes."

"I'm sorry, but you're most needed here. People are hungry, and someone needs to keep them fed."

"But—"

"You don't know the terrain, and you don't have the equipment to deal with snow. You'd be a hindrance, not a help." Tom looked over at Maggie, then back at Justin. "Help your girlfriend, that's what's needed."

A sharp pain struck her gut.

Justin walked back to his station and began slicing. It was as if she was looking at a stranger who didn't quite fit in.

Taking the platter, she carried it to the serving table, checked what was needed, then went back to encourage and cajole people to keep working.

As she did so, she kept up the silent prayer she'd been making since the news first got to her.

*Please bring my daughter home safe.*

# Chapter Thirty-One

Tom trudged up the trail with the search and rescue canine team. He'd delegated the command center role to his deputy sheriff. The passive position had gotten to him. He needed to be out searching.

The night sky was clear, throwing a benevolent light from the clusters of stars and the half moon. All around them, the air was still and cool. Even in June, the nights could chill quickly in the mountains.

The girls were probably not dressed for this weather.

He couldn't think about that.

When they reached the edge of the avalanche, they stopped.

"Everyone get their snowshoes on," Elizabeth said. "The work will get a little trickier from this point on. It's not a level surface. There's a lot of debris ahead. The choppers scanned the area before they lost the light but couldn't make out anything. Our best bet in finding someone alive is either on this section before the worst of the chute, or on the other side. We've already searched this side thoroughly. I'm not going to lie to you. It's going to take a lot out of everyone to cross that debris. If you want to turn back, now's the time to do it."

No one said anything.

"Alright. Here's what we're going to do." He assigned them in a fanned-out position. They each had heavy duty headlamps, leaving their hands free to help them navigate the rough terrain. Two of the searchers carried bright orange rolled-up stretchers on their backs. Once again they set off, this time at a slower pace.

As they walked, they listened. Every once in a while the leader would call out for them to stop, then yell the names of the girls. They would strain their ears, hoping for an answer, but none came.

Memories flowed through Tom as he walked: Teagan as a little girl when he taught her to swim for the first time. Maggie had tried, but her own inability to do much more than a dog paddle had kept her from getting very far.

They'd spent a lot of time at the lake, just the three of them. All through that time he'd hoped he could be more than a friend of the family, but nothing he said had ever changed Maggie's mind.

He'd find Teagan, but then he was giving up. He'd been a fool for waiting this long.

His foot slid partway down a chunk of icy snow, and he lost his balance.

"Easy there," one of the team said steadying him.

"Thanks, buddy." He needed to keep his mind on the job at hand. He wasn't going to be of any use if he twisted his leg.

Then he'd be as worthless as Justin.

"This next part is the worst of the snow pack. It picked off a number of large trees, so watch your step. Pair up. Don't be heroes. Help each other out."

All around Tom tree trunks and large limbs were scattered like a bunch of Lincoln Logs. It was going to be heavy going.

"Pair up?" the man who'd helped him before asked.

"Sure."

Together they maneuvered through the chunks of snow, some as hard as the rocks they contained, others so soft only snowshoes kept them from falling through. More than once they removed their snowshoes and clambered over the trunk of a ponderosa pine, its still-green needle-laden limbs draping the snow around it.

Finally, they reached the opposite end of the snow pack.

"We didn't see anything. Could they have been buried?" asked one of the younger volunteers.

"If they're in there, it's doubtful they survived. But let's not dwell on that. As of now this is still a rescue mission and will be in the near future."

Tom refused to think of any other possibility. He took

several chugs of water, then continued northwest on the trail with the others.

Another half hour passed.

He heard something. He stopped to listen more closely.

A shrill blast came again.

A second. Then a third.

"Do you hear that?" he shouted at Elizabeth.

"Yes!"

It came again and he raced to the sound.

Soon he made out two figures in the dimming light. One was on the ground, the other standing and waving.

As he got closer, he recognized the standing figure.

"Teagan! I'm coming!" he called out, his chest squeezing the words out.

As soon as he reached her, he grabbed her in his arms. "You're okay. You're okay. Thank God. Oh, kid, I'm so glad you're safe."

# # #

"Where did you get the whistle?" Tom asked after the others arrived and started to assess the situation.

"You stuck it in my stocking one Christmas," Teagan said. "I think I was about thirteen. You told me to always carry it when I went hiking. And you taught me how to use it. Three long blasts. Wait and listen. Then three more blasts. So that's what I did."

"Good for you. I can't believe you kept it this long."

"It seemed important to you." She leaned against him, her emergency blanket crinkling. "I'm glad you're the one who found me. Where's Mom?"

"Back at the center. Making sandwiches with your grandmother."

"That's her job," Teagan said, then started to cry.

Tom held her close.

"We're going to get the other girl on a stretcher," Elizabeth told him. "She's got a sprained ankle—pretty bad. Do you think she can walk out? We're going to have to make a trail to the road. We can't bring them back over the slide."

"What do you think?" he asked Teagan.

Teagan nodded.

"I'll stick with her," Tom said.

"Good."

While some of the volunteers readied the stretcher, others looked at topo maps and compasses to strategize the best way down the mountain.

Elizabeth radioed the good news, and they all grinned as a cheer was broadcast over the walkie-talkie.

Then they headed down the mountain.

# # #

When they finally got to the road, Tom helped Teagan into a waiting ambulance.

"I'll let your mom know where they're taking you," he said. "Be brave. She'll be there soon."

"You, too?" Teagan asked.

"Probably not right away. I have things to clean up."

"But you'll be there."

"I will. I promise."

The girls were loaded and the ambulance took off.

His heart ached from the adrenaline it had taken to find them and his gratitude they were alive. It could have turned out much worse.

"Command?" he said into his walkie-talkie.

"Zeke Bilyk."

"Can you let Maggie and Rebecca's parents know they'll be at Logan Health in Kalispell? Rebecca's got a twisted ankle, but other than being cold for a long time, Teagan appears fine."

"Roger that," Bilyk said.

"I'll be there in about twenty minutes."

"Yes. See you soon."

In reality it was only around ten o'clock, but Tom's body insisted it had to be the wee hours of the morning. He settled into the back of the van that had come for the volunteers and promptly fell asleep.

### # # #

It was close to midnight when he entered Teagan's room. Her small figure was wrapped in blankets to her neck, except for the hand that was exposed for an IV drip. She also had an oxygen feed in her nose.

A lump in the chair nearby stirred.

"How is she?" he whispered to Maggie.

"Getting there." Maggie grabbed her phone and led him to the hallway. "They've got her on warming fluids and air as a precaution, but they're not worried about hypothermia. She wasn't that cold."

"And Rebecca?"

"The same except for the ankle. They're two healthy young people in good physical condition. It could have been worse," Maggie said, her voice breaking a little as her brave face faltered.

"Far worse. I'm glad she's okay." He stared at her for a moment, longing to take her into his arms and comfort her, just as he had Teagan. "Are you staying all night?"

"Yes."

"Is Justin with you?"

"I sent him home. My mom will come spell me in the morning. They may let Teagan out tomorrow or the day after. It depends on how well she's doing."

"Do you need anything?"

She looked up at him.

Tension sparked between them.

Her lips parted and for the first time in his adult life, he felt it might be okay to kiss her.

Her phone buzzed, and she looked down at it.

"Justin," she said.

He stepped back. Nothing had changed. She was with the man who could give her everything the world thought mattered.

"I'll check in tomorrow," he said. After a last glance at the slim figure in the bed, Tom walked away from the woman he loved.

## Chapter Thirty-Two

Maggie's footsteps dragged as she took her coffee to the back porch early Sunday morning. Slowly lowering herself into a chair, she stared at the chaos of the garden, too tired to even care.

Teagan was safe. The drumbeat echoed faintly in her head.

Her little girl had used her head and kept both her and her friend alive. She was on the mend. Although Teagan protested she was fine, her eyes frequently drifted shut as she lay on the couch in their living room.

*Thank God.*

Pieces of the future garden came into focus. The pond was a dug out hole and the rock garden a stack of interestingly arranged stones. In the butterfly garden, weeds were thriving.

She closed her eyes and raised her face to the sun. Soon she'd have to open the store, but for now she could simply be still and drape herself in gratitude.

Birds chattered in the trees, and hummingbirds droned as they jockeyed for position around the feeder Teagan had gotten her one Mother's Day.

Tom had helped save her girl. He was always there for her—for them. And Maggie had turned him away every time he wanted to take their relationship further.

She'd been a fool.

That moment in the hospital hallway had proved that. She touched her lips. If only Justin hadn't called.

She'd finally felt that spark she'd been waiting for half her life. It had always been there between them, but she'd been looking for flash and glitter, not realizing that a deep connection between two people provided dynamite for a bigger explosion when it happened.

*Spring in Promise Cove*

Had Tom been touched by the electricity, too? Or was she fooling herself?

She needed to talk to him. Soon. She had to convince him to give them another chance.

But first she had to do something about Justin.

What a mess she'd made of things.

She checked her phone.

No time to try to straighten it out now. Work beckoned.

# # #

"How is Teagan doing?" Betsy asked as she paid for her weekly groceries.

"On the mend," Maggie replied.

"You look tired."

"I am, but we're a little short-handed right now. Greg and Sandy both have the afternoon off, and Mom's cleaning up the kitchen from the lunch rush."

"You need to take care of yourself, too. That was a lot of stress. There's nothing worse than standing around waiting. It's exhausting."

"It is," Maggie agreed, returning Betsy's change to her.

"How is Teagan doing?" another woman asked, sidling up to the counter with her quart of milk.

"Fine," Maggie said. Almost everyone in town seemed intent on coming into the store and asking how her daughter was doing. They meant well, and she loved the townspeople because they cared for each other, but the constant questioning was wearing her down.

Nonetheless, she continued to handle each customer as they came, rote actions accompanied by a smile.

Her mother came to relieve her at one point, but the fine lines around Elaine's eyes and mouth were exaggerated, demonstrating her total exhaustion. Maggie sent her upstairs.

Sandy and Greg returned together, smiling and laughing.

"We decided you needed a hand," Sandy said, walking behind the counter.

Greg looked at the boxes piled up in the back of the store. "I'll start stocking shelves."

"Oh. Okay. Thank you," Maggie said, relieved with their kindness on their day off.

They made it through the rest of the day. At the end Greg had cleared away all the boxes and prepped for the morning's breakfast.

"Thank you," Maggie told Sandy again as they were closing up. "I don't know how I would have done it alone."

# # #

The trip to Justin's didn't take as long as Maggie had hoped. She'd texted him to let him know she was coming, and he'd said he was working but should be ready to take a break when she got there.

"Hello," he said as she climbed the stairs. "This is an unexpected surprise."

"Hi," she said as she reached the top.

He gave her a quick kiss. "Have a seat. It's a beautiful night. How is your daughter doing?"

"Teagan's on the mend," Maggie said. "It will be a few more days, but she's already complaining. That's a good sign."

"It sure is. Can I get you something to drink? I have a pinot noir open."

"That would be nice."

She settled uneasily into a chair and ran through all the ways to begin the conversation they needed to have. By the time he returned with two large-bowled glasses filled with garnet liquid, she'd been totally unable to come up with an opening line.

As she'd learned to do in his presence, she swirled the wine, sniffed, and then took a generous sip.

The whole ritual felt pretentious and fake.

They sat quietly for a few moments, but it wasn't the easy companionship it had been in the past.

"What's up?" he asked. "Not that I'm not happy to see you, but I have a feeling there's something more on your mind."

"This isn't going to work."

"This?"

"This relationship, or whatever we are doing here."

"Ah," he said.

"I'm sorry," she said. "I thought—well—that we—that I—I'm not doing this well." She stared into the wine for a few moments. "I mean. I'm a small town girl at heart. Corporate jets, skiing with the rich and famous, Paris—it sounds wonderful. But I wouldn't know what I'd do in that lifestyle. I don't know who I'd *be*."

"Change can be difficult," he said, leaning forward. "You've never had the chance to learn, to see what it would feel like beyond Montana. You can still be a small town girl at heart and explore all the world has to offer. There is so much out there. And you could achieve anything you set your mind to. I'm going to bet it will be more satisfying than running the family store, or even being mayor."

She was throwing away the chance of a lifetime. What if Tom didn't want her? Would she still be happy in her roles?

"If I went with you, what do you see happening?"

He leaned forward and took her hand. "We'd start by exploring the great cities of the US: New York, Chicago, LA. I'd treat you to the best restaurants and shops. You could spend a day or a weekend at an exclusive spa. Then I'd teach you about the work I do. We'd find a spot for you in my company, or another job if you wish."

"Would we live together?"

"If you wanted. No pressure. You know I want to make love to you. You're beautiful." He traced a finger down her cheek. "I thought that's what you wanted too."

"But nothing permanent."

He sat back and let go. "No. I'm not a marrying kind of guy if that's what you mean. I told you that. But we can have a lot of fun, Maggie. Who knows how long it might last?"

"But not forever."

"Probably not. And you wouldn't walk away empty handed."

"A necklace from Tiffany's?" The snark appeared in

spite of herself. Two days ago she would have leapt at what he described.

Two days ago she hadn't realized she was in love with Tom.

"Don't be like that," Justin said. "I'm talking about a good, well-paying job and exposure to some of the most amazing treasures on the planet. Isn't that worth something?"

"I'm sorry," she said, really meaning it. Justin had been nothing but honest and nice to her, but she had to see how it played out with Tom. She'd never forgive herself if she didn't. "You're right. It would be wonderful."

"But you're not going to do it."

She shook her head. "I can't." She gave him a smile that felt sad to her. "I'm the mayor. How can a mayor leave town?"

Pushing aside the glass, she stood. He immediately followed suit.

"Thanks for everything. It's been wonderful knowing you," she said. "Good luck with your new project."

"I enjoyed you," he said. "I hate to see you slip away. But you need to choose what's right for you. I hope you find what you're really looking for."

"Me too." She gave him a little wave, then headed down the deck stairs.

# # #

Monday, Teagan insisted on going to school. "There are only three days left. I graduate Friday night! I can't believe it!" She squealed.

And last Friday night she'd almost died. Maggie took a deep breath.

"Okay, go. But no running."

"PE is a study hall. They've given up on us." Teagan grabbed her backpack with a grin and hustled down the stairs.

Her daughter's childhood had gone by way too fast.

Maggie finished her routine and headed down to the

store. The morning regulars would be waiting impatiently for her to get the coffee brewing, chatting with each other and descending on Charlene when she arrived with whatever baked goods she was bringing.

Another day in paradise.

Her paradise.

She'd slept untroubled last night, reaffirming that ending it with Justin was the right thing to do.

Would Tom come in today? Teagan said he'd texted her to check in, but Maggie hadn't heard anything from the man. She could invite him over to work on the backyard this weekend. He'd promised to help with the pond, and she'd hold him to that.

She almost skipped down the stairs, ready to set her life back on track. George should be finished with his paying job soon, which meant work on the performing arts center could start up again. The summertime festival was in good shape.

And it no longer mattered that her mother was going to Paris.

Humming, she started the coffee urns, pulled up the shades, unlocked the front door, and turned the sign to open. In the back, she could hear her mother clanking pots and pans as she readied the grill for eggs, bacon, and sausage.

Soon people trickled in, and the Monday rhythm began. While people still talked about the dramatic rescue on Friday, they put less pressure on her and handled the gossip among themselves.

Every time the bell rang, she checked the door for Tom's entry. Her heart beat a little faster when she saw a man in a sheriff's uniform enter.

But he was a familiar stranger—someone she'd seen around town, but had no idea of his name. The uniformed man waited until there was a lull in the traffic at the counter, then approached her.

"Hi," he said. "I'm Zeke Bilyk, deputy sheriff. I'm doing some follow up for Tom. Have you had any more things stolen recently?"

"No, not that I'm aware of."

"Have you seen any of these people in here lately?" He showed her a list with about five names.

"These two come in regularly. This one was here Sunday. But the other two I haven't seen in about a month. Why? Is one of them responsible?"

"I'm afraid I can't reveal that, ma'am."

"Maggie, please call me Maggie."

"Okay. Maggie. Also, please don't talk about this to anyone else. Tom said you could be trusted."

"I won't say anything. Where is Tom by the way?"

"He's taken some time off. I'll be covering for him for the next week."

"Oh, okay." Her heart hammered with fear. Tom had never been gone for that long. Teagan had given him a ticket for her graduation. She'd be disappointed if he wasn't there. "Thanks for letting me know."

"Ma'am." Zeke touched his hat and turned to go.

"Maggie," she whispered to his retreating back.

Throughout the rest of the day, Maggie did everything she could to tamp down her rising fears. What if Tom found another job somewhere else like the rumor mill had suggested. He'd never know how she felt.

As soon as she closed up the store, and everyone left, she slid into the worn chair of her tiny office.

Maggie: Where are you?
Tom: Livingston
Maggie: Why are you there?
Tom: It's complicated. I'll explain when I get back.
Maggie: I broke it off with Justin.

Silence. She swung back and forth on the swivel, ignoring its squeal of protest as she stared at the phone. Finally she couldn't stand it any longer.

Maggie: What do you think?
Tom: It's none of my business.

She twirled some more. How did she get him to

understand?

>Tom: I've got to go.
>Maggie: Come back soon. It's different. I need to talk to you.
>Tom: I don't think there's anything to say.
>Maggie: But I left Justin!!!!
>Tom: So?

"Agh!" How could men be so thick?

>Maggie: I want to go on a date with you. I've been stupid. I'm sorry.

No response. She got up from the chair and paced. It only took five steps—small steps—in each direction.

>Tom: I don't think so.
>Maggie: Why not?
>Tom: You made your choice and forced me to move on. It's better this way. I don't need the runner-up title. Gotta go.

Maggie slumped back into the chair and bawled.

## Chapter Thirty-Three

"I miss this in the winter," Kelly said, leaning back into her chair.

"It *is* beautiful," Maggie agreed.

"Peaceful," Alex concluded.

The lake visible in the glow of the firepit was painted a deep blue gray by the late setting sun. Seagulls whirled on the edges, their crisp outlines dark against the western sky's palette of pinks, blues, and pale yellow.

Maggie took another sip of her margarita, then reached for a couple of chips from the bowl on the small table between her and Kelly. Ryan had painted the Adirondack chairs and tables in preparation for the retreat that began in a few weeks. Everyone was moving forward with their lives.

Everyone except her.

"He dumped me," she blurted out.

"Who? Justin?" Alex asked. "Good riddance."

"No. Tom." Maggie gave a little hiccup of a sob but managed to gain control before she fell apart again.

"Well, that's what you get for waiting so long," Alex said.

Kelly glared at Alex. "Are you sure?"

"Yes. He told me—he told me—he didn't want to be my second choice. And he's in Livingston. He's looking for another job. I know it. There's no other reason to go down there."

"There's a lot of reasons to go to Livingston," Kelly said. "It's a really neat town. Maybe he just needed some time to himself. That rescue took a lot out of him, too."

Maggie shook her head. "What am I going to do?"

"What do you want to do?" Kelly asked.

"I have no idea."

"I see."

How could Kelly see when Maggie's vision was so

clouded it was like a dust storm had combined with drifting smoke?

"What about Justin?" Alex asked.

"I broke up with him."

"Why? I thought you were preparing to run off into the sunset with him."

"I couldn't do it." She bit into another chip with a loud crunch.

"We should eat," Kelly said.

"Suits me." Alex stood and went to the solid wood table Ryan and his friend Larry had built for Kelly. A colorful woven runner stretched across the gleaming pine, and ceramic bowls filled with a chicken taco mix as well as all the trimmings perched on its top. "Looks wonderful. I keep thinking I'm going to learn to cook someday, but by the time I'm done with work, popping something into the microwave looks like the only game in town."

"It's the problem with raising children," Kelly said as she handed Alex a plate. "They want to be fed."

"Maggie raised a child, and she can't cook either."

"I can, too," Maggie protested. "My macaroni and cheese tastes great."

"And it comes from a box."

"But I add things to it. I'm cooking."

"Elaine is such a good cook, it must be hard to compete," Kelly said.

Maggie nodded, letting Kelly soothe the waters. "When Teagan was little, Elaine insisted on feeding us every night. As I took over the store more and more, it became the norm. Actually, I've been lucky. Being a single mother was terrifying enough."

"And now Teagan's graduating," Alex said, sitting down with her full plate.

"Hard to believe," Maggie agreed. "Did you get your tickets? She was only given five tickets. Sorry I couldn't get one for Ryan."

"He understands."

"So one went to your mom," Alex said. "Who got the last one?"

"Tom," Maggie whispered. "I'm not sure he'll be there. Teagan will be crushed. He took her to the father-daughter dance, remember?"

"He'll be there," Alex said. "Tom is one of those loyal and true kind of people. There's no way he'd disappoint Teagan."

"I agree," Kelly said. "I don't think you need to worry about that."

"Only everything else."

"Look," Kelly said. "I haven't wanted to put any pressure on you about coming to the retreat—Alex has been doing enough of that. But I still have a spot for you."

Automatically, Maggie started to protest, then stopped. What did she have to lose?

"I don't have any artistic talent. How can I fit in? Who else is coming?"

"So far I have a jazz singer from Philadelphia, an actress from LA who is seeing her roles dry up as she ages, and a poet from Denver who feels she doesn't have time to write."

"I can relate to that," Maggie said.

"Besides, I think you do have an artist's viewpoint," Kelly continued. "Anyone who can hold a vision in their head and make it come to life is an artist in my book. And you can certainly do that. Look at what you're doing with the garden."

"The garden is a mess."

"Art is messy."

"But I can't take all that time off," Maggie protested.

"Let me get this straight," Alex said. "Your mother is leaving for a summer in Paris, your daughter is going to college, and you can't take a week off before all that happens? What about Sandy? You said she's doing a great job."

Maggie toyed with the idea for a few moments. Sandy was capable of running the store, but she'd do things differently from the way Maggie had always done them.

Did it matter?

What did anything matter without Tom in her life?

"Even if I come for a week, what am I going to gain? My life has still got a big hole. Going to a retreat isn't going to bring Tom back."

"Neither is sitting around crying," Alex shot back.

Maggie opened her mouth to remind Alex she hadn't really moved on since her husband died years ago. But she shut it. She couldn't be that cruel to anyone. Alex had rough edges, but she would move heaven and earth to help her friends if she could.

"Sometimes," Kelly said. "Sometimes it's good to take a look inside to figure out what's going on outside."

"What do you mean?"

"Let me ask you a question first. Why did you go out with Justin?"

"Because he was fun. I wanted something different. You know, sometimes it feels like Promise Cove is closing in on me, and I have to escape or I'll explode," Maggie said.

Kelly nodded. "I get that. What else attracted you about Justin?"

"I hate to be shallow, but the fact that he could spend money with ease didn't hurt. I'm always on a budget, saving for this or that, praying something major doesn't happen with the house or car that's going to sink us back down into the financial hole."

"Is that why you read all those billionaire romances?" Alex asked.

"Those belong to my mother," Maggie said with a smile. "I don't have time for a book. It's all I can do to watch a rerun of one of the Law and Order series without falling asleep."

"Having money is nice," Kelly admitted. "It isn't everything, or even the most important thing, but it sure helps make other things easier."

Silent agreement ensued. Maggie stared into the flames, unsure where this conversation was going. What did it matter why she went out with Justin? It had been a fun time. Sure, she'd hoped it would turn into something more, but when she thought about leaving everything she'd known, panic had set in.

It was totally stupid. She'd thrown away her chance at something more and now she was going to be stuck—loveless—in a small town for the rest of her life.

"Justin was pretty easy on the eyes," Alex said.

"Yeah," Maggie admitted.

"How far did you go?"

"Geez, Alex! Pry much?"

"Sorry. I should have filtered that."

"Would have been nice. Especially since all I did was kiss him."

"Too bad," Alex said.

Maggie shook her head but grinned anyway. Alex was always willing to express what everyone was thinking, but no one else had the courage to say. While it was one of her less endearing traits at times, it kept things real.

She looked at her plate. There were only a few shreds of cheese left. "This was really good."

"I can give you the recipe. It's pretty easy."

"That would mean a need to cook."

"Like I said earlier, it's hard when there's a good cook in the family," Kelly said. "But maybe once Elaine leaves, you can try some things."

"Once my mother leaves, I'm going to starve," Maggie said.

"It won't be that bad. You'll adjust."

"I hope so." It was going to be a big change. Followed by a bigger one in August.

"How is the summer celebration coming?" she asked.

"We're doing okay," Kelly said. "You gave us a lot to work with. Nearly everyone you had set up for booths last year has agreed to come again."

"Except for the pony man," Alex said. "He had another engagement."

"Fine with me," Kelly said. "I am not a fan of cleaning up horse poop."

"That's why I always had the volunteer fire department do it," Maggie said.

"I'll keep that in mind for next year."

"What about the auction items?"

"They're coming in," Alex said. "I don't think we're going to score like Kelly did last year."

"Ryan's working on a big quilt," Kelly said. "And

Makaila's offering some web package, but Betsy isn't parting with anymore Hollywood treasures. She's saving them for Henry."

"How's he doing?" Maggie asked.

"Seems okay. He's living with Betsy now."

"She must be glad to have him back," Alex said.

"Funny, I saw Betsy at the store and she didn't say anything," Maggie said.

"You know our postmistress," Alex said. "She knows everyone else's business, but is very closemouthed about her own."

"True," Maggie said. "That's good news about Henry, though. I'm glad for Betsy."

"Me, too," Kelly said. "What about the performing arts center? Do you think the opening will be postponed until next year?" Her voice was hopeful.

"Nope. You can't delay your debut. George assures me everything will be ready for the fall opening in September," Maggie answered.

"Rats."

Maggie laughed. It felt good. Far better than the tears she'd shed. Joy almost made her feel hopeful. If only she could share it with Tom.

But he might be gone for good, and it was her own fault.

She was going to have to learn to adjust to a dramatic new reality: mother in Paris, daughter in college, and the man she loved somewhere else in Montana.

"Okay. You've convinced me," she said. "I'll go to the retreat."

# Chapter Thirty-Four

Thursday morning there was a full staff of people at the store. Elaine was back in full form, bossing Greg around in the kitchen, Sandy was checking in supplies and making lists of what needed to be ordered, and Teagan, finally done with school, was at the register.

They didn't need her.

Maggie shifted a few things on the counter, then moved a stack of paper from one corner of her desk to another. She turned on the office computer, stared at the lack of things that needed attending to, and turned it off. Picking up her mug of coffee, she went out to the back porch.

The shrubs she'd planted along the back wall were thriving, but a puddle was developing where water dripped off the eave. Rainy season was almost done, so it wouldn't be much of a problem until next spring. It would be nice to have a system all set up to capture melting snow. Maybe there'd be enough in the budget to put everything in place by fall.

What if Tom never returned?

She'd have to create her vision by herself. It wouldn't be impossible. All her life she'd been figuring out how to create something from not much. All it would take was some cash, a number of hours viewing internet videos, and sweat.

The morning was free. She'd ignore the pond for now, leaving it as a silent plea that, at the very least, her friendship with Tom could be restored.

A hummingbird buzzed her, then returned to hover a few feet from her face.

"Okay. I get the message," she told it.

There were clouds in the sky, and morning drizzle was expected, but it was supposed to clear up in the afternoon, leaving the ground as perfect as it would ever get for pulling weeds. Spring was an opportunity to embrace hope, no matter how dark the winter exile might have been.

Maggie picked up her mug, told Sandy she'd be gone for a few hours, and headed down to Whitefish.

"Hi, there," Peggy said as Maggie walked onto the grounds. Peggy turned off the hose she was using to water the flats of annuals that brightened the front of the shop.

All that color lifted Maggie's spirits.

"I don't know if you remember me ..." Maggie began.

"Of course I do," Peggy said. "You're Jack's daughter. Ready to do another stage of your project?"

"Yes. The hummingbirds are back and letting me know they're hungry."

Peggy laughed. "They are the fiercest little birds." She pointed to a feeder that hung off one of corners of the building. A dozen of the tiny critters buzzed around it, jockeying for position, and chasing each other off a coveted spot.

"They may need to wait a while at my place. I have a space I want to plant with things that butterflies, bees, and hummingbirds like."

"Wonderful. There's a new book out on creating a pollinator-friendly garden. Have you seen it?"

Maggie shook her head. "We have a copy at the counter. Let's start there. Did you bring your plan with you?"

"It's not much, just a few sketches."

"That's all you need," Peggy said.

For the next half hour they poured over Maggie's design and the book's suggestion, finally coming up with a selection of plants. Anchoring the garden with snowy buffaloberry, they came up with Maximilian sunflowers, wild bergamot, large beardtongue, showy milkweed, and a few other fillers.

"You want to plant dense," Peggy said. "They seem to prefer it that way."

"What about a crook and a couple of hanging plants?" Maggie asked. "Maybe petunias or something like that for the hummingbirds."

Peggy nodded. "Good idea." She tapped her finger on Maggie's plans. "You have a natural talent for this. Have you taken classes?"

"No. I was going to get my MBA ... eventually ... but life intervened," Maggie said.

"What a waste," Peggy said. "We need fewer people chasing money and more of them creating useful beauty." She held up her hands. "Just my opinion."

"Most of my life has been running the general store."

"The one in Promise Cove? Love that place. People need feeding, too. And you've made it an attractive place to be. You must have an artist's soul."

"Oh no. We have lots of real artists in the area."

"I've never understood that term," Peggy said. "What makes an artist 'real'? Isn't a creatively knitted top just as real? Or a colorful meal? How about a comfortable nook in a house or library?" She gestured at the plants around them. "Or a garden that delights us and nature? You need to expand your definition of art, because you *are* an artist."

Maggie didn't have any answer to the questions Peggy raised.

"Um. Thank you."

Peggy nodded. "Let's get these plants loaded so you can head home and create."

# # #

Maggie's phone buzzed while she was waiting in her car to get to the coffee shop window. She clicked the text message from an unfamiliar number. Expecting spam, she was ready to hit delete when she realized it was from Paul.

> Paul: The DNA results came in. Teagan is my daughter, but you already knew that. I'm sorry again I was such a jerk.

Maggie stared at her phone. Even though nothing had changed, everything had changed. Paul knew. More than that, he acknowledged. Tears sprang to her eyes. Teagan could know who her father was.

And what a rotten man he'd turned out to be!

She should leave things the way they were.

Paul: I want to see her. I don't have much time left. Can I come in two weeks?
Maggie: No. She's been fine without you all these years. Leave it be.
Paul: She deserves to know.
Maggie: Your opinion.
Paul: My right.

She didn't know how to answer that. A car moved up, and she was finally at the window. Completing her transaction, she drove to the end of the parking lot, took a sip, and drove onto the highway home.

For the first part of the trip her phone buzzed away, and her mind tumbled through her options. Ultimately, Paul was correct. He did have the right to see Teagan. Maybe not a legal one, but a moral one. And her daughter deserved to know who her father was. What Teagan did after they met was up to her.

The answer was obvious. Maggie would need to let him come. She'd even talk to Gabriella about providing a room for him.

Two weeks. That's all she had left to have Teagan all to herself.

# # #

Maggie and Elaine settled into the stadium seats next to Kelly and Alex.

"You didn't need to bring those," Maggie said, pointing to the box of tissues on Kelly's lap.

"Oh yes, I did," Kelly said. "I've seen my kids graduate. Like weddings and newborns, it produces lots of tears."

"She's right," Elaine said. "I still remember your dad and me watching you on this very same field."

Maggie took her mother's hand. Her own graduation had seemed so long ago. She was eager to throw off her small town life and go for the gold.

Her future life ended when she became pregnant.

But had it?

The empty waiting chairs on the field seemed to mock the thought. They awaited a new set of human beings, ready to make their mark on the world. Raising a child to be a young woman of promise in this day and age was an accomplishment. And, with her mother's help, she'd provided Teagan with a good life, maybe not everything she'd wanted in physical goods, but the important things had been there in spades.

"Thanks, Mom," she said.

"You're welcome," Elaine said. "We did a good job."

"Yes."

"With a little help from our friends."

"That, too. I'm lucky." She released her mother's hand and stood as the band began "Pomp and Circumstance."

Immediately, the tears began to fall.

Maggie reached out a hand to find a tissue ready and waiting.

She was blessed.

# # #

The ceremony had been far too brief. She'd screamed herself hoarse when Teagan was presented with an award Maggie didn't know about, again when the top students were recognized. And finally when her daughter raised her diploma in her fist in triumph.

Kelly's tissue box was nearly empty.

A few times Maggie had searched the stands to see if Tom had arrived but hadn't been able to see him.

Once the ceremony was complete, they made their way down the stands to where the graduates gathered, a bevy of black sparkling with the bright colors of dresses worn underneath robes as students starred in family gatherings, dinners out, and, later, parties where hopefully some adult would keep track of what was going on.

Before they could reach Teagan, a man in a beige shirt and dark brown pants approached her, extending a bright red bouquet of pink and white carnations. Teagan screamed and flung her arms around the man.

Tom had made it, and Maggie's heart turned over with regret.

She slowed her pace. Next to her, Alex glanced over, then looked back at Tom. "You can do this," she said. "You're the strongest woman I know."

Maggie took a deep breath and continued on.

When they reached Teagan, she pulled her daughter close. "I'm so proud of you," she said. "I love you."

"Love you, too, Mom." Teagan squirmed a little, and Maggie released her. "Look what Tom brought me! Aren't they pretty?"

"That was very nice," Maggie said, turning to Tom. "Thank you."

"It's a big day," Tom said. His eyes, hidden behind dark sunglasses, couldn't tell her a thing about what he was thinking.

"Sure is."

"We're having a family dinner in the back of Mike's," Elaine said. "You're welcome to join us. Alex, Kelly, and Ryan are coming, too."

"Thanks, but I need to attend to some other things tonight," Tom said.

"Mom," Teagan said, looking up from her phone. "There's a party tonight at Avery's. Can I go? It's going to be awesome. And Avery is so cool. Rebecca's parents said she could go."

"Who is Avery?" Maggie asked, wondering if the name belonged to a girl or boy.

"Her parents own a big house on the lake," Teagan answered. "Please?"

Automatically, Maggie looked at Tom.

He nodded. "They're good people. They'll keep a lid on things."

"Okay, I guess you can go."

"You're the best!" Teagan hugged her again. "I have to tell Rebecca." She dashed over to a clump of girls, leaving Maggie to face Tom.

"Paul's coming," she blurted out.

"Here?"

"Yes. He wants to see Teagan. He knows he's her father. He's dying. Cancer."

Tom nodded.

Silence strained between them.

"I hope it works out. I've got to go. Enjoy your dinner." He gave a friendly wave to the others, then turned and walked away.

## Chapter Thirty-Five

A few days later in the mid-afternoon Tom drove up the dirt road to Ryan's quilt studio. It was the first story of the cabin Ryan had lived in before he'd married Kelly. The top floor was rented to a handyman who was away on a job for a month.

Tom and Ryan had been allies of a sort in high school, both pining after girls they'd wanted, but couldn't seem to make the right connection with. Kelly's parents had stopped coming to Promise Cove when she'd been a teen, and Maggie thought Tom was great as a friend, but nothing more.

He should have given up long ago. A smart man would have. And now he was finally ready to let go.

At least he thought he was.

He pulled the car to a stop and got out, a six pack of beer in his hand. The door to Ryan's studio was open, so Tom pulled open the screen door and went in.

A riot of color and pattern blazed from the right-hand wall where stacks of fabric filled clear plastic pins. Beyond them, on a far wall were more shelves with plastic bins and spools of thread perched on pegs. At the center of the space was a large table with a complicated-looking sewing machine on one side.

Ryan was sitting on a stool next to the table. A good-sized quilt lay across the surface, and he was working on a corner, long fingers pushing and pulling a needle Tom could barely see through the fabric. The quilt itself pulsed with the colorful life of a woodland, small critters to large, and several realistic birds flying across blue themed fabric.

"That's amazing," Tom said.

"Thanks. It's for the raffle."

"But you could get thousands for it, couldn't you?"

"Probably." Ryan looked up from his sewing. "The fire

department saved my house last year, along with a bunch of others. All the proceeds from the raffle go to them. It's the least I can do."

"Gotcha." Tom held up the beer. "Want one?"

"In a few. I want to finish this section, but go ahead and start without me. When I'm done, we can go sit on the deck. With Larry gone, it's free for me to use again. It's the one thing I miss about living here."

"How's it going at the retreat center?" Tom popped the top of the beer and put the cap in his jeans pocket.

"It's still a work in progress. When someone's lived by themselves as long as I have, it takes some adjustment, just like when I quit being a cop and returned here from New York City. But those experiences let me know just how long the process can take. And Kelly is worth every moment of figuring it out." Ryan looked up at Tom and smiled.

"I'm happy for you."

"Heard you went to Livingston," Ryan said.

"You and everyone else. It was actually north of there—Paradise Valley. They're looking for a deputy. It'd be a step down, but the pay's good, and there's more opportunity."

"I see."

"It's time to move on."

Ryan didn't say anything but kept stitching, his gaze focused on the handwork in front of him. He pulled the thread through the fabric a few more times, then picked up a tiny pair of scissors and snipped the thread. He slipped the needle into the threads of the spool and placed it to the side.

"I'm ready for that beer. Let's head upstairs." Ryan walked to a cabinet near the stairs, pulled out some chips, then reached into a small fridge nearby and pulled out a bowl. He held them up. "Kelly heard you were coming. She has an ingrained need to feed people."

"I won't object."

They headed back outside, then up the staircase to the deck.

Tom had forgotten how amazing this view was. The cliff in front of the house dropped off enough so he could see the outline of the lake miles below. The soft blue sky flattened the edges of everything, making the scene almost dreamlike.

The sound of a cap being flipped off a bottle made him turn around. He lowered himself into one of the chairs and took a sip of his own beer. For a few moments they sat there in companionable silence.

"Why Livingston?" Ryan asked.

"Pay's good. It's a nice place to live. I might get to meet someone and get lucky like you did."

Ryan laughed. "Luck was a small part of it. And I almost blew it." He settled his beer on the table. "Like you're about to do."

"Maggie doesn't want me."

"Uh-huh."

Maggie must have told Kelly about his text message. It was such a dumb way to break up a friendship, or whatever it was they had between them. His better angels would even suggest it was cruel.

He needed to fix that before he left. If he left.

"What am I supposed to do?" he asked, his throat aching a bit from the shrillness of the words. "I watched her date everyone else in high school. I was ready to move on when she left for college, but then she was back, and pregnant, and so scared. She needed someone around."

Ryan nodded but didn't comment.

"So I was there. Not Paul. Not the guy who was Teagan's father, but me. I took that kid to the father-daughter dance, showed up for all the school plays and assemblies. I was at the hospital when she had her appendix out, and gave her a shoulder when she had her first breakup. I was like a father to her."

Tom shook his head. "And no matter how many times I asked her out, no matter how many 'family' dinners I was part of, Maggie always turned me down. Yet when a man shows up in town—someone just like Paul—she immediately starts dating him." Tom gripped the bottle. "I've been a fool all these years for waiting around. She doesn't want loyal and steady. She wants flashy and rich."

"It does appear that way. But I heard she sent him packing."

"Yeah." Tom's guilt about the text churned his stomach.

"Sounds like, from what Kelly said, that she may have woken up to what's in front of her."

"It's too late." Tom stood. "I'm going to get another beer from the fridge. Want one?"

"Sure." Ryan pulled open the bag of chips and took the plastic lid off the container. "There's a roll of paper towels on top of the fridge. Bring those up, too, okay?"

"Sure."

Tom trotted down the stairs and grabbed the bottles. Before climbing back up, he took a couple of deep breaths. Who was he really angry with? Maggie for ignoring him or himself for being such a heel when she finally came around?

When he returned to the table, he ate some chips and dip. Something needed to be in his stomach to soak up the beer.

"Paul's coming back," Tom said.

"Really? Why?"

"Apparently, he's finally gotten around to acknowledging his daughter." Tom gave a short, brittle laugh. "Maggie said he's dying and wants the chance to meet her. I don't know. Maybe. Or it could be a con."

"You've been a cop too long. What could the man have to gain? I think it's probably as simple, and as sad, as what Maggie told you. Imagine spending your whole life missing an extraordinary girl like Teagan."

"She's certainly been one of the blessings in my life."

Tom relaxed back into his chair as he thought about the young woman he'd helped raise. He would probably never have children of his own, but he'd done something real to help the next generation get started.

Paul had definitely missed out.

"You're probably right." He grabbed a few more chips and loaded them with dip. "Man, Kelly can do it right."

"I've gained ten pounds over the winter living with her," Ryan said with a chuckle. "I need to do something to get back in shape."

"It gets harder every year," Tom said. "Remember being a teen and stuffing as much as you could find into your stomach?"

"Uh-huh. And I'd still be hungry."

"I'm still hungry," Tom said, nabbing another chip.

"It's probably not food you want."

"So what would you do? I mean, so what if she's let Justin go. What happens if the next out-of-towner comes through town offering her everything she's ever dreamed of? Why wouldn't she turn her back on me and move on."

"It's your job to make sure she doesn't."

"What's that mean?"

Ryan stared at the label of the bottle and picked off a corner with his fingernail. "Women need to be romanced. Not just at the beginning, but the whole time. They need to know they're still important as themselves. Life gives them a beating, demanding they be everything to everyone."

"I've been there for her," Tom protested.

"Yes. *As a friend.*"

"Not fair. She won't go out with me."

"Have you told her how you feel?"

"Of course."

"Was she paying attention?"

"Huh?"

"Was it a separate moment? Did you tell her everything about how you felt, that you couldn't live without her? Or was it just, 'You know I love you?'"

"Women need all of that?"

"Apparently. Some over-the-top concrete exhibition of that love is required as well."

"Is that what it took for you?" Tom asked.

"Yep. I had to find a way to stop her and make her listen to me."

"But I've done tons of things for her."

"And she's come to expect them. It's normal."

"So I need something earth-shaking."

"About sums it up."

Tom shook his head. "I'm not real good at this."

Ryan laughed. "No kidding. None of us are. It was easier when they were younger. Things seemed to happen naturally. But now that they have experience under their belt, it's a lot more complicated."

"That's for sure." Tom opened the second beer. "But is it worth it? I mean, she can still reject me in the end. Still tell me all she wants is a friendship."

"Yep. But after all the time you've put in, isn't it worth one more try?"

Tom sipped his beer and studied the pines around the house.

The offer in Paradise Valley was a good one. There might be a chance for love, someone he didn't have to work so hard to get.

But there was one thing Paradise Valley didn't have.

Maggie.

# Chapter Thirty-Six

Maggie towed the kid's red wagon loaded with her duffle bag to the cabin she'd been assigned: Athena. The goddess of art. Hah!

But it was the only one left. The jazz singer was housed in Euterpe, the actress in Melpomene, and the poet in Terpsichore. Each cabin was named for one of the goddesses of the arts.

Maggie still wasn't sure what she was doing here, but her life had been turned upside down, and she couldn't think of anything better to do. Teagan and Elaine had both urged her to go, and Sandy had assured her she'd call if any major problems arose.

Then Kelly had taken her cell phone. "No phones for the first twenty-four hours," she'd directed.

"You are such a dictator," Maggie said.

"It's for your own good. Now off with you."

As Maggie walked into the cabin, tranquility seemed to wrap its arms around her. The cabin smelled of lavender, and fresh wildflowers were centered on the bureau. Thick towels and fragrant soap bars—this time with a citrus aroma—lay on a shelf in the bathroom. Shower gel, shampoo, and conditioner were also supplied.

It was like landing in a five-star resort.

Except for the additional room.

Kelly must have taken extra care here. A drafting board dominated the center of the room. Next to it was a table that contained all manner of plastic rulers and templates. Mechanical and artists pencils filled a beautiful ceramic cup. Drafting paper was stacked next to it.

A bookshelf off to the side held a dozen books on native Montana plants and garden design.

Maggie wandered through the room, touching and

caressing the tools and books, ending at a desk set up overlooking a view of the lake, similar to the one they viewed from the firepit.

She returned to the living area, put her clothes away, and stood in the middle of the room.

Now what?

She was used to being active.

Rereading the schedule for the day Kelly had given her, she was bothered to see there was nothing scheduled until gathering for drinks and supper at five. That gave her two hours with nothing to do. She hadn't even thought to bring a book.

She opened the cabin door. There was no one else around.

May as well take a walk. Henrietta, Kelly's grandmother, had planted beautiful gardens that changed as the short growing season progressed. A path beckoned.

Maggie followed it, slowly putting one foot in front of the other, like Dorothy at the beginning of the yellow brick road. Each step brought a new rainbow of color. Greens, from bright lime to dusky gray, mingled together, gave way to yellows and oranges pressing to the sky. A cluster of stalks mourned daffodils that had gone by, but new buds on a neighbor plant promised a replacement. Bushes gave shape to the garden. Tiny purple flowers served up nectar to buzzing customers. A limb of exquisite pink bells hung over the dark green leaves and white bells of lily of the valley.

It took her a half hour to walk the path, that short amount of time to realize how little she knew about plants, and how much she wanted to learn.

But where would the time come from? Being mayor and running a store took up all of her time.

She wouldn't think about that now. Instead, she continued her walk around the other side of the garden, ending at the fire pit where she stared out, not really thinking, but letting the sounds and sights wash over her.

Footsteps crunched on the pebble path.

"Oh, I'm sorry. I didn't know anyone was here." A middle-aged woman with thick black hair and a vaguely

*Spring in Promise Cove*

familiar face stood by the chairs.

"There's plenty of room," Maggie said.

"Thank you. I'm Carolee, by the way."

"Maggie."

"Good to meet you, Maggie."

As Carolee settled back into the chair and closed her eyes, Maggie tried to place her. She was probably the actress. Maggie didn't follow jazz artists, and poets were known more for their lines than their faces.

She'd know eventually, but for now, closing her eyes and dreaming of plants seemed like a perfect way to while away the time.

# # #

"Welcome, everyone," Kelly said as they gathered together in the large meeting space. Soft music played in the background, and an array of appetizers, wine, and soft drinks lined the wall. A pot of coffee brewed as well.

"I hope you've had a chance to unwind from your travels. This part of Montana isn't always easy to get to."

"I'll say," said a woman with sparkling eyes and an easy smile. "I was worried I was going to have to get on a horse at the end."

Kelly smiled. "We've come a ways since then."

"It is beautiful," Carolee said. "I'm glad to be here."

"Me, too," the last woman said. She had an angular body and a sleek haircut.

Maggie would bet she was the jazz artist.

"This evening is to break the ice," Kelly said. "Let us get to know each other a bit more."

"Oh, but we already do," the smiling woman said, who by default must be the poet. "We all went to college together."

"Yes," Carolee said. "We all majored in theater, but as you can see, our paths diverged."

"I knew you were friends, but I didn't realize you'd known each other that long," Kelly said.

"I don't think our resumes went back that far," the poet

said. She turned to Maggie. "But you don't look familiar."

Maggie shook her head. "I didn't go to college with you. I'm a friend of Kelly's."

"So you're helping out?" the jazz singer asked.

"No, she's here, just like you are, to do some thinking about what's next for her," Kelly said.

"What's next is a glass of wine," the poet said. "I'm Midge, by the way," she added.

"Hi. I'm Maggie."

"Wendy here," the jazz singer said. "And I'll join you for that wine."

"And we've already met," Carolee said. "We're happy you're joining our merry band this week."

"Wine?" Midge asked Carolee.

"I'll pass," Carolee said and headed for the soft drinks.

"Okay. How about you, Maggie?"

"Gladly." It was as if she'd been thrown into an alien world. Not only were these women accomplished in their fields, but they had an easy comradery because of a shared youth. She looked at Kelly with a silent plea of *Help!*

Midge brought her back a glass of wine, then indicated two of the comfortable chairs Kelly had placed around the space, giving it a homey feeling. "Let's get to know each other. I love meeting new people."

Carolee and Wendy settled into another pair of chairs where Kelly joined them.

"So tell me about yourself," Midge commanded.

After a sip of wine, Maggie began her tale. Midge was a skilled conversationalist, and soon Maggie had told her far more than she'd intended. The poet was equally open.

"I love writing poetry," she said, "the more scandalous, the better!" She laughed, a deep throaty sound. "But it does *not* pay the bills. For that I suffer young adults who are of that age where either they think they know everything about everything, or are scared to death they'll never know anything."

"Oh, don't let her fool you," Wendy said, approaching them. "She's one of the most loved professors on campus. And a few of her students have gone on to acclaim in the poetry world."

"You haven't done too shabby yourself," Midge said.

"It hasn't been an easy road."

"They never promised the arts would be easy," Carolee said, joining the group.

"I don't think they mentioned money at all," Wendy said.

She had sharp edges that reminded Maggie of Alex. It would take a bit to get to know her.

"Getting rough in Hollywood?" Midge asked sympathetically.

Carolee's features finally clicked into place. She'd won a Golden Globe for an impactful drama about the second wave of feminism and had gone on to several other meaty roles before taking on lighter fare over the years. Although Maggie hadn't seen her in anything in the last five years or so.

"Dinner is ready," Kelly announced, pointing to the chafing dishes set up on a side bar.

Maggie waved to Ruth, the woman behind the serving bar. Although Kelly had given Ruth's catering business its start, it had grown steadily over the last six months.

They filled their plates with thin chicken breasts in a savory sauce, a vegetable filled rice, and grilled asparagus. Salad fixings and dense wheat rolls also waited for them to choose.

"Save room for dessert," Kelly said. "Rumor has it we have fresh apricot and blueberry crumble."

"There goes my diet," Wendy complained.

"You and your diets," Carolee said. "Remember when you had us eating a whole grapefruit for lunch every day?"

"Not one of my better ideas."

"Diets are overrated. And evil," Midge declared. "Food is definitely one of the finer things to enjoy in life."

The banter continued through dinner. Fully sated, Kelly invited them to follow her to the firepit area. Each of them clutched a last beverage as they walked down the path.

As she stepped on the familiar flagstones, sobriety settled on Maggie's shoulders. She was embarking on a path that could potentially change her life. Up to this point, everyone else had dictated who she was and what she was to do.

Now it was going to be up to her.

They settled in the chairs and spent a few moments talking about the scenery laid out before them. Then Kelly started to talk.

"This retreat is a gift you've given yourself. You may think it's simply an excuse to get together with good friends, you may have a strong idea of what you want to accomplish, you may have no idea what you are going to do with this week. This time will be transformational, tearful, joyful, and frustrating. You will cavort, cry, create, and curse at times. The lessons will take you places you don't want to go, you long to go, you need to go."

She rose and walked to the table at the edge of the space where she picked up a stack of books.

"These are journals for you to use," she said as she handed one to each of them. They were exquisite books with pebbled covers in different swirls of color and a soft binding so the journal could be laid out flat. A matching ribbon provided a way to mark a place.

"Borrowing a concept from Julia Cameron, I'd like you to write at least three pages in them every morning while you are here. It can be writing about anything you wish. Some people start with lists of chores if they can't think of anything else."

"I've got lots of lists like that," Midge said with a grin. "The problem is I don't seem to be able to check off any of the items."

"Know that one," Carolee said.

"However you get started, you still need to do three pages," Kelly said. "There will be other assignments, but we'll discuss them tomorrow morning when we gather for breakfast." She paused. "There is only one rule for this retreat." Kelly paused and held the gaze of each of them in turn. "All I ask is that you be honest about yourself and your emotions. We are all adept at hiding our true selves. As artists and public figures, you are better at it than most. I'm asking you to drop the mask. Drop it here and now. At the end of our week together, you are free to pick it up again, or perhaps you'll fashion a new one. Can you agree to that?"

"Absolutely," Carolee said.

"I'll give it a whirl," Midge said.

Wendy hesitated, fidgeting with her earrings and brushing her hair behind her ear.

"Maggie?" Kelly asked.

"Um ... well, I don't know if I have a mask. But I'll do my best to live without it." With a forced laugh Maggie acted as if she was taking off her face and tossing it into the fire.

There was a moment of silence, then they all laughed. When it was over, Wendy nodded. "I agree."

"Thank you," Kelly said. "The other tradition we've developed is to start our retreat with a group hug and end it the same way. If you would, ladies." Kelly stood.

They formed a group and put their arms around each other.

It was the most awkward thing Maggie had ever endured.

## Chapter Thirty-Seven

The next morning started early, but the strong coffee and pastries Charlene had delivered made up for it. Maggie had written her required three pages, a jumbled meandering of things she needed to take care of at the store, her frustration with herself, and longing for Tom to give her a second chance.

Once they'd finished, they gathered in the chairs Kelly had rearranged, and she began.

"I'd like you to give us a brief sketch of the biggest thing that may be holding you back from the life you want to lead," she said. "It doesn't have to do with your art or music—it can be a place where you feel stagnant in your life. I believe everything we think, feel, or do influences everything else."

Holding her back from what? Maggie had no idea what direction she needed to go in. How was she supposed to know what was holding her back?

The others seemed equally stumped.

"I'll go," Carolee volunteered. "It's a pretty simple answer: Hollywood. The industry, no matter how much we've moved forward over the past few decades, still has few real strong roles for woman who are older. Men can get grizzled and gray, but they want ingénues to play the plucky heroines, no matter how old the man they're playing against."

"Thank you," Kelly said. "We're not going to solve the problem right now, but state it. Who's next?"

"I feel like I've been on a hamster wheel most of my adult life," Midge said. "I love writing my poetry, and I love my students, but I'm exhausted. If I don't teach, I don't have enough money to live. If I give up my poetry, I lose my soul."

"What would be ideal?" Kelly asked.

"Marrying a billionaire," Midge quipped.

"Unfortunately, I'm totally in love with my husband, so that's a non-starter."

"Midge, be serious. She's trying to help," Carolee said.

"Okay." Midge put her coffee cup down with a thud. "I'd like to have a life where my day job doesn't suck up all my creativity. Then I think I could write some phenomenal poetry."

Kelly nodded. Then she pointedly looked at Maggie.

"Me? I have no idea what the life I want to lead even looks like. I gave up my dreams for other people, and now they're all leaving."

"So not knowing what you want to do with your life means you can't make it ideal," Kelly said gently.

Maggie ran the sentence around in her head a few times. "I guess so."

"Makes sense to me," Midge said. "We've got a lot in common, you and me." She grinned at Maggie.

Maggie was starting to like this woman a lot. She'd definitely need to read some of her poetry.

Everyone looked at Wendy.

"Oh, I don't have any problems. I just came to spend time with my friends," Wendy said brightly. "My career is going great, my voice is holding its own, and there's plenty of money in the bank. Oh, and I love what I do."

Kelly didn't say anything. Even Maggie could hear the false note in the statements.

"Wendy," Carolee said and shook her head.

"What's going on?" Midge asked. "What don't I know? C'mon, we're supposed to be best friends."

"Nothing I want to talk about," Wendy said sharply.

Fear froze Maggie. She was the interloper.

But she wasn't alone. All of them sat in the moment, dealing with the awkwardness of secrets not everyone knew.

"It is up to each participant what they want to share," Kelly said. "I hope you gain more than renewing old friendships in this week. But sometimes that's exactly what we need." She looked at Maggie with a smile. "I know that from experience."

Kelly went to a small whiteboard set up on an easel. She

wrote: Hollywood, time to create, what to do, and a question mark. "Let's explore these for a moment. What strikes you?"

Maggie stared at the phrases. "Some of them have to do with other people," she said, not entirely sure what she meant.

Kelly nodded.

"I get that," Midge said. "Hollywood is what it is. Carolee, as brilliant as she is, won't be changing that industry anytime soon."

"The music industry isn't a whole lot different," Wendy said. "A lot of the small clubs where I like to perform are owned by men. And like it or not, men like to fill the stage with young women. Jazz has a bit more respect for older voices, which is why I can still do what I do."

"I don't know much—make that anything—about the movie industry, but aren't older women starting to make their own movies?" Maggie asked.

"That's true to some extent," Carolee said. "But they aren't making the money the big networks are. And I really have no interest in directing or producing. I want to act. I want juicy roles."

"There's always Lady Macbeth," Midge said.

"I'd rather be Margaret of Anjou in the Henry plays," Carolee said. "Now there was a woman who knew how to work the power system."

"Isn't that what you have to do?" Maggie asked. "I mean ... well ... can't you decide what role you want to play and somehow make it happen?"

Carolee stared at Maggie.

"Sorry. I guess I don't know what I'm talking about," Maggie said, wishing she could take back her words as easily as editing them out of a film.

"On the contrary," Wendy said. "You have a valid point."

Carolee nodded. "I need to think on that."

Kelly smiled at Maggie.

"What about this one?" she asked the group, pointing to "what to do."

"Maggie, can you give the other three a little background, so we know where we're starting."

Maggie summed up her adult life: Dad's early death, taking over the store for her mother, unplanned pregnancy, mother and daughter both on their way out of town.

"Maggie is also our mayor," Kelly added.

"A turning point," Midge said.

"What do you mean?" Maggie asked.

"It seems that circumstances have dictated what you had to do in your life up to now. In your words, other people and their actions have been controlling it. But now, your life is up to you."

"Well, I still have to run the store."

"Do you?"

Maggie opened her mouth to say, "Of course," but stopped. Did she have to run the store? Part of her had been willing to run away with Justin and abandon everything. What would have happened to the store then?

"Often there is a tension between obligation and desire," Kelly said. "Our job is to figure out what truly is an obligation and which desires are concrete enough for action."

"Wow," Midge said. "That's something I need to think about, too."

"That might be on my list," Wendy said quietly. Her face, normally animated and alive, had a pallor of weariness that spoke of a profound sadness.

Carolee reached over and squeezed her hand.

Midge shifted uncomfortably.

Maggie glanced at Kelly, who put down the marker and rejoined the group.

"How is everyone feeling?" Kelly asked. "Should we take a break? Perhaps a long one where you can reflect in the way that makes most sense to you?"

"I think that would be good," Carolee said.

Midge nodded.

"I'd like that," Maggie said.

They all looked at Wendy, who gave the smallest of smiles and said, "Sure."

"Lunch will be ready at 12:30," Kelly said before she walked back toward the coffee table. Maggie rose and joined her, leaving the three friends to sort through whatever was going on.

"Is it always this intense?" she asked.

"There are always moments like these."

"I don't know how you do it."

"A lot of self-care when you all aren't around. Ryan helps. He pretty much takes over when I'm done with the week."

The pain Maggie was growing accustomed to feeling in her heart zapped her.

"I think I'll go back to my cabin."

"One thing before you go. Behind your cabin is a patch of earth Ryan dug up for you to work if you want. There are some rocks out there, as well as a few plants. If you want something specific, let me know, and Ryan will pick it up. Tools are in the yellow shed."

"Really?" Maggie's spirit lightened.

"Yes."

"You guys are amazing." Maggie set down her coffee cup and headed out to work the earth as much as her heart desired.

# # #

Tom explained to Elaine what he wanted to do.

"That's a wonderful idea," Elaine said. "And Maggie will love it. But are you sure? It sounds like a commitment. Are you ready to make it? Last I heard you were making a plan to move to Livingston."

"That was the plan, but it's changed."

Elaine placed her fist on her hip. "She's finally figured out she's in love with you. From what I've heard, you told her you weren't interested."

Small towns. Nothing was sacred.

"It's complicated."

"Love always is … until it isn't. That's when you know it's the right thing."

"I've always loved her. You know that," Tom said. "But she never wanted anything to do with me. She wanted bright lights, and all I had was a home fire." He shifted, his cop's eye caught by something he wasn't quite sure he'd seen. He turned his gaze back to Elaine. "Someone pointed out I've been a little too passive in telling her how important she is to me. I owe it to her, to both of us, to show her what I can give her."

Elaine was quiet for a moment. Then she nodded. "Okay, go ahead." She smiled. "Maggie's going to love it."

"I hope so. Thanks. Now I need to go check on something." He left the counter area and headed toward the far corner of the store. Standing out of sight behind a row of shelves, he watched the nondescript woman moving from one display to another. Finally she stood in front of a shelf containing sunscreen and insect repellent. She gave a quick glance around, then slipped a small green can into her large tote and snapped it closed.

Nancy Smith continued down the row, then walked toward the front desk where she purchased a cup of coffee and one of Charlene's pastries.

Tom watched as Nancy sat at one of the tables, pulled a small laptop from her tote and began to type.

He'd found his thief but wasn't sure how to approach her. Did she even know she was stealing?

# Chapter Thirty-Eight

Maggie returned to the cabin, selected one of the design books, and took it to the space behind the cabin. The turned earth was a rectangle about six feet long and four feet wide. She stuck her hands in the dirt, mashed it, then let it drift through her fingers, like a child in a mud puddle. Not only had Ryan dug it, he'd added some compost to make it more receptive to whatever she put in there.

She walked around it, then sat on a chair that overlooked the raw earth and the descending tree line beyond. Standing back up, she approached it from different angles, until she felt she had the area so firmly in her mind it had seeped into her bones.

After washing her hands, she made a cup of coffee and returned to the space, picked up the book, and started reading.

By the early afternoon, she had an idea of what could be done with the garden, but no clue about what could be done with her life. Lunch had been subdued, everyone deep in their own thoughts. Afterward, Kelly had released them with an instruction to go play.

So she took another walk through the gardens, then down onto a path through the woods of fir, pine, and aspen that surrounded the property, making it feel like it was isolated in a faraway corner of the world, not a few minutes from town.

What if she invested the time to show Sandy how to do everything connected with the store? The young woman was bright and willing to work. She could find another person to run the counter. She'd have to do that anyway with Teagan leaving in the fall.

Her mother could participate however she wanted.

Maggie laughed as a thought struck her. After her dad

died, she'd taken on the store for her mother's sake. But Elaine had made it clear she'd run the store for Jack. Her passion was painting.

There was no need for Maggie manage the store unless she wanted to do so. She could walk away from it any time.

Then what?

Her passion in high school had more to do with leaving Promise Cove than anything else.

A desire to move from one place to another wasn't enough to sustain a life.

What about love?

She'd missed that boat. There was still hope that Tom would change his mind, but she couldn't count on that. People said time mended a broken heart. She might need to find out if the saying was true.

The path ended on a small knoll overlooking the inner part of the cove. A series of roofs indicated the few streets of the town, and the shape of the two-story store was evident. Across the street, smoke rose from the timbered top of ART. Someone must have felt a need for a fire. Next to it, the rough outline of the performing arts space seemed more solid than ever.

By fall she'd be able to hear Kelly play her first concert.

It was something Maggie had done. No, she hadn't built the structure, but it was her dream and perseverance that made it happen.

Justin had told her she was a good manager who could work with a diverse set of people, a skill that was very needed in most businesses. Tom had admired her outline for the backyard, willing to help it come to life.

She looked at ART and the building coming to life next to it. What if her artistic talent was in developing attractive living spaces? With a little—okay a lot—of effort, she could make the front of ART so enticing it could increase traffic to the town's centerpiece. She could do the same for the store.

She could also develop a brochure to be handed out at both cash registers.

With a new eagerness, she left the knoll and raced up the path to start designing her own life.

### # # #

"Here's your list," Maggie said to Kelly when she strode into the conference room near dinner time. The others were already there, enjoying a glass of wine and snacking on savory treats. Maggie grabbed a cheese stick and bit off a chunk.

She was starving.

"I'll get Ryan to pick these up tomorrow," Kelly said, stuffing the list in her pocket. "Looks like you had a good afternoon."

"The best. I have so many plans. First—"

"Wait until we're all together," Kelly said. "The others have news to share, as well. Now get your wine and let me go help Ruth in the kitchen."

"Okay." After pouring her wine, Maggie piled a plate high with snacks and joined the others in the cluster of chairs. "Hi! How is everyone?" She glanced around as she said it.

Carolee smiled at her but definitely didn't have her enthusiasm. Wendy nodded, but her expression of sadness hadn't changed during the day. Only Midge seemed animated.

"Good," Midge said. "And you look bursting at the seams. Give. What have you figured out?"

"Well, I haven't figured out all of it, but here's my plan." Maggie explained her ideas. All three women nodded.

"Sounds good," Carolee said. "But will you be able to make a living doing that?"

"Oh, don't be a wet blanket," Midge said. "It's a great idea. Maybe we all need to go down and play in the mud for inspiration."

"Sounds wonderful!" Carolee said.

"What about everyone else?" Kelly asked, joining them.

"I've been thinking about what Maggie said this morning," Carolee said. "She's right. I'm not going to be able to change how Hollywood works. There are a lot of people knocking at that door, but until the leadership changes, particularly at the big studios, movies are going to be safe repetitions of formulas that worked in the past. Look at all the sequels they do. And how long it took for *Black Panther* and *Wonder Woman* to emerge from the pile of white male Marvel characters."

"And even those had stereotypes galore," Wendy added.

"If all of that is true," Kelly said, "what are you going to do to get the roles you want?"

"Well ..." Carolee looked into her glass of wine for a moment, took a sip, then put it on a side table. "I think I need to change my idea of what success looks like."

"Ahh," Kelly said.

The words sunk into Maggie's consciousness as the quiet deepened around her. Who defined success? Had she spent most of her life dreaming about society's idea of what was important: corner office, latest fashions, and a yearly vacation at an exotic location?

"What does success mean?" Maggie asked. "Who gets to say if you're successful?"

"Excellent question," Kelly said. "And one that would be a great topic for our fire chat later. For now, let's eat."

# # #

The next few days were filled with questions, scribbles, and research. Maggie planted the small garden, using bright flowers that would spell out the word, "Peace," against a green perennial background. The annuals would need to be replaced each year, but she suggested to Kelly it might give some retreat guest satisfaction to get her hands in the dirt and nurture the plan to life again.

Maggie also spent time drinking coffee and talking with Midge. She told her new friend about the long friendship with Tom and its apparent end. The poet sorted through her own definition of success.

"I realized," Midge said, "that I've built my ideas on what my parents had: a house they owned in suburbia, two kids they sent through college, yearly vacations, and a retirement to Florida. My husband and I had one kid, and we struggled to help him with any part of his college tuition. We own our home in the 'burbs, but the taxes go up every year, and we're barely making ends meet. I've been saving for several years to be able to do this with my friends, but it's the only vacation I've had in years."

"Doesn't sound easy," Maggie said.

"It isn't. Worse, I'm not even sure it's right."

"What does your husband do?"

"He's a cop. I know, odd combination, but it's worked for us. We make each other laugh. And that's the greatest gift we could ever give each other." Midge's smile of affection tore at Maggie's sore heart.

"What if you sold the house?"

"Rents aren't any better these days."

"It's difficult," Maggie agreed.

"But it's an idea. If we threw away that anchor and opened up the possibilities, who knows what could happen?" Midge grinned. "Thanks!"

# # #

It was almost the last day when Wendy finally let go of her grip on her secret. They'd spent the afternoon in a pampering session, masseuses and manicurists descending on their cabins to ease sore muscles and pretty up nails. Maggie had fallen asleep on the massage table, finally letting go of everything.

Being indulged left her feeling vulnerable, open to new possibilities. It appeared to do the same for the rest of the group, because when they gathered in the room for a late-afternoon session, the women had seemed to melt into their chairs.

Carolee began with her ideas of how she was going to reframe her life in terms of the roles that were important to her. "I'm blessed. I don't need the money. Both my husband and I have done well. There are good roles out there for women my age. And people are producing them. I may have to give up my dream of an Academy Award, but how important is that anyway? Isn't it more important to inspire or comfort someone who is struggling by what I can help bring to the screen, no matter how big that screen is?"

"Yea, you," Midge said. "I love it!"

"Yes!" Wendy said. "You are awesome." She looked around. "You all are awesome." Her gaze lingered on Maggie. "I'm glad you came. It kept us from being insular and too focused on our past glories."

"Thank you," Maggie said, unsure if it was the right thing to say.

"It's been good to be here." Wendy held out her hands. Her fingertips were colored a variety of pinks. "I love my sparkly new nails. They're happy, and I ... I ... well ... I'm not." She dropped her hands to her lap. "I've wrestled all week with what to do ... and I still don't know." Her voice fell to a whisper.

Maggie waited. Kelly had taught them the value of silence in deep conversation.

"My husband had an affair."

"Oh, Wendy," Midge said.

Like the others, Maggie felt grief flow through her, sorrow for the depth of the other woman's pain.

"He wants another chance. Says it was bad judgment, and I want to give it to him." Wendy raised her head, her dark eyes luminescent with unshed tears. "But I don't think I can ..."

"What do you want?" Kelly asked.

"You mean, other than turning back the clock to before it happened?"

"Yes. Besides that."

"That's the problem. I don't know. My mother told me once that my dad had been with other women. His job took him away from home a lot. It was just the way it was, and she accepted it." Wendy shook her head. "But she was miserable. I know she was. I don't want that in my life. But I feel I owe it to him, to our marriage, to try again."

"Can you truly do that with your whole heart?" Kelly asked.

"That's the question, isn't it? I find myself going over our married life—twenty years—and seeing places where it may have happened before. Times when he'd been checked out, like he was when this was going on."

"Marriage needs trust," Midge said.

Wendy nodded.

"What do you need from us?" Kelly asked.

"I needed to say it out loud," Wendy said. "What I don't need is lots of questions if that's okay."

"Sure," Maggie said. Everyone else nodded.

"Thanks."

# # #

The last night arrived.

Maggie stared at what she'd written on the paper. There had been so many things rambling around in her mind it was difficult to pick just one to begin, like trying to decide which end to pull from a tangled ball of yarn. But finally she'd chosen what she planned to do first.

"I'll go first," Carolee volunteered. "My job involves research. I'm going to find out who's doing what in town. I've always focused on the big studios, but it's time to go beyond that into indies and some of the new production companies doing streaming content." She stood, crumpled the paper, and threw it into the fire. With her chin raised, she went back to her chair, looking every bit the accomplished actress she was.

"I'd like to go next," Wendy said, her voice low. "I did a lot of soul searching last night. I put aside what I thought I *should* do and went for what I needed to do for me." She took a deep breath. "I'm going to ask my husband for a trial separation when I get home." She pushed herself up from the chair, placed her paper in the fire, and watched it burn. There was no triumph when she went back to her seat, only bittersweet determination.

Maggie wanted to go next, but she didn't want to interrupt the silence honoring the huge decision that had been made.

After a few moments, Midge spoke. "I'm going to talk to my husband about what the next part of our life should look like. He's almost ready for retirement. I could leave teaching behind. If we sold the house, there'd be money to invest in other things. We could have an entirely new adventure!" Midge rose and flung her crumpled paper into the fire, then turned back to them with a huge grin.

Midge's cocky attitude tickled Maggie and she chuckled. The others joined in. Then they all turned to Maggie.

"I have lists and lists," she confessed. "And it took a long time to figure out what I could do first that would mean the most. I almost wrote down that I'd try to talk to Tom one more time, but then I realized I was making my happiness dependent on his decision." She paused. "I really do want to try to reach him, and it will be painful to live life without him, but I need to start." She took a deep breath. "My first task is to have a conversation with my mom about creating a management team for the store so I can free up my time. She's co-owner with me, so I need her agreement. I don't think it will be a problem." Maggie stood. Neatly folding the paper, she bent down and watched the flame catch the thickest corner. As it did, she sent up a silent prayer that her future held success and a little bit of room for true love.

# Chapter Thirty-Nine

Home. Maggie felt like she'd gone across the continent instead of up the street. For a few moments she stood in front of the store, envisioning the changes she'd make to the front. Before she began that, she'd talk to Elaine about hiring someone to repaint it and check the roof. It was time.

Not wanting to drag her bag through the store, she headed to the garden gate so she could go up the back stairs. She walked through the gate and dropped her bag as her mouth dropped open.

Much of the space was like she'd left it: a mess of work in progress. But the center had changed.

Leaving her bag, she walked toward a small island of grasses. In the middle, a rock cairn, just as she'd imagined it, spewed water down a cascade and through a broken urn, before trickling to a place she couldn't make out.

She stepped closer, filled with the joyous sound as she followed a stone path closer. When she got to the end, she gasped again.

To the left of the stone-covered pump, a small leafy tree threw its shade over the small area beneath, shading both dense grass and part of the water. More grass and shrubs surrounded the entire pond, except for one area where an iron bench perched. She followed the path to the bench and sank down.

Her pond.

There was only one person who could have done all this.

Between some of the grasses on the other side, a turtle head poked out.

"Oh!" She rose, then laughed. It was a brass sculpture, not the real thing.

Her gaze rested on each stalk and leaf, noticing the subtleties of color and substance. It was exactly as she'd planned. Not only had Tom done the backbreaking work, he'd been loyal to her vision.

A painted rock caught her eye.

Rising, she walked to it and picked it up, along with the folded paper beneath it. The rock had a heart painted in red, with two sets of initials: MM and TG. She set the rock back down, then unfolded the piece of paper.

> *Let's fall in love*
> *At the same time*
> *For the first time*
> *TG*

Tears spilled from her eyes, and she covered her mouth with her hand.

"It's not supposed to make you cry," Tom said from behind her.

She whipped around.

He was standing at the edge of the grassy area.

She ran down the path and threw her arms around him. He pulled her to him and held her tight.

"I'm so sorry," she said between streams of tears. "So sorry."

"Shh," he said. "It's okay. We've got it right now."

She stayed there in his arms until she was cried out. Then she looked up at him.

"Thank you. It's just as I imagined. Even a turtle." Her giggle held a little hiccup.

"Not a real one. I figured you'd want to pick him—or her—out yourself."

She nodded.

"Was it good? The retreat?"

"Yes." She untangled herself from him. "I have so many amazing ideas. I want to tell you all about them."

"I want to hear them."

"Just like you always have."

"Yes."

"I love you," she said.

"And I love you." He pulled her close again.

Kissing him was the natural next step. As she leaned into his embrace, the spark she'd been waiting for flamed into true love.

# # #

They spent the rest of the afternoon talking to each other. She told him all the plans she'd made at the retreat. He talked about his interview in Paradise Valley. They talked about nothing. And they talked about everything.

"Let's get a burger," he said. "I'm starving."

"I should help my mother close up."

"I have a feeling she won't mind," Tom said, taking her hand and heading to the store.

"Hi, Mom," she said. "I'm home."

"You've been home for a while ..." Elaine said. "Couldn't even come say hello?"

The attempted frown cracked Maggie up.

"I had something else to do."

"So I see." Elaine put her fists on her hips and stared at Tom. "Are you going to do right by my daughter?"

"Of course."

"Well then. I approve." She looked at Maggie. "And it's about time you grew some sense."

"I'm taking her to Moose's?" Tom said. "Can we get you anything?"

Elaine dropped her pose. "Nope. You've already given me everything I've ever wanted. Now get out of here."

"Way to go!" Mike said loudly when they walked into the saloon. Laughter from some of the other patrons followed.

Tom shook his head and followed Maggie to a corner table. She took the seat next to the wall so she could see everyone who came in or out.

"I guess we're 'out' now," Tom said.

"No doubt about that."

They ordered beers, burgers, and fries, then went back to catching each other up on everything and anything.

"Did you ever figure out who was stealing things?" Maggie asked.

"Yep. My problem is I'm not sure what to do about it."

"How come?"

"I don't think she's doing it consciously. I know kleptomania is rarer than television shows would have you believe, but I believe it's true in her case."

"Throwing her in jail wouldn't solve the problem."

He shook his head.

"Can you find a judge who will sentence her to counseling?"

"Maybe. The county judge is a bit of a stickler for sentencing regulations. He doesn't like to get creative."

"Maybe if she had an advocate? Someone in addition to her defense attorney?"

"Like who?"

"I was thinking maybe Kelly," Maggie said. "She had so much insight during the retreat. I was amazed at how good her questions were."

"Or maybe she'd be willing to talk to the woman herself?" Tom asked. "It's a little irregular, but since I haven't done anything official, it's possible. Thanks for the tip. I'll talk to her." He put his hand on hers. "I've missed this. You were always the best person for me to talk things over with. I'm glad we'll be able to do this again."

"Me, too." Light brightened the interior as the door opened. A young man, someone Maggie didn't recognize, walked in, his upright carriage denoting former military. "I wonder who that is."

Tom twisted to look. "Don't know. Probably passing through."

"Probably." One of the realities of Montana life was that people of color who were non-Native American made up a minute percentage of the population. The military man's darker skin tone made him part of that percentage.

Tom shrugged. "Just one more stranger passing through."

"Yep." She took a sip of her beer and put her hand on Tom's arm. "I love you. I'm sorry I didn't know it sooner."

"Stop apologizing. We've got this now." He grasped her hand.

"Burgers?" the waitress asked.

With a giggle, Maggie untangled herself from Tom to allow space for their plates.

"Need anything else?" the waitress asked.

"Nope," Tom said. He chomped into his burger like the starving man he'd claimed he was, and she did the same. Never had anything tasted so good.

"What about Paul?" he asked.

"He's coming next week. I talked to Teagan about it before I went to the retreat, so she's prepared."

"How does she feel about him?"

"I think she's a little nervous, but told me whatever he said, it wasn't going to make much difference in her life." Maggie smiled at the man she loved. "She told me as far as she was concerned, you'd always been father enough for her, and that's the way she planned to keep it."

Tom coughed, sounding like he was choking on the fry he'd just bitten into.

"You okay?" she asked.

"Better than okay," he said when he'd gotten it under control. "There's nothing more I could wish for."

"Me either." She reached for his hand again, and he grasped hers, recharging the connection that had always been between them.

Promise Cove wasn't the bright lights and big city, but it was home. There was no need to go searching for anything else. Everything she needed was right here: a career, a community, and love.

The End
# # #

Now that Maggie and Kelly are paired up, is there anyone who can get past Alex's prickly exterior? Find out in *Hope in Promise Cove*, available at your favorite online bookstore or your local bookstore can order it through IngramSpark.

# Author's Note

In my twenties, I lived in E. Glacier Park, MT, a place that is almost as remote now as it was then. The Blackfeet called the town "White Man's Heaven," because most of us who wanted to do good—teachers, medical professionals, architects—lived there. The place was blessed with two tiny groceries that served roughly three hundred people in the winter and hordes of tourists in the summer.

Most of us got paid once a month, and the day after payday, the town was empty as we headed to Kalispell, roughly ninety miles west. That worked well for the first two years I lived there, but in the spring an avalanche took out one of the essential bridges on Highway 2. We were forced to go two hours east instead.

That avalanche has always been part of the stories I tell about that rugged but beautiful land. So when I needed something dramatic for this story, what better than an avalanche?

Search and rescue teams are essential in the wilderness and most of them are volunteers. I am grateful to Julie Balch of North Valley Rescue Association for providing information to keep my story as accurate as possible. Any mistakes are my own.

I am also thankful for my three college friends—Carolee Boger, Wendy Simon, and Midge Guerrera for allowing me to use their names for my retreat, although the details of their lives have been totally changed! We majored in theater together but have traveled different routes from our time at Montclair State. Wendy is an accomplished jazz singer (and happily married!) in Philadelphia. Midge just released her first book, *Cars, Castles, Cows and Chaos*, about her travels in Italy. And my dear friend, Carolee, while working full time, has earned her PhD navigating the medical system and providing incredible support to those of us who need her.

Thank you, ladies!

And thank you, my dear readers!

Sincerely,
Casey Dawes

# Hope in Promise Cove

**Her widowed life revolves around work. He loves loud music and fast dancing. Can the sparks that fly between them turn into love?**

Alex Porter believes she'll never love again. A well-regarded artist of wood furnishings, she's created a solitary life in Promise Cove. Although her friends complain she can be prickly, life is just the way she likes it.

Until he moves in next door.

After a traumatic childhood, Sal Rivas keeps life casual. He travels the country in his converted van, picking up work as a casual laborer, and spends his evenings crafting poems and short stories. He's not opposed to a carefree romance, but not with his neighbor, a woman with wide eyes and vulnerable heart.

She wants him to go away, but there's something about the angles of his face that draws her closer. He wants to know what makes her tick, but if they get too close, both of them will get burnt. Can they make it past their differences and open their hearts?

She wants him to go away, but there's something about his energy for life that draws her closer. He wants to know what makes her tick, but if they get too close, both of them will get burnt. Can they make it past their differences and open their hearts?

Set in the glorious country of western Montana, this heart-warming story will delight fans of clean small-town, seasoned romance. Get comfortable in your favorite chair and become lost in love's promise.

Follow me on Amazon or BookBub to be notified when Hope in Promise Cove is available.

# Excerpt from Hope in Promise Cove

Alex lost herself in the colors of the bowl she was scraping. The wood had a lovely grain, the result of a twisting and tortured lifetime on a high cliff. Once she smoothed and polished, it would be the perfect addition to someone's sideboard.

Maybe she'd charge a little extra for this one. Start saving for the next round of quarterly taxes.

A loud rumbling seeped into her workshop. The rhythmic thumpa thumpa took over her nervous system, interrupting the flow of her movements.

She put down the bowl and scraper. Whatever that noise was, it had to stop now. The house next door was empty—she was supposed to be keeping an eye on it while the couple who lived in it were off working in Colorado.

Stomping out the back door, she went around to the front of the house.

A large red van with a yellow and orange flaming stripe down its side was smack in the middle of the neighbor's drive. The noise suddenly stopped, and she could finally hear the crows protesting from the nearby pines.

The driver's door opened, and a man stepped out. He wasn't much taller than she was, but his longish hair was a dark brown, except where the sun glinted off streaks of gray. His skin was the light brown of a freshly peeled Doug fir.

He took his sunglasses off, giving her the same frank gaze she must be giving him.

This must be the man Maggie warned her about. But her friend had failed to mention the dramatic lines of his face: His wide eyes, framed with eyelashes it seemed only men could grow, contrasted with a sharp nose, and full-lipped mouth. It was not a handsome face, but her fingers itched for the right piece of wood.

She could see it in her mind's eye, a high-grain surface, carved with all the right angles ...

"Are you done?" the man said.

"Who are you?" She widened her legs and planted her

feet firmly.

"I thought I was about to be dinner, the way you were looking at me." He grinned, and her interest—which was purely artistic up to that point—took a turn to something else. Something she refused to examine too closely.

"Who are you?" she repeated. She'd left her phone in the studio, playing the soft jazz she used for bowl scraping.

"You're obviously my new neighbor." He took a step toward her and held out his hand. "Salvadore Rivas. My friends call me Sal."

"That house wasn't sold," she said, refusing to believe what he was saying. Her neighbors were quiet and frequently gone on one adventure or another. She did not need this man, with his bright van and loud music next door.

He shrugged and dropped his hand. "I'm house sitting."

"You can't be. They asked me to look after the place. They would have told me."

Salvadore ...Sal ... whoever ... held up a key. "It's legit. David Brisbois—he's my new boss—checked with them. They said I could housesit for the summer."

"They didn't tell me."

Again Sal shrugged. "Don't know what to tell you."

"You can't move in."

Sal's face hardened. "And why is that?"

In her mind's eye, she could see him as a character in a street gang movie. It took everything she had not to take a step back. "I'm an artist. I need quiet." She gestured at the van. "You're too noisy."

He stared at her for a second. "Too noisy?" Then he began to laugh, a big, deep, not caring if anyone was watching, laugh.

His face transformed again, the menacing look gone. When he finally got ahold of himself, he shook his head. "I've been told to leave for a lot of reasons, but being noisy is a first."

"Sorry. But that's the way it is."

He shook his head. "I guess you're going to need to learn to live with a little Latin," he said. "It will be good for you. Loosen you up." He looked her up and down in an exaggerated and non-sexual way. "You're a little tight."

"And you are obnoxious. I can't believe David hired you. I thought he was a better judge of character."

"I think he liked my van," Sal said. "So here I am. We should get to know each other. I'd offer you a beer, but I have to go shopping after I get my stuff unloaded. Maybe later?"

"Not happening. I have work to do. Work requiring sharp objects."

"Maybe later then. The offer stands. When you're done with sharp objects, that is."

"I don't think you're funny."

"I suspect you don't think much is funny." His smile disappeared. "Okay. I'll stay out of your way, and you stay out of mine."

"Don't play your music so loud."

"Oh, no, *amiga*. I'll play my music as I like it. Loud with a beat. Get some earplugs." He grinned again. "Or you could learn to like it. Come by, drink a beer, and I'll teach you to dance." He waved. "Got to get it done before that nice lady at the general store closes up for the night." He disappeared around the back of the van.

Of all the nerve.

She stomped back to the workshop, her heavy boots thudding on the wooden walkway.

Here? He was moving in here? Where was the justice in that?

This was becoming the most frustrating day in her year so far. First, Gower called to pressure her into submitting some kind of artistic piece—the kind of work she hadn't done since she'd left his studio.

And now this hip-hopping rude man had moved next door.

A man who'd sparked something within her, an unexpected twinge that felt like an emotion she'd known long ago. A feeling that meant disaster.

# Other Books by Casey Dawes

### Promise Cove Romance Series

*Return to Promise Cove*
*Spring in Promise Cove*
*Hope in Promise Cove*
*Winter in Promise Cove*
*Promise Cove Wedding (coming spring 2023)*

### Beck Family Saga

*Home Is Where the Heart Is*
*Finding Home*
*Leaving Home*
*Coming Home*
*Starting for Home*
*Finally Home*

### California Romance Series

*California Sunshine*
*California Sunset*
*California Wine*
*California Homecoming*
*California Thyme*
*California Sunrise*
*California Coast Romance Series (5 books)*

**Stand Alone Stories**

*Keep Dancing*
*Chasing the Tumbleweed*
*Love on the Wind*
*Short Stories for Women (And Some Men)*

**Christmas Titles**

*A Christmas Hope*
*Sweet Montana Christmas*
*Montana Christmas Magic*

# About the Author

Casey Dawes writes non-steamy contemporary romance and inspirational women's fiction with romantic elements.

Her women's fiction series, Rocky Mountain Front, explores the five siblings from a ranching family living in Montana, the people who love them, and the characters in the small town in which they live. Previous to that she wrote a five-book contemporary romance series about friends and family on the Central Coast. Her latest series features love between "seasoned" heroes and heroines in a small Montana town.

Currently, she and her husband are traveling the US in a small trailer with the cat who owns them. When not writing or editing, she is exploring national parks, haunting independent bookstores, and lurking in spinning and yarn stores trying not to get caught fondling the fiber!

*Are you enjoying Promise Cove? Go to*
**https://bookhip.com/VAKFSWN**
*to get a free novella set in Promise Cove! You will be added to my newsletter mailing list: On the Road to Your Next Read ...*